Chapter 1

The mid-morning sun lay warm and heavy across Jay Baysinger's back. He peeled off the tweed jacket and slung it over his shoulder, hooking a thumb through the hanging strap. The jacket was wrinkled, the lining damp with perspiration, as was his shirt. He wore no tie. Why not? he wondered. He always wore a necktie to work. Where was it?

He couldn't remember. Well, it would come to him. Probably took it off down at the lab and left it lying there somewhere. It would not be the first thing he had forgotten. When he was involved in a project he tended to become absent minded, much to the amusement of his fellow researchers. Who was he working with today anyway? Ah, no matter, he was on his way home now. Had to learn to leave work behind. That's what had caused the problems between him and Kristy—bringing the work home.

Baysinger trudged on up the slight grade of Lemon Grove Street. With the tips of his fingers he massaged his upper forehead, right at the hairline, where there was a feeling of tightness. Not a headache, exactly, just a slight, unsettling pressure. He raked fingers back through his scrubby hair. Bad haircut. He was going to have to find a new barber.

It would be good to get home and relax. Home

to Kristy. Baysinger smiled, conjuring a mental picture of his wife. Pert and slim with short glossy black hair and Irish blue eyes. He resolved to start showing her more attention, as when they were first married. The growing distance between them was his fault, he would admit that. They still enjoyed their good days, but those were getting fewer. Well, that was going to change.

He told himself this would be one of the good days. Kristy would sit him down in his favorite recliner and stroke his head and put a tall, icy drink in his hand. She would listen to his recitation of the day's problems, and make him smile with stories of her work with troubled children. A very special woman, Kristy Baysinger. He resolved to make her know that he appreciated having her to come home to after a tough day like this one.

And this *had* been a tough day. Hadn't it? Oddly he could not recall the details. A combination of the slight headache and the heat had muddled his mind.

He stopped, shaded his eyes with a hand, and looked up at the sun. It was almost directly overhead. That did not compute. Why was he coming home in the middle of the day? Damned if he could remember. What was the matter with his memory?

The first chill of apprehension hit him. He had an odd sensation of floating off and up, enclosed in a sealed pocket, watching himself walk up Lemon Grove Street somewhere below. And at the same time he was down there, being watched. The dual point of view made no sense. He started off again at a quicker pace, up the street toward his home.

Lemon Grove was a long, straight street lined with tall coconut palms. The street ran from the Golden

HEAD GAME

DO YOU KNOW WHO YOU ARE?

GARY BRANDNER

Copyright 2021 © Gary Brandner
All Rights Reserved.

The characters and events in this book are fictitious.
Any similarity to real persons, living, dead or undead is
coincidental and not intended by the author.

No part of this book may be reproduced in any form or by
any electronic or mechanical means, including information
storage and retrieval systems, without permission in writing
from the publisher, except by a reviewer who may quote
brief passages in a review.

Cover art and design by Christian Francis.

Encyclopocalypse Publications
www.encyclopocalypse.com

State Freeway all the way up to the rolling green spread of Brand park where the white Grecian library nestled in the embrace of the Verdugo foothills. It was a nice, clean, comfortable street in Glendale, California. A street where life was pleasant and predictable.

Baysinger smiled as he quickened his pace, remembering the excitement He and Kristy had shared when they signed the papers four years ago making them first-time home owners. The house was carefully chosen after two years of budgeted living in a Van Nuys apartment. They got a good buy on the house, which the owners had abandoned to move to Arizona. Neighborhoods to the south and the east had deteriorated, and gang graffiti had spread like a fungus outward from Los Angeles. However Lemon Grove Street had stayed much as it had been in the 1950s.

A troubling new perception slowed his steps and brought him to a stop. He knew this street as well as he knew his own face. He had walked it many times, the three long blocks from his house to Gilbert's liquor store-delicatessen down on the corner of Glenoaks. That walk was, embarrassingly, almost the only exercise he got these days. In the car culture of southern California, nobody walked anywhere unless he had to.

But why was he walking now? He carried no package from Gil's. Returning from work? But that was wrong. He always drove to and from the job, Monday through Friday, and sometimes Saturday. For that matter, what day was today? What the devil was wrong with his thinking process?

A growing anxiety prickled the hairs on the back of his neck. He frowned in concentration, taking a hard look at his surroundings. There was something *different* about Lemon Grove Street today. Something *wrong*. These were the same houses—1950s ranch models and tile-roofed Spanish bungalows. And yet they were... *different*. The shrubbery was wrong—too bushy, or too bare, or in some cases not there at all when it should be. The tight feeling at his hairline increased.

Baysinger started walking again. He crossed Cypress Avenue, the last street before his own block. There was a construction barrier set up where a trench ran the length of the block. When did they dig that? There was no trench there when he left the house. Was there? Why was it so difficult to remember?

A soft buzzing began inside his head. Like the stirring of a distant swarm of bees. He *really* needed to get home and relax.

He walked faster, eyes shifting from one side to the other as he registered the subtle but unmistakable changes in his neighborhood. A fence surrounded the Carney's lawn where there should be no fence. Children's toys lay scattered on the grass. Frank and Emma Carney were a quiet couple in their late 60s who never had children, never wanted any. And across the street yellow-brown patches marred Terry Williams' lawn. To proud gardener Terry Williams, a dead patch in his beloved dichondra would be unthinkable.

Baysinger began to sweat. Finally he was home. He turned eagerly up the walk to his front door. And stopped. Planted in the grass to the left of the walk was a Century 21 real estate sign. *For Sale*. And a little tag hung underneath the sign: *Sold*.

Sold?! What the hell was going on? A joke? Not funny. And yet somebody had jammed a For Sale sign into his lawn between the time he left the house and now. What time exactly *did* he leave the house? The bees swarmed closer.

A clang of metal behind him spun him around. Two men were carrying furniture up a loading ramp into the back of a large truck. On the side of the van was the red shield of the Salvation Army. Baysinger walked back out to the curb and looked at the chair the men were horsing into the truck's interior. It was his familiar and beloved recliner.

"Hey, what are you people doing?" he said.

The two men turned and paused with the chair halfway up the ramp. The younger looked to the older man to answer.

"We're making a pickup." The tone of his voice said that much should be obvious.

"That's my chair."

The man sighed as though he'd run into this situation before. "You'll have to talk to the lady. She called for us to pick up the furniture. It's all signed for."

"I didn't sign anything."

"Mister, the stuff is all loaded."

"Well you can just unload it."

"Can't do that, friend. You'll have to call the downtown office."

"Then I'll damn well call them."

While the men watched him with long-suffering expressions, Baysinger marched up the walk to his front door. He grasped the brass doorknob, turned it and shoved. The door did not budge. Locked. He dug in his pocket for his keys. Not there. He checked his other pockets, the jacket. No keys. He *always* carried his keys in their neat leather case. They were as much a part of his clothing as the wallet on his hip. But what the hell?! The wallet was gone too.

Behind him in the street the truck engine ground to life. He turned to see the Salvation Army rumble away carrying his recliner. Damn! What could have gotten into Kristy? She was going to have some explaining to do.

He thumbed the mother-of-pearl button set into the stucco wall beside the door. From inside he could hear the familiar *bing-bong* of the chimes. He must have put his keys down somewhere before going to the store. Sure. And he forgot to change his wallet from one pair of pants to another. Easy explanations. Everything would be lying right there on the bureau, and he would feel like a fool. He and Kristy would have a good laugh at his absent-mindedness and make jokes about the early onset of Alzheimer's.

No! This was not funny. What about the truck? And the *For Sale* sign? And the wrong look of the whole neighborhood? Too many things were out of place here. His pulse raced, the surging blood pounded in his ears. The swarming bees droned ominously.

The door opened. Jay Baysinger's knees turned to water.

Chapter 2

A tall, thin young man Baysinger had never seen before barred his entrance. Baysinger looked him up and down. The boy's hair was pale and short. He was cultivating a hopeful moustache, He wore faded jeans and a T-Shirt with a cartoon character Baysinger did not recognize.

"Well?"

Words clotted in Baysinger's throat. He looked past the young man into the living room. *His* living room. But it was not his any more. Half the furniture was missing. Not only his recliner, but two other chairs, a pair of end tables, the desk he always used at home, and a large bookcase. Cardboard cartons were stacked along the wall. Clothes, clothes, were piled on the floor, separated into jackets, pants, shirts.

Of remaining furniture he recognized Kristy's piano, the coffee table, and the couch with the floral pattern he had never liked. Two tall glasses and a pitcher of iced tea sat on the coffee table. Across the room Kristy, his wife, sat on the couch looking at him. There was nothing in her face to indicate she knew him.

"What's going on?" The words came out of him in a pinched whisper.

"You want something?" The young man in the doorway was looking at him warily now.

Baysinger frowned at him. "Who are you?"

The boy turned to Kristy, who shrugged, then back to Baysinger. "I think the question here is, who are ___?"

His patience was about used up. "I'm the guy who lives in this house and bought most of that furniture they just trucked away." He took a step forward, and when the boy put out an arm to stop him, angrily pushed it away. He focused across the room at Kristy. "Somebody better tell me what the hell's going on here?"

His wife stood up and faced him. She wore a man's blue work shirt and tight white jeans. "I think you've got the wrong house, mister."

For a terrible moment Baysinger felt his sanity tremble. Could he have somehow made a dreadful mistake? Even knowing it was impossible, he took a step back outside and read the bronze metal numbers screwed into the wall beside the door. Numbers he himself had put up there. *1436.*

"If there's a mistake here," he said, "I didn't make it." His voice gained strength as some of his confidence returned. "I live here. This is my house." To the young man he said, "I don't know who you are, sonny, but you," pointing at Kristy, "are my wife." His words lost some of the intended power when he was swept with a wave of vertigo and stumbled against the door jamb.

The other two exchanged a look. The boy stepped forward, ready to catch him.

"Hey, are you all right, man?"

"I... I... I don't know," Baysinger got out. The room wavered in and out of focus.

"Maybe you'd better sit down."

"I don't want to sit down."

But he allowed himself to be led into the living room. Kristy cleared a stack of newspapers from one end of the couch, and he sagged onto the cushions. A hard, cold knot began to grow just under his diaphragm.

He looked up into the faces of the two people in his living room. The boy was standing disconcertingly close to his wife. Kristy's expression, gentle concern, still with no sign of recognition, chilled him to the bone.

"I'm Jay Baysinger," he said, feeling foolish. "I live right here at 1436 Lemon Grove Street in Glendale, California. You are Kristy, my wife. I don't know your friend. Now how about an explanation?"

Kristy approached him warily. "Either this is one ugly joke, or you are a very confused man. Apparently you know my name, and my husband's name, and you have the address right. That doesn't prove anything."

"I don't see that l have to prove anything."

"Suppose you just start by proving who you are."

"My name is Jay Baysinger." He bit off each word and spat it out. "You prove I'm not, if you can."

Kristy faced him, her shoulders squared. "My husband, Jay Baysinger, has been dead for two years."

It was like a punch in the stomach. *"No!"*

Both Kristy and the boy started at his vehement denial. The boy looked toward the door as though for reinforcements. Kristy took a step toward the table that held the telephone.

"Wait a minute," he said. "Maybe you're right. Maybe I am confused. Let me try to sort all this out." While his wife and the young blond man moved closer together and watched him, Basinger looked around. This was *his* living room. *His* house. *His* furniture, what was left of it. The pictures on the walls were familiar. The hole was still in the wall where he had knocked out a chunk of plaster when he carried in the new television set. The place even smelled the same—lemon furniture polish and that floral stuff Kristy used on the carpet when she vacuumed. And yet, like the neighborhood, nothing here was quite right. The bees were back, humming in circles in his head.

He took a closer look at Kristy. She was maybe a bit thinner, and her hair was longer than it should have been, but beyond any possible doubt she was his wife. There could be no confusion about that. Baysinger became aware that the young man was talking to him.

"My name's Ross Newland. I work with Kristy sometimes down at the clinic." He paused, letting the implied familiarity sink in. "We've known each other almost a year. I know what he looked like. I've seen pictures of her husband. You are not anything like Jay Baysinger."

He looked back at Kristy. She slowly shook her head, watching him carefully.

"Look, something weird is going on here. I don't know what it is, but I do know I live here and Kristy Baysinger is my wife. We've been married six years. Or is it seven?" He turned on the couch and looked over his shoulder. "There should be a picture of you and me, taken on our honeymoon in Hawaii, right there on the piano."

Kristy stared at him. "How did you know that?"

"I know it because I live here, damn it. Because it is our honeymoon picture. Can we please knock this off?"

Kristy took a few seconds before answering. "There *was* a picture there. Of Jay and me." She chewed on her lower lip. "Just a minute."

She walked over to the row of cartons, dug through one of them, came out with a square, tissue-wrapped packet. With her eyes on Baysinger, she pulled away the tissue and dusted off a framed enlargement of a color photograph. She stepped forward and handed it him.

He saw a young man and woman in luau shirts smiling into the camera. They stood on a white sand beach with their arms around each other. Picturesque palm trees leaned into the cloudless sky behind them. The woman was a slightly younger version of the Kristy who stood now watching him. He remembered the beach, the trees, the warm day, even the silly shirt he was wearing. But the fair-haired, slightly plump young man with his arm around Kristy was a stranger.

Baysinger looked up from the photograph. "This isn't me." Kristy took the photograph from him. "I know. That's Jay Baysinger. My husband."

He looked to Ross Newland for some sign that this was all an elaborate hoax. The boy gave him none.

Baysinger lurched to his feet. He walked unsteadily to the gas fireplace and stared into the mirror above the mantle. The face that looked back was still his—gray eyes, high cheekbones, stubby brown hair. Definitely not now or ever was he the honeymooner in the photograph.

Kristy said, not unkindly, "If you're feeling all right now, I think you'd better go."

A lump, cold and hard like congealed grease,

seemed to constrict his breathing. He swallowed hard and clenched his hands, digging the nails into his palms.

"This is... wrong. What are you doing to me. Who is that in the picture with you, Kirsty?"

She answered him gently, "I told you. That's my husband, Jay Baysinger. nine years ago. where he worked. The picture was taken right after we were married Two years ago Jay was killed in an accident. That's all there is. That's the end of the story."

"What about the *For Sale* sign out front? The... the Salvation Army truck?"

"I've had the house listed for a year. The real estate market is bad, and it took until last week to find a buyer. The deal is in escrow now. I'm starting my packing and getting rid of a lot of things I should have dumped long ago so I'll be ready to move."

The swarming bees grew louder and became a rushing wind. The light in the room dimmed and brightened and dimmed again. With an effort he brought everything back into sharp relief. Anger flowed in to cover his confusion.

"All right," he said through clenched teeth, "game's over. You two have had your fun. I want an explanation, and I want it now!"

Ross Newland reached for the telephone. "That's it, man. Either you're out of here or I'm calling the police."

The mention of the police froze him. Why? Jay Baysinger had never been in trouble in his life. He had no reason to fear the police. And yet the threat was powerful enough to grab hold and push him across the room and through the front door.

The boy followed and stood in the doorway. "And don't come back."

Kristy watched him from across the room. "You really should get some help."

Baysinger stood for a moment just outside the door of his house with the warm sun overhead and his wife inside looking at him like a stranger. He bit down hard on the knuckle of a forefinger, as though to wake himself from this nightmare.

"You got a problem here, Kristy?"

Baysinger started at the sudden male voice behind him. He turned to see his neighbor—fat, friendly Howard Denbo. Howard did not look friendly now. His right hand gripped the handle of a heavy hedge clipper.

"Howie, for God's sake, tell these people who I am."

"I give up, pal. Who you?"

Baysinger could only stare. Howard took a firmer grip on the hedge clipper.

Kristy came to the door to stand beside Ross Newland. "It's all right, Howie. The man made a mistake. He's leaving now."

Baysinger took a last searching look at the three stony faces, saw no softening. He took two faltering backward steps, then wheeled and walked stiffly toward the street. Behind him the door to his house closed with a thump. The dead bolt lock clacked into place. At the sidewalk he turned and headed down the street the way he had come. He did not look back at his home or at his good friend and neighbor, who stood watching him, the hedge clipper held ready.

The familiar neighborhood took on a surreal look as he continued down the block where he and

Kristy had lived together. The houses were too sharply defined. The sunlight too bright, the grass too green, the patches of shadow too dark. Everything stood out in painful relief.

Baysinger mentally replayed the scene he had just been through. None of it made any sense. It was not conceivable that this was a cruel joke. Kristy was not the kind of a woman to do such a thing. And yet she had looked him straight in the eye and betrayed no hint of recognition. Told him Jay Baysinger was two years dead. And there was that photograph taken on their honeymoon with a strange man standing in his place.

His mind rebelled. This was not happening. *Could* not be happening. A boy he had never seen before was sitting in his living room, apparently helping his wife pack up to move out of their home, which had a *For Sale* sign out front. And how could he explain his friend and neighbor Howie Denbo? Good old Howie, with whom he'd drunk beer, watched football, shared do-it yourself projects. Howie had stood ready to eviscerate him with a hedge clipper. If this is some insane dream, he thought, please, *please* let me wake up.

He walked more swiftly down the inclined street, his mind a kaleidoscopic jumble. Clutching his rumpled jacket in one hand, he began to jog, then to run. The tall palms bounced forward to met him. Baysinger ran on. He ran as though demons were chasing him. His hard-soled shoes banged the concrete sidewalk, each step sending a jolt up his shin bone, through his knee, upper leg, and into the pelvis. His arms pumped, the breath blasted in and out through his gaping mouth. The palm trees, the parked cars, the houses with their neat lawns, the cloudless sky, the relentless sun all blurred into a rushing diorama.

On and on he ran, heedless of the children who stopped their play to watch the wild man galloping down their street. He gave no thought to what he was running from. Or to. Only the physical act had reality. If he ran fast enough, maybe he could outdistance the terrible dark shadows of his mind.

Chapter 3

California State Prison at Folsom has an inmate population of 6,400, give or take a couple of dozen. It opened in 1890, and is the second oldest correctional institution in the state.

Folsom is considered a high-risk, maximum-security institution. Hard time. Christmas comes on time every year, even to Folsom and its 6,400 souls. From the outside the walls, you wouldn't know it.

Inside, a tiny plastic Christmas tree with half a dozen cheap ornaments did little to cheer up a cubicle used for interrogation of prisoners. The walls were a depressing institutional beige, stained tobacco brown up near the ceiling.

Outside the heavy steel mesh of the room's single window a steady drizzle darkened the afternoon. Inside, unshaded fluorescent lights brought out the harsh lines and deep shadows in the faces of the two men sitting at opposite ends of a library table. The men looked unflinchingly at each other and ignored the Christmas tree.

One of them was tall and lean, with powerful sloping shoulders, dressed in the gray prison uniform. He slouched in his chair, silent and watchful. His bony face betrayed no emotion. The pale gray eyes were alive behind his half-lowered lids.

Facing him was a loose-jointed man with the red hair, freckles and guileless expression of a kid in a Norman Rockwell painting. The eyes, however, belonged to a man who had seen things Norman Rockwell would never paint. He wore a Red Sox warmup jacket over a navy sweat shirt. Every few minutes a prison guard peered in at them through the bulletproof view plate in the locked metal door.

The two man had been sitting mute for several minutes.

Neither seemed in a hurry to speak.

It was the red-haired man who finally broke the silence. He was Merlin Ryan. He carried credentials Identifying him as an agent of the Federal Bureau of Investigation. The FBI, however, did not include Ryan's name on its official roster, nor did it keep accessible records of his activities. When he finally spoke, his voice was low-keyed and casual.

"You know, Lou, even if you did manage to beat the gas chamber, there is no possible way you're ever going to get out of here. Have you added up the years of your sentences, even figuring you get the absolute minimum?"

"Two hundred and seventy-seven years," said the prisoner. A corner of his mouth twitched in what might have been a smile.

His mouth was not one to which a smile came readily.

The prisoner's name was Louis Matchek. He killed his first man when he was sixteen. It happened during an argument over a parking place. The other man called Matchek "son of a whore" in Spanish,

Unfortunately for the man, Matchek understood the words. Even more unfortunately, the description of his mother was accurate, and was a particularly sore point with young Lou Matchek. When a crowd finally pulled him off, the other man, four years older and twenty pounds heavier, had broken ribs, missing teeth, multiple contusions, and a fractured skull. He died a day later bleeding from the brain.

Matchek served a year in prison for that one. It was the only time prior to the current incarceration that he had been locked up. It was also the only time he had killed for purely personal reasons. The others, rumored to total more than a dozen in the past twenty-one years, were strictly business.

"And I hope you're not foolish enough to think about escape," Ryan continued. "There are people who would like to see you try it, just for the opportunity to shoot you down."

"Something I've been wanting to ask you," Matchek said. His eyes were the luminous gray of a threatening dawn.

"Go."

"Why don't you dress like other FBI men? Where's the conservative dark suit? The snowy white shirt? The tasteful tie? You look like you're trying out for a role on *Cheers*."

"I'm in Special Projects," Ryan said. "They let me bend a rule here and there."

"J. Edgar must be spinning in his bulletproof coffin. Or is it true that you've got him in deep freeze somewhere waiting for a comeback?"

"Let's get on with it, okay?"

"You're just wasting your time and mine,"

Matchek said. "You could be home with your family now singing carols and trimming the tree. I could be back in the shop stamping out license plates. We both know what you want from me, and we both know you're not going to get it."

Ryan leaned back in the wooden chair. "What is it with you, Matchek? Have you been watching old Warner Brothers prison movies? This hard-guy code of silence is a bunch of crap. Nick Tenzi put you in here as surely as if he'd walked into the court room and fingered you. You were set up, Matchek. You're the fall guy. You don't owe Tenzi a damn thing. Certainly not loyalty. He's living high and free, while you grow old looking at the world through steel bars."

"Hey, I'm doing useful work in here. Besides license plates we also make trash receptacles for the state parks. Doing my part to save the environment."

"By God, I believe you're developing a sense of humor."

"I laugh a lot when nobody's looking."

Ryan got serious. "Lou, Nick Tenzi is slime, and we both know it. He's living in a fantasy of the past when the mafia carried real clout on the Coast. All that's left now are a few little hoods in their shrinking little islands. Their power is all in their imaginations. I want to clean up what's left. And what's left is Nick Tenzi."

"If you know so much about him and his operation, what do you need me for?"

"Dates, places, names. You've got the information that will nail him right now. We'll get him eventually, so why not do yourself some good and cooperate. There's no percentage for you in protecting him."

Ryan pulled out a package of Marlboros, lit one, offered the pack to Matchek.

"Do I have to tell you every time that I don't use those things."

"Oh, right, you don't drink, don't smoke, don't write on walls. No bad habits. Except, maybe the one that put you in here."

Matchek ignored the dig. "Isn't this where you offer me something for helping you people do your job?"

"You know how it works, Lou. We don't expect anything for nothing."

"So what's the bait this time, a condo in Florida and a new identity?"

"Hunh-uh. Not for killers. But we could make life a lot easier for you. There are softer places than Folsom to do your time. You cooperate and the Bureau could pull some strings, get you transferred to a medium security prison. You're never going to walk, but you don't have to spend you life on a metal stamping machine. You've got a little education. You could be doing nice clean work in nice clean surroundings. Play a little tennis, swim in the pool."

"Tennis is for faggots, and I never learned to swim."

"You're stubborn, Matchek. Worse than that, you're stupid."

The killer eyed the FBI man, focusing on the precise spot below his earlobe where a sharp swift blow could kill him. He said, "I may be all that, but I'm not a snitch."

With a sigh Ryan got up and walked to the door.

He rapped on the metal and nodded when the guard's eyes appeared. While keys jangled outside he turned back to Matchek.

"We'll get Tenzi, you know, with you or without you. This might be your last chance to help yourself by helping us."

Matchek answered him with a yawn.

The guard keyed open the door and let the FBI man out. Two more guards entered, cuffed Matchek's hands behind him, and led him back to his cell block.

* * * * *

The office of Warden Elmore Getchell considerably more festive than the interrogation room. Saucer-sized snowflakes were sprayed on the windows, inside the steel mesh. A holly wreath hung from the coat hook on the door. Christmas cards marched across the top of the row of file cabinets. Outside, the gloomy drizzle continued.

The warden himself had the ruddy cheeks and twinkly eye of a Dickens reveler. However, he was frowning now as he faced Merlin Ryan across his desk.

"So he still won't go for it," the warden said, in a dispirited voice.

"I'm afraid not. I've gone about as far as I can go with him."

"Damn. Having Lou Matchek in my prison is like having a ticking bomb. This was my second chance this month to get rid of him, and I lose again."

"Second chance?" Ryan repeated.

Getchell flicked his hand across a manila folder that lay on his desk. "The latest request from Fairhaven for volunteers specifically asked for Matchek. Don't ask me why, but I'd have been more than happy to comply, if only he'd gone along.

Naturally he didn't."

"What's Fairhaven?"

"It's an experimental facility down the coast run by Armand Vespa. We get requests from him occasionally for volunteers for some experimental program. So far no takers on this one."

"The name Vespa is familiar."

"He did a lot of work with traumatized Vietnam vets. Developed new procedures for rehabilitation. Got a congressional citation and a big federal grant to continue his work."

"What's he doing now?"

"All they gave us is a sketchy description. Something to do with brain implants. Now that I think about it, I can't really blame the cons for not signing up. Nobody wants some doctor poking around in his brain." The warden permitted himself a tiny smile. "Some of the comments we got back on our request forms were pretty funny."

"I wonder why they wanted Matchek specifically."

"Search me. He wasn't buying it for a minute."

"I'm not surprised," Ryan observed. "He may be a rotten human being, but the man is no fool. How does Vespa qualify for taking prisoner volunteers? I thought they weren't doing that any more."

"Political clout. His work for the V.A. made him powerful friends in Washington. We're really getting pressured to provide guinea pigs for him. Nobody seems to know exactly what he does down there. I hear it's easier to get into CIA files than into Fairhaven."

Ryan stubbed out his cigarette and stood up. "Happily, that is not one of my problems."

"Lucky you," said the warden.

* * * * *

"Merry Christmas."

That night Lou Matchek lay in the bottom bunk of the two-man cell and stared up at the sag of Clarence Robinson's fat black butt ten inches away. Something, he reflected, really should be done about overcrowding in the prison system.

He thought about Merlin Ryan and the offer he could never accept. He thought too about Nick Tenzi, 44 years old, short, cocky, still playing the gangland boss to an ever-dwindling audience. Today was not the first time someone had hinted that Tenzi set him up. And not for the first time Matchek wondered seriously how much truth there was in the accusation. If ever he found out for sure, Tenzi would die. One way or another Matchek would get out, find Nick Tenzi and kill him.

There was evidence, but no proof. You could not kill a man on a hunch. Once again he replayed in his mind the chain of events that had landed him in here.

The target was Ira Niedenfuer, a small-time union collector and professional rat who was in a position to do serious harm to Nick Tenzi. Matchek had collected his fee in advance, as he always did, and selected his own time and place for the job. To his surprise, somebody else got to Niedenfuer a short time before he did and dispatched the little fink using Matchek's favorite method, a bullet through the eye. To his even greater surprise, when he walked out of the house more cops than he had ever seen in one place converged on him, daring him to go for his gun.

True, Nick Tenzi would have been in a position to finger him, but why would he? Matchek was no threat. He was a well-paid craftsman, taking pride in his work, content with what he did. He had no ambitions to move into management. And yet his concentration shattered as Robinson rumbled into his cell-shaking snore. Matchek kneed him in the butt, and Robinson rolled over on his side with a grumbled protest. It was another hour before Matchek slipped into a dreamless sleep.

The line for breakfast the next day was enthusiastic.

During Christmas week the food was better than usual, the servers actually smiled occasionally, and the cons were as close as they could come to entering the holiday spirit. Matchek took no part in the general low-key conviviality. He did not like people in general, and he liked his fellow prisoners less than most. And knowing his reputation on the outside, most of them were content to leave Lou Matchek alone.

Up at the head of the line there was a sudden clatter of metal as somebody dropped a loaded tray. Voices were raised curses shouted. The men standing toward the rear of the line surged forward to get a better look. Matchek eased out of the line and made his way back through the pushing bodies away from the disturbance. He wanted no part of somebody else's trouble.

As he watched from the perimeter of the action, he sensed somebody moving in close behind him. Too close. Before he could turn a voice breathed in his ear, "Nick says hello."

The blow hit him just above the right kidney. It was something like a punch, but did not have the force behind it. An instant later the red-hot pain hit him and Matchek knew he had been stabbed. He whirled in time to see Vin Faccio draw back the prison-made shank for another thrust.

With the pain lancing from his kidney area down his right leg and up into his shoulder, Matchek locked his hands behind Faccio's greasy head and pulled his head down hard at the same time as he pumped up his left knee. The cartilage of Faccio's long, pointed nose crunched like a walnut shell as Matchek's knee drove it back into his skull. Faccio let out one high-pitched squeal and went limp. Matchek kneed him once more in the face and let him drop like a sack of manure.

Just before he blacked out, Matchek's mind clamped onto a single picture. A year and a half ago, on one of his rare visits to Nick Tenzi's home in the Hollywood Hills he had bumped into a man coming out who he hadn't seen around before. A greasy haired, long nosed hood named Vin Faccio.

Nick says hello.

Chapter 4

Gradually Jay Baysinger fought down the panic and slowed his pounding run to a jog and finally to a walk. He stopped when he reached the intersection of Lemon Grove and Glenoaks Boulevard.

He leaned against the rough stucco wall of a cleaning shop. To his surprise he was not even breathing hard. A man who took as little exercise as he should be exhausted by running a quarter of a mile, even downhill. Nothing was as it should be today, not even his own body.

He took the time to check his body. Lean, firm, well muscled. Why had he assumed it would fail him? Questions upon questions.

He stepped away from the wall and looked back up Lemon Grove Street. No demons followed, reaching for him with bloody talons. No monster stalked into view. No beast was chasing him. No threatening black limousine. There was nothing to hide from.

Nothing but himself.

Now what kind of a crazy thought was that? If he was going to make any sense out of this nightmare he was going to have to straighten out his thinking. He would have to take control of his life and knock off the panic attacks.

He pulled the sweaty shirt away from his skin

to give the air a chance to dry it. When he felt in control once more he shrugged into the jacket and began walking along the street, striving to look like a casual stroller. It took a mighty effort of will not to look over his shoulder to see if some fiend might yet be following.

The store fronts that lined the street were a monotonous collection of small shops—appliance repair, bargain furniture, video rental, auto parts. On the other side of the boulevard one sign triggered a memory. It was a colorful depiction of a cat holding a cocktail glass, done in neon tubing. The neon script below the cat read: *El Gato.*

He stopped in mid-sidewalk and stared over at the cinder block building. Mental gears hummed and meshed.

El Gato. The name meant nothing to him. But he knew the place. It should have been *Ernie's Kit Kat Grill.* Same street, same building, same neon cat. Wrong name.

Ernie's was as close as could be found in north Glendale to a typical neighborhood bar. It was a funky hangout where the white-collar residents between Glenoaks and the park could go and act like truckers relaxing between runs. It was a man's bar with deep ashtrays, free peanuts, a satellite dish for sports, and an air of good fellowship. The drinks were generous, the sandwiches were thick, the juke box was stocked with non-threatening oldies.

For Jay Baysinger, a moderate social drinker, Ernie's had been a refuge for the times when he and Kristy had one of their senseless fights. Such times, he realized, had been increasing lately. He could go into Ernie's, sulk quietly at the bar, and listen to the good natured banter around him until he felt better. By the time he got home, while nothing was solved, at least he and Kristy would be past the shouting stage.

But why the new name? When had that happened? He probed his memory and came up empty. Ernie could explain. Even though he owned the place, he spent more time behind the bar than he did at home. Ernie knew all the latest jokes and could settle bets on any sports event. Today maybe he could nudge Jay Baysinger's life back into balance.

The crowd would be mostly regulars. Ken Taylor, the commercial artist, John Forsmark, the high school coach, Lloyd Spears, the auto sales manager. *Somebody* in Ernie's was sure to know him. Somebody would provide a clue to what had gone wrong with his life.

He trotted across the boulevard at mid-block, ignoring the angry bleat of auto horns. The door into El Gato was offset slightly from the street and gave the impression you were entering a cave.

Inside the light was dim, accented by illuminated beer signs: *Miller Lite, Coors, Budweiser, Old Milwaukee.* Baysinger stood for a minute just inside the entrance, letting his eyes adjust to the gloom and trying to figure out what was different about the place. As the interior of the bar came into focus he realized that damn near everything was different.

The setup was the same—bar along one wall, booths on the other, juke box to the left of the door, restrooms all the way back and to the right. But nothing else was as he remembered it. There should have been a cozy dining area with the little square tables beyond the arch at the far end of the bar. Instead there were two pinball machines, three arcade video games, and a quarter-slot pool table in the center of the room, Two players interrupted their game of eight-ball to watch him. One was tall and whip-thin, the other blocky with the muscular build of an iron pumper. Their eyes were cold and speculative.

Tending the bar was not good old Ernie, the friendly sports authority, but an unsmiling Latino with a snake tattooed on the back of one hand. The juke box thumped with the Latino rock music called salsa.

Half a dozen men sat at the bar—dark-eyed, long-haired, dressed in T-shirts and jeans. The floor was sticky with spilled liquor. Cobwebs were visible in the shadowy corners. Like his street, his house, his own wife, the neighborhood bar was definitely not as he remembered it.

One of the men at the bar nudged his neighbor. Both turned to look at Baysinger. The look was not friendly. He wanted to shout, *Hey , I belong here! Who the hell are you?* He willed his muscles to relax, and crossed to the bar. There he took a stool well apart from the others. The tattooed bartender approached him.

"You want something?"

"What happened to Ernie?"

"I don't know no Ernie,"

"He owns the place. Or used to."

"No Ernie here. You want something or not?"

"Uh... uh ..." It was crazy, but he could not remember what he usually drank. He had been in here many times, and as recently as... damn, he couldn't remember that either.

"You okay, man?"

"Yeah. I'm fine. Give me..." His eyes flicked over the advertising signs. "a Bud."

The bartender hesitated a moment, studying him, then moved off to the cooler. Baysinger chewed his knuckle, tasted salty perspiration. He stood up and walked back along the bar to the men's room. At least that was still where it was supposed to be. He could feel the eyes of the pool players and the men at the bar following him.

The men's room was a welcome island of familiarity in the sea of skewed perceptions. Two urinals, a toilet stall, and a sink in the men's room. The odor of pine disinfectant was strong enough to make his eyes water. Baysinger stood at the urinal trying to bring his thoughts into some kind of order. Places, faces, recollections were not coming together. He finished and washed his hands, scrubbing at them with the pink powder dispensed by the wall-mounted canister.

He took the opportunity for a good look at himself in the mirror. He half-feared his face might have changed too, but it was familiar enough. Lean jaw, slight squint to the pale eyes, flecks of gray showing in the cropped brown hair. Yes, he knew the face. Why didn't his wife know it? Or his neighbor? Why didn't anybody know him. Jay Baysinger, age 34, born in Medford, Oregon. Attended UCLA, belonged to Delta Chi fraternity. Worked as ...

The bees stirred to life. What the hell was his job?

Something to do with a laboratory. He should remember that. He had been on his way home from work. Hadn't he? What the fuck was going on?

He cupped his hands under the cold water faucet, splashed his face. The bees quieted, but the tight feeling in his scalp did not go away. He dried his face with two paper towels and leaned closer to the glass. Using both hands he parted the hair where it began high on his forehead. On the scalp was a tiny scratch in the shape of a diamond. Half an inch by an eighth of an inch. No, not a scratch, a scar. The area around it was tender but not painful. *A recent injury of some kind?* The scar looked too precise to have been made by accident. Surgery?

Impossible. Baysinger's only operation was an appendectomy at age 15.

Frowning, he unbuckled his belt, pushed down his pants and briefs. The skin of his stomach was flat and smooth. No scar. But there *had* to be a scar. A red line as long as his thumb.

Baysinger had lived with it for twenty-two years. He ran the flat of his hand over his bare, unmarked stomach.

No scar.

The door to the men's room opened and one of the men from the bar came in. He *gave* Baysinger a suspicious glance and locked himself in the toilet stall. Baysinger hastily pulled up his pants and rebuckled the belt. He left the men's room and returned to his place at the bar. A sweating bottle of Budweiser sat in front of his stool with a glass.

"Dollar-fifty," the bartender said.

Baysinger nodded and reached for his wallet. Damn, he had forgotten, there wasn't any wallet. In a side pocket he found a crumpled wad of bills. He peeled away a pair of ones and lay them on the bar. He stuffed the rest of the bills back into his pocket and felt something else in there. A credit card. He pulled it out and squinted at the card in the dim light of the bar.

Not a credit card, a bank card. The kind used in an automatic teller machine. The name on the front in raised letters was Elliot Porter.

Elliot Porter?

He turned the card over. Written on the plastic in pencil was a four digit number. *6256.* It meant nothing to him. On the signature strip the same name was spelled out in a handwriting that was definitely not Baysinger's. *"Elliot Porter?"*

"You say something?" The bartender was looking at him strangely.

Baysinger shook his head, embarrassed that he had spoken aloud. He poured beer into the glass and took a long swallow. The taste was unexpectedly bitter, and he shuddered as it went down.

A hand touched shoulder. Beer splashed out of his glass onto the bar. He spun around on the stool, hands raised, ready to fight.

Chapter 5

"I'm sorry. I didn't mean to startle you."

"Kristy!"

She was wearing the same man's shirt and white jeans she had on at the house. Her eyes were soft and worried.

"I spoke, but I guess you didn't hear."

"No... I didn't."

"For a minute I thought you were going to hit me."

He looked down at his hands as though they belonged to somebody else, and lowered them to his lap. "Sorry. I thought. I don't know what I thought."

"Can we... talk?"

Baysinger nodded without speaking. Kristy sat down on the stool next to him.

The bartender came over and mopped the bar in front of her. "Something for you?"

She looked at Baysinger, then down at his glass. "I don't care. Give me one of those." She waited until the bartender returned with the beer, paid for it with a five dollar bill, then looked at Baysinger. "I'm sorry about what happened back at the house."

He glanced at the other drinkers, who had fallen silent. "Maybe we'd better move to a booth."

They picked up their beers and walked across the room. The bartender watched silently. The men at the bar resumed their conversation.

Baysinger settled uncomfortably on the scarred red vinyl seat and watched the woman across from him, waiting.

"First I want to get several things clear."

"Such as?"

"I do not know you. As far as I can remember, I've never seen you before. One thing for sure, you are not Jay Baysinger. Jay Baysinger is dead."

"So why did you follow me."

"There's something about you... something I can't explain. You know things you shouldn't know. That photograph. I took it off the piano years ago. I don't know when you could have seen it."

"Years ago?" he repeated.

"Yes?" she prompted.

"That's impossible. It was there just this ..."

"I was going to say this morning, but suddenly it didn't sound right." He chewed on a knuckle.

"You don't look anything like Jay, but in certain ways you remind me of him."

"What ways?"

"This place, for one. This was where Jay always came when we had a fight. It used to have another name."

"I know."

She reached across the table and tapped the knuckle of his right forefinger, lightly dented by his teeth.

"That's another thing. Biting your knuckle. It was a mannerism of Jay's when he was nervous. You did it just before you left the house. And again just now."

He stared down at his own hand. "I didn't know I was doing it. So what do you think it all means?"

"I don't know. At first I thought you were on something, or were some kind of psychotic."

"And now you don't?"

"No. You've got trouble of some kind, that's for sure, but you're no doper. And you're definitely mixed up, but you don't look psychotic to me."

"How can you be sure?" he asked.

"I can't with absolute certainty, but I do have a degree in psychology."

"I know that," he said. "UCLA."

She studied him closely. "How do you know that?"

He took a sip of beer and shuddered. Like everything else in his upside-down world today, the beer did not taste the way it should.

"That's where I met you," he said.

"No, you did not," she said firmly. "I met my husband at UCLA, but you are not my husband. I have no idea who you are."

"Okay. Let me give you a brief bio. My name is Jay Baysinger. I'm thirty-four years old. I was born in Oregon, moved with my parents to Los Angeles when I was 13. I went to North Hollywood High School. Straight-A student. Lousy in sports. Scholarship to Cal Poly, where I majored in psychobiology. Went to work when I graduated for IBI, International Biotech Industries."

He stopped abruptly and stared at her. "That's funny. A minute ago I couldn't remember where I worked."

"Go on," she said.

"We met while I was working at UCLA on a research project and you were a senior psych major. We were married right after your graduation, six years ago. Honeymoon in Hawaii. Lived in a series of apartments on the west side and in the Valley for a couple of years, then moved into the Lemon Grove house. Then I took a job... a job with ..." He faltered. "That's where it fogs up. "I'm not working at IBI any more, am I."

Kristy waved a hand impatiently. "Tell me about me," she said. "Jay Baysinger would know things about me."

"You're a California native, born in Encino. Your father was a dentist. Mother moved to Florida to live with her sister when he died." He looked down at her glass, "You drink an occasional beer, but prefer white wine. You like the ballet, studied dance when you were little. Love Clint Eastwood, hate Eddie Murphy. You drive a white Pinto, you're a registered Democrat. Want more?"

She shook her head. "I don't know what to think. You've got the facts basically right on Jay, except for your confusion about his last job. And you know a lot about me, but your time span is off. Jay and I were married nine years ago, not six. We moved into the house seven years ago. I haven't had the Pinto for two years. I'm still a Democrat, but in the last election I couldn't bring myself to vote for Dukakis."

"Who?"

"Michael Dukakis? Democratic nominee for President?"

"Wasn't that Mondale?"

She looked at him a long time. "What year do you think this is?"

"What?"

"Just tell me, what year is this?"

"Nineteen eighty-seven?"

"My friend, somewhere you went and lost three years. This is 1990, Sunday, March 11, 1990,"

"Oh, shit." The bees swarmed in his head again.

Kristy reached across the table and touched his hand. He looked up quickly. She smiled, but withdrew the touch.

"Let's see if we can't figure out what's going on with you. Where those three years went, and how you happen to know so much about Jay and me."

He chewed the knuckle of his forefinger, caught himself doing it, and grinned sheepishly, "Where do you want to start?"

"Anywhere you like."

He walked to the bar and paid for a second beer. He raised the bottle in a question to Kristy. She shook her head, no.

He came back to the booth, sat down, and began to talk.

Haltingly at first, then more freely he told of the first little signs that things were not as they should be. The street, the houses, his own house. Then the shock when he saw the *For Sale* sign and walked in to find a strange young man and a wife who didn't know him.

He paused to take a drink, shuddered, and pushed the glass away as a wave of dizziness passed over him.

"The beer isn't going down well for some reason."

"Maybe you'd better leave it alone."

"Tell me something, Kristy. Why are you here? Why did you come after me?"

"I told you. You need help."

"That's nice. Very humanitarian. But why me? Why a guy you never saw before who swears up and down he's your husband. A husband you tell me was somebody quite different. And has been dead a couple of years."

Kristy cocked her head and looked at him seriously. "Oh, you're different, all right, but in some ways you are like Jay. The Jay I remember from our happy days, before the marriage started going downhill. It's there in little mannerisms—the way you talk, the way you scrape the label off your beer bottle."

He looked down and saw he had indeed dug a furrow through the Budweiser label with a thumbnail.

"Sure, I want to help you if I can," she continued, "but I've got my own reasons for being curious about who you are and what your connection is or was... to Jay."

"So... got any ideas?"

"Nothing that makes sense. How about you?"

"Amnesia?"

"Doesn't hold water. That could explain the missing three years, but not the fact that you don't look anything like Jay."

"Plastic surgery," he suggested.

"Hunh-uh. They can do a lot of things, but they can't change the shape of the head, and they can't lengthen your legs. Anyway, what would be the purpose?"

"You got me. Trying to hide something that

happened three years ago?"

"What happened was that Jay Baysinger died."

"That, now, is damn hard to accept. How am I—is *he* supposed to have died?"

"An accident. There was an explosion and a fire where he worked. Jay was the only one in the room at the time. There was supposed to be an investigation, but nothing ever came of it. I've never been completely comfortable with that."

He was silent for a long time, then he said, "I can think of one other possibility."

"Well?"

"This whole thing is a conspiracy, and you're all in on it. You, the kid in the cartoon shirt, Howie Denbo."

"And all the other neighbors? And the Salvation Army?" She stifled a laugh. "I'm sorry, I know it isn't funny, but that conspiracy idea is just so outlandish. What in the world would be the motive?"

She giggled again, and it was so infectious he found himself honestly grinning for the first time since he'd found himself on his curiously changed street. "Maybe you want to have me committed so the lot of you can split up my fortune?"

This time she laughed out loud. "I don't know about you, but Jay Baysinger never had enough money at one time to get a month ahead on the car payment."

He sobered. "About that kid, that Ross Somebody, who is he?"

"Just who he said he is. Goes to school at Occidental, puts in a couple of nights a week at the clinic."

"He was acting pretty protective."

"Why not? He's got a crush on me. Nothing

serious. But I'll tell you something, Jay would never have noticed." She was thoughtful for a moment. "That brings up a point—I can't call you by his name. It makes me feel queasy. Is there something else you'd like to go by?"

He shrugged. "All I've got on me is a plastic card belonging to an Elliot Porter. I don't feel like an Elliot Porter."

"You don't look like one, either." She pursed her lips. "How about Jack? Just until we find out who you really are. It's close to Jay, but it doesn't carry any memories for me."

He tested it. "Jack. I guess can live with that."

"Any choice for a last name?"

"Gannon. It was my mother's maiden name." Kristy stared at him.

"What's the matter?" he said.

"Jay's mother's name was Hauser. Where did you come up with Gannon?"

He blinked. "I don't know. It just popped out. Now when I think about it, the name doesn't mean anything to me."

"Well, it's our first breakthrough. From now on, until we find out different, You're Jack Gannon."

"Call me Jack."

Kristy looked him over. "This is it."

"Do you have any other clothes?"

"You're a little taller, and thinner, but I think you can wear some of Jay's things. They were going to be the next load for the Salvation Army. Unless you object to wearing a dead man's clothes."

He gave her a tight smile. "As far as I'm concerned, they're clothes, remember?"

"Then let's go home and you can try them on."

He closed his eyes suddenly as a wave of nausea swept over him.

"Are you all right?" she asked.

He pushed out of the booth and stood unsteadily. "Excuse me for a minute."

He headed back toward the men's room, his stomach cramping, the floor undulating. Kristy watched him with a worried frown.

The two young men at the pool table also watched. As he made his way unsteadily through the door they nudged each other and smirked, then switched their attention to the booth where Kristy sat.

"Did you check out the ass on that one when she came in?" said the taller of the two pool players.

"In those stretchy white pants? I couldn't hardly miss it, man." He grabbed at his crotch. "Speaking of hard, I got something here that would fit nice and snug in that ass."

The taller one lay his cue carefully across the table.

"Let's go say hello."

His companion, shorter and solid in a black muscle shirt grinned and nodded. He carried his cue with him as they swaggered toward the booth.

Chapter 6

"Can you hear me, Matchek?"

The words of the warden filtered to him through a haze of pain and medication as he struggled back to consciousness in the prison hospital.

Getchell's Dickensian face, round and ruddy and happier than a sickroom visitor should be, looked down on him.

He had managed a nod and gagged on something. He blinked and saw a rubber tube that taped to his forehead to drain fluids out through his nose.

"I hear you." His voice gargled with phlegm. He tried to clear his throat and fell into a coughing spasm.

"Well, listen good because mine may be the last voice you hear." The warden made no effort to disguise his festive mood.

"They tell me there's a better than even chance you're going to die."

Matchek grunted a noncommittal answer.

"If it makes you feel any better, Vin Faccio has preceded you to the great beyond. Not that it matters now, but killing Faccio wouldn't have counted against you. Enough people who saw it tell us you crunched him in self-defense." Getchell winked. "That was a nice move, by the way. Where'd you learn it?"

Matchek made a gargling sound. He was starting to feel the pain through the anesthetic fog.

Warden Getchel tried for a sad face. "We've done all we can for you here, with what we've got to work with. Budget cuts and all. You know how hard it is these days to pry money for prisons out of Sacramento."

Matchek tried to turn his head away, and groaned with the effort.

"Hurts, does it?" Getchell said. "I'm not surprised. Faccio was no amateur. He knew what he was doing. Put the blade right into your kidney, nicked the iliac artery. If he'd severed that sucker the way he intended, you'd have died before you hit the floor. Never would have had a chance to shove his nose back into his brain." The warden shook his head in admiration. "That was some move, all right."

Matchek summoned his small reserve of strength. "Go to hell."

"Sure, Lou, I understand. You'll want to be alone at a time like this. I just stopped in to say goodbye." The warden started out the door, then halted and came back, as though he had just thought of something else. "Like I say, you're probably going to die. Unless ..." He let it hang.

Matchek could not hold back. "Unless what?"

"Unless you want to think about the Fairhaven Project. We still have that request for you from Dr. Vespa."

"The brain fucker."

"Hey, call him what you want, but he's got all the modern medical facilities down there that we can't afford. You might die anyway, but at Fairhaven you'd have a chance. And you'd be a whole lot more comfortable."

"Chance for what?"

"To stay alive, Lou. When you come right down to it, that's what we're all scrambling for, isn't it. The most miserable dirt bag on Death Row would a thousand times rather live out his days there than eat chlorine gas in the San Quentin Green Room." He waited for some sign of affirmation from Matchek, finally went on anyway when he got none. "I'll be honest with you. Vespa is having a tough time getting a volunteer for this one."

"Too bad."

"If it wasn't for that, and the fact that he specifically asked for you in the first place, they'd never consider taking somebody in your condition."

"Why me?" Matchek got out.

"Damned if I know. But why look a gift horse in the mouth? At Fairhaven you'd get top quality care. Be one hundred percent healed before they phased you into the project."

"Fuck with my brain."

"If you want to call it that. Hey, I'm only bringing it up as an option. A way for you to stay alive. The whole thing is completely voluntary. The choice is yours, Lou. Maybe your last."

The pain had hold of him now like a lobster claw clamped onto his lower back. He ground his teeth.

"Hurts I'll bet." said Getchell. "Nah. I like it."

"Tough guy to the end, eh?" The warden checked his watch. "The doctor will be along in ten or fifteen minutes. Maybe he can give you something for the pain. Try to hold on. Well, I'd better be getting back to work."

"Warden!" It came out like a bark. "Lou?"

"I'll do it."

The warden nodded solemnly, trying to conceal the grin as he went out. "I'll get the papers together."

In a few minutes the doctor came in and shoved a hypodermic needle into his arm. Matchek relaxed and let his mind float as the lobster claw loosened its grip.

* * * * *

When Getchell had first approached him about the Fairhaven Project he had treated it as a grim joke, an attempt by the warden to cut down the prison population by one hard case. The other inmates were no more receptive. Long-timers who would let them pump unknown substances into their blood streams in exchange for a few years off their sentence wanted no part of Dr. Armand Vespa. The project was spoken of as some kind of Frankenstein experiment where your brain would be scooped out and something else plopped into your cranial cavity.

Lou Matchek knew, of course, that this was an exaggeration, still he had not the slightest intention of letting anybody tinker with his head. He would stay in Folsom and take his chances. Vin Faccio's misdirected shank had drastically altered the situation.

In the few minutes the warden spent talking to him in the prison hospital Matchek weighed his options, such as they were.

He knew Getchell was telling the truth about his chances of dying here. He had seen too many sorry results of prison surgery. If he did live, he would likely spend the rest of his days as a pain-wracked cripple. It was worth a shot to go to Fairhaven. Once he was there he would let the doctors patch him up, play the game as long as he could get away with it. Meanwhile, he would look for a way out of the place. It had to be easier to crack than Folsom. Getting out was an obsession now. He had a big, big score to settle with Nick Tenzi, and he couldn't do it while he was inside.

The way he added it up, he had nothing to lose. If worse came to worst and he could not make it out of Fairhaven, he still wasn't going to let anybody mess with his head. Before they came at him with the skull saw he would just say he'd changed his mind.

The system was not going to let them fuck with a man's head without the man's permission. Like most cons, Lou Matchek knew how to use the system when it suited his purpose.

Within an hour of his talk with the warden the consent papers were brought to his bedside. He scrawled a signature, and before nightfall he was bundled into the back of an ambulance heavily sedated, and driven south to Santa Barbara and the Fairhaven Facility.

* * * * *

The first few days there were spent in a pleasant narcotic haze. People came, people went, his sheets were crisp and clean, all his needs were taken care of. Gradually he became more aware of his surroundings. He was in a small, antiseptic room with fresh flowers on a stand and a soothing landscape print on the wall. There was an array of electronic gadgetry attached to his body that provided a continuous readout to a monitor screen at the head of the bed. His body was immobilized to keep in place the various tubes and electrodes. All things considered, he was not uncomfortable.

His first shock came when, after a dreamless sleep, he opened his eyes and saw Death.

That was his first impression of the tall, skeletal figure with the skull face, that stood silently at the foot of his bed. Then Death spoke.

"Good morning, Mr. Matchek. I am Dr. Armand Vespa."

The rush of relief was so exaggerated that Matchek smiled at himself.

"Did I startle you?" the doctor said. "I thought you were somebody else."

"We are going to start reducing your medication, so you may be feeling a bit more pain, but I'm pleased to tell you that the prognosis is quite favorable."

"I'm not going to die?"

"You are not going to die."

"So what... is. going to happen to me?"

"We will discuss that as recovery continues. your job is to get better."

Meanwhile, sedated though he was, Matchek caught the false ring of Dr. Vespa's attempt at a warm bedside manner. "You do your job," he said, "I'll do mine."

Matchek's recovery was not easy, but it was steady. As he became more alert he grew to appreciate his second floor room in the infirmary building at the Fairhaven Medical Complex. It was a comparative luxury after the months spent cramped in with Clarence Robinson at Folsom. It did not matter that he was still a prisoner. That situation, he assured himself, was temporary.

On an evening in February he lay stretched

out on the narrow hospital bed, making himself as comfortable as he could lying on his stomach. The pain of the wound in his back had eased to a dull interior ache, but the scar had been slow to heal.

According to the surgeon, there would be recurrent bouts of pain from nerve damage, but the kidney tissue would regenerate. All things considered, Matchek felt he got off lightly. An experienced blade man like Faccio seldom missed.

His chin was propped on the pillow in a position that allowed him to watch a small television he was given a week after his arrival. Currently on the screen was the manic host of a popular game show. He was grinning fit to kill as a female contestant bounced up and down in orgasmic glee at winning several thousand dollars.

Matchek hit the *Mute* button, silencing the woman. It gave him a feeling of control that brought great satisfaction. At Folsom he had no choice but to watch what his fellow inmates wanted to watch. That was invariably mindless cartoons or cop shows during which they would cheer enthusiastically for the bad guys. Yes, he decided Vinnie Faccio had done him a favor when he slid that shank into his kidney.

The medical treatment here, as Warden Getchell had promised, had been first class. At Folsom Matchek had stayed religiously in shape, working out daily in the weight room and running in the yard whenever he had the chance. Now his physical condition aided in his recovery, which, after two months, was almost complete. Time now to quit wallowing in the soft life and start planning his escape.

His plans were intensified by an encounter

one evening in his room. Matchek had been doing his stretching exercises when a square built man with heavy black eyebrows and moustache entered without knocking. He wore a plain dark suit, but might as well have had *COP* stitched across his chest. Outside the open door stood two men in sharply pressed tan uniforms. One was a tall, blond athletic type, the other a chunky black man with the scars and the grace of an ex-boxer. They remained watchful and silent, mean looking black batons clipped to their belts.

Matchek lay back and looked at his visitor. "You don't know me, do you," the man said. "No."

"My name is Gunther Tork. I'm captain of security here at Fairhaven."

Matchek's eyes narrowed. He sensed that was not going to hear good news.

"Name doesn't register either, huh?" A shake of the head.

"What about Ismael Quierdos?"

Then it all came together. Four years ago Quierdos was a high official in the Panamanian government. He supplemented his considerable salary by cooperating with a Columbian cartel that helped supply the U.S. demand for cocaine. When he got too greedy the Colombians decided to erase him. Quierdos heard about it and fled to Miami where he contacted the Drug Enforcement Agency with a proposition. He would finger some important dealers in this country and Panama in exchange for protection and asylum. The DEA agent charged with protecting Quierdos was Gunther Tork.

"I see you're making the connection," Tork said.

"Doesn't mean a thing to me," Matchek lied.

"I don't expect you to admit it. You were never

charged with that one, but I know damn well it was you who blew Quierdos away. It had your trademark. One shot through the eyeball."

Matchek gave him a blank look.

"Someday I'd like to know how you got to him."

"I don't know what you're talking about."

Actually, it had not been all that difficult. A small bribe here, a diversion there, and he had walked into the hotel room dressed as a waiter, carrying the magnum of champagne Quierdos had just ordered for himself and his girlfriend. The job was completed so neatly that the girlfriend, preening in the bedroom, didn't realize what had happened until she found her lover with an empty eye socket and the waiter long gone.

"Maybe someday you'll feel like telling me." Tork's smile had no humor.

A sudden thought hit Matchek. "Did you have anything to do with bringing me here?"

Tork showed his lower teeth. "You're not complaining, are you?"

"Just asking."

"Enjoy it while you can, gunman. In the meantime, I'll be watching you."

It was the last conversation he was to have with Gunther Tork until much later.

As he continued to improve, Matchek was allowed considerable freedom within the grounds. Not that they were so careless as to let him walk around alone. Not while Gunther Tork was Captain of Security.

A medical aide named Elliot Porter was assigned to accompany him whenever he left the hospital building. And always, floating at the edge of his vision, was one or both Tork's constant watchdogs. The tall blond one, he learned, was named Barry Spencer, The stocky ex-pug was Leon Krebs. They were under orders not to fraternize, but over the weeks an subtle bond grew between the guards and the prisoner.

Elliot Porter, under no such restrictions, was thrilled by the assignment to hang out with a real life hit man. He was an eager, balding young man who chattered on oblivious to the fact that Matchek barely responded. While giving minimum attention to his companion, Matchek used the walks with Porter to inspect the facility and the grounds, paying special attention to the security system. As he suspected, it was designed to keep people out rather than keep them in. Despite the surveillance by Spencer and Krebs, Matchek foresaw little trouble when he was ready to go. He discovered early that one of Vespa's rules was no visible guns in the complex. He considered that a gift for which he would someday thank the good doctor.

The entire Fairhaven Facility covered maybe ten acres.

There was an administration building with offices and laboratories, the fully equipped infirmary, a gymnasium, living quarters for the staff, and several smaller structures. The grounds were well tended with artfully spaced groves of trees and flower beds. A man-made stream wandered through the shrubbery.

The main gate was guarded 24 hours and locked electronically. The perimeter, as much of it as Matchek could see in his daily walks, was marked by an eight-foot masonry wall. It would be no deterrent to a man in good physical condition.

Lou Matchek was a careful planner. In his business to be impetuous would be folly. Thus, it was his intention to work out a careful blueprint for escape before making his move. His intention, however, was derailed by a combination of events that occurred during one of his late afternoon strolls with Elliot Porter.

They were following a path along the bank of the stream, Porter babbling away as though they were old friends. The concept of friendship was foreign to Matchek, but he let the young man rattle on. No purpose would be served by puncturing his fantasy that they were pals.

With Porter's conversation mentally tuned to a low drone, Matchek turned his attention to a cinderblock building across the stream and beyond a shielding grove of aspen. It was notably isolated from the rest of the facility. He had wondered about it before, but Porter had never offered an explanation. As he watched now, the door burst open and a man in a white shirt and dark pants ran out and headed for the trees waving his arms wildly. Even from this distance Matchek could see the man's mouth gaping wide, but his screams were muffled by the lapping of the stream against the smooth stones along the bank.

Matchek turned to Porter, but the younger man was deep in describing some movie he had seen, oblivious to the events taking place two hundred yards away. When he looked back he saw two uniformed security men charge around the side of the cinderblock building and overtake the running man. They closed in, one on each side of him. One of the guards gripped his hand in a pain compliance hold and they led him back toward the building.

Porter was now watching too. "What goes on?" Matchek asked.

Porter looked away quickly and tugged at his arm. "That's the North Annex. Come on, we don't want to get in the way of the guards if somebody's acting up."

Matchek held back and watched the guards hustle the now docile man inside.

"Let's move along," Porter said.

"Who was the guy they yanked back into the building?"

"Nothing to worry about. One of the droolers just got excited. They'll calm him down."

"Droolers?"

Porter clapped a hand over his mouth. "Forget I said that. That's what the staff calls them, but Dr. Vespa hates the term. We get a lot of charity patients in here. Some of them can be helped, some can't. The North Annex is a ward for the incurables. The ones who are beyond anybody's help."

"The droolers," Matchek said.

Porter winced. "Actually, they say it's the most comfortable ward of any on the grounds."

"Yeah, I saw how comfortable they were making that guy."

"Let me give you some advice, Lou," Porter said seriously.

"Forget what you saw."

Chapter 7

Matchek shrugged to let Elliot Porter know that he had already forgotten the incident of the North Annex, but he tucked the whole scene away in a corner of his mind for possible future use.

As they started back across the lawn toward the main cluster of buildings Porter said, "You know, Lou, I'm going to miss these walks and our little rap sessions."

A warning signal sounded in Matchek's head. "You leaving?" he said, deliberately casual.

"No, I just mean after Wednesday I'll be assigned somewhere else and you'll, well, you'll be, well, you know," he finished lamely.

"No, Elliot, I don't know. What's going to happen Wednesday?"

The young man looked pained. "God, I'm really talking too much today. I just assumed the doctor told you."

"Told me what, dammit?"

"You're scheduled for the O.R. on Wednesday. God, I shouldn't have said anything."

So soon? Matchek was reminded of the method of execution by guillotine. The prisoner was marched out and positioned with his face against a vertical plank. While he was still wondering what the plank was for it tilted violently forward, carrying the prisoner with it and dropping his neck under the descending blade. *Bang!* It was all over and the poor wretch never had a chance to worry about it.

He said, "Oh, sure, Vespa told me about that. I just didn't think about you being reassigned."

"Well, that's just automatic considering," Porter grew vague, "...considering..."

Matchek's mind whirled. *Considering the fact that he might very well die on Dr. Vespa's operating table.* There would be no time now to work out the detailed plan he wanted. If he was going to do anything, it had to be at the first slight opportunity. It had to be improvised, and it had to be now.

He clutched his side just below the rib cage and gave a convincing impression of a man trying to suppress a cry of sudden pain.

"What is it?" Porter said, alarmed.

"I don't know. Something... Aaaahhh!" He sagged and seemed about to go to his knees.

Porter reached out to catch him. "Here, hold onto me, Lou. I'll help you up to the clinic."

Matchek flinched away from his touch. He shook his head and make little moaning sounds as he bent sharply at the waist.

"Adhesions," Porter said. "Hang on, I'll go get help." He took off at a run across the lawn toward the infirmary.

Matchek waited, still doubled over, until Porter had turned once and looked back. When he ran on toward the main building Matchek straightened up, whirled, and sprinted in the opposite direction.

He splashed through the stream, which was no more than knee deep at the middle, and scrambled up on the opposite bank. He glanced back, saw no sign of Elliot Porter or any pursuit, and pounded on toward the aspen grove. As he reached the trees he heard a series of short, sharp beeps on an air horn that could only be an alarm. Too soon. He had hoped to make it to the wall before they came after him, now he was trapped inside.

Through the trees he could see men running toward him from the main complex. He recognized Krebs and Spencer among the leaders.

Nothing to do now but go on. He burst out on the other side of the aspens and headed for the brush out behind the North Annex. There he might find some concealment while he worked his way toward the perimeter wall.

He ran in a crouch along the windowless side of the building. Ahead of him a loud rushing sound overpowered the alarm horn. He pulled up suddenly at the sight of a man in a tan security uniform. Too late. He had been seen.

There were two of them. Probably the pair he had seen grab the running man a few minutes ago. One of them held the nozzle of a fire hose while the other stood by. The loud stream of water battered a cowering figure in dark pants and white shirt—the runner.

Lined up along the back wall of the building were more than twenty people. They were mostly men, mostly young, but a few elderly and women were included. All wore the same black and white outfit as the man under the hose.

They were arranged in two ragged ranks in front of an open back door, to witness the punishment. The bodies of some jerked or drooped from lack of muscle control. Emotions they could not express distorted some of the faces. Some smiled witlessly at a secret joke. Merely empty.

Other faces, the most unsettling of all, were The droolers.

One of the guards shouted and gestured toward Matchek. The other cut off the water. Matchek wheeled back in the direction he had come and saw the pursuers bursting from the trees and pounding toward him. Calculating the odds against him, he spun back and ran at the two guards who stood between him and the wall. They had their batons ready now and were advancing to meet him.

He veered off and headed for the two rows of watchers. With all other avenues cut off, he shoved his way through them and into the building. As though he had given a signal, the people followed him in.

Someone hit the metal door at the rear of the building and it swung shut with a hollow clang. Matchek stumbled to the center of the room, where he came to a sudden stop.

He was in a single high-ceilinged room like a gymnasium with a reinforced door at either end. A jumble of furniture—couches, chairs, stools, hassocks—was scattered about in no discernable order. Along the two side walls were narrow wooden cots, maybe twenty on each side. The people who had followed him in formed a semi-circle facing him.

Matchek turned slowly, searching the faces for one with the light of reason. A man began to laugh in a high-pitched out-of-control voice. Another took it up, then another until the room echoed with mindless clattering laughter.

Someone outside began to pound on the door at the front. At the sound the droolers began to move toward him. Instinctively he backed away until his shoulder blades hit a wall. Shuffling, limping, sidling, stalking, they came on. A woman with bright red hair and no upper teeth reached him first. She plucked at his sleeve, her face close to his. A pale, soft looking young man with an unlined face gently took the woman's arm and pulled her away. The others gabbled senselessly and closed in.

"Hey!" Matchek shouted, surprised by the smallness of his voice in the big room. "Hey, hold it!"

They answered him in a chorus of whimpers, grunts, growls, giggles, snorts, and moans. Like some hellish Broadway chorus they closed around him, their arms reaching, fingers wriggling.

With a crash the front door burst open. Spencer and Krebs burst in and jumped to either side of the doorway. Spencer blew a long, shrill blast on a whistle.

The people circling Matchek stopped. The reaching hands fell away and they retreated. Their wordless mutterings changed in tone but were no more comprehensible. In their mad, unreasoning eyes flickered some primal emotion. Anger? Fear?

Matchek had no time to wonder about it as the two guards who had been out in back charged in past Spencer and Krebs. They rushed forward and seized his arms. Matchek struggled in their grasp as one raised his baton.

"Hold it!" The basso voice of Leon Krebs froze the guards and silenced the droolers. More softly he said, "You just come along quiet, Mr. Matchek. Doctor don't want you all marked up."

Matchek knew there was a time to fight and a time to give it up. Krebs and Spencer took charge and hustled him out of the building without resistance. The two fire hose operators stayed behind to deal with the droolers.

He was taken back through the grove of aspen trees, across the stream, and back to the infirmary. As they led him inside he saw Elliot Porter standing off by himself, his eyes hurt and accusing.

*****

They took Matchek back to his room in the infirmary with no conversation from anyone. Left alone, he stretched out on the bed, folded his hands on his chest, and waited to see what would happen next.

Nothing happened. Not until the sky outside his screened window began to darken. Then the door opened and Dr. Armand Vespa entered. The chief of Fairhaven wore his habitual long white lab coat and white shoes with silent rubber soles. His hair was combed straight back, accentuating his widow's peak. He produced what passed for a smile, showing long yellow teeth that only made his bony face more skull-like.

"You gave us quite a little excitement this afternoon." Matchek said nothing.

"I deduce, from your exertions today, that you are feeling better."

"Improving slowly," Matchek said.

"Maybe a little faster than that," Vespa said. "Your wound was a complicated one, but two months is more than adequate for convalescence."

Matchek gave him a shrug, waiting for the man

to get to the point.

"They tell me you were quite athletic in your little adventure."

"Do they?"

"You displayed some acting ability too. Young Mr. Porter. was convinced you were having a seizure of some kind. Apparently I overestimated his competence. Or perhaps I underestimated yours."

Matchek had enough of the game. He said, "I hear you scheduled me for the operation."

"Well, yes, tentatively. Will next Wednesday be convenient?"

Matchek ticked off the days on the calendar in his head.

This was Friday. They would surely be watching him more closely now, but he still had four days for to watch for the one mistake that would leave him an opening.

"Why ask me?" he said. "You're the doctor."

"Because you are a volunteer, Mr. Matchek. In spite of your little, um, excursion today, we must remember that you are here on your own volition. I believe you were given a copy of the papers you signed."

"Oh, sure."

"So you know nothing here will be done without your consent."

"Got it," *You lying bastard, you're up to something.* "Of course, should you now decline to continue, we would have no option except to return you to Folsom. I suspect Warden Getchell would not be pleased."

I care a lot about what pleases Warden Getchell, Matchek thought.

He said nothing.

"I will take your silence to mean that we still have your consent. Therefore, it is time for us to discuss the operation you will undergo. In general terms for now. Later we can get into the details. I want you to understand exactly what we hope to accomplish here."

Matchek knew what he wanted to accomplish, and it had nothing to do with Dr. Vespa's Frankenstein dreams. He assumed an attentive expression and let the man talk.

The doctor's long articulate fingers moved incessantly, tracing the edges of his lab coat, stroking each other, slipping in and out of pockets as he spoke.

"The surgery itself is simple and safe. We make a small incision in the scalp, open a tiny aperture in the frontal bone. Then a minimal curettage, microscopic implantation, and it's all over."

"That sounds like a lobotomy."

Vespa's restless hands tensed. The black eyes sparked deep in their bony sockets. "It is *nothing* like a lobotomy. Prefrontal lobotomy is a crude, antiquated operation we have never considered, will *never* consider at Fairhaven. I want that thoroughly understood."

"Right. No lobotomy." He would have to be careful, Matchek thought. Armand Vespa acted like a man who could be easily nudged over the edge.

The pale hands resumed their restless wanderings. "There will be certain, er, modifications in your behavior pattern." The skull smile blinked on and off. "In your case I think we can agree that almost any change would be considered a definite improvement."

Matchek kept his face expressionless. He wanted Vespa to go away so he could concentrate on getting out of here. Still, he was curious about the weird operation they had planned for him, the operation he had no intention of submitting to.

"What kind of... modifications are we talking about?"

"That is something we can discuss in the days before the operation. Right now I just want to sketch in the overall picture."

"How about sketching what's in this for me."

"You, my friend, stand to benefit enormously. If we succeed to the extent I anticipate, the professional killer Lou Matchek will effectively cease to exist."

"Say again?"

"The psychopathic personality that the state of California saw fit to lock up forever will be gone. Vanished. Kaput."

"Dead?"

The skull smile flashed again. "Interesting you should say that. As far as the outside world is concerned, Louis Matchek is exactly that. Dead."

The emphasis he put on the word made Matchek shiver. "Maybe you could explain?"

"We felt your notoriety might attract unwelcome publicity to Fairhaven. So we worked it out with Warden Getchell so the news was released that Louis Matchek had succumbed to wounds received in a prison fight. The story had the necessary grain of truth, you see. When no relatives came forward you were buried in the prison cemetery."

"Not funny," said Matchek.

"Trust me, it is no joke."

"What the hell did you do that for?"

"It will be to your eventual benefit," Vespa

said. "If we are successful, you will be, for all practical purposes, a new man."

Matchek's mind raced. If he was officially dead, the threat to send him back to Folsom was a hollow one. Likewise, these people had no intention of letting him opt out of the project. He spoke quickly before Vespa could realize he had made a slip.

"Are you talking witness relocation? New name, ID, that stuff?"

"Much more than that, Mr. Matchek. Much more. The important thing in your case is that there will be no reason to hold this new man in prison."

"You're saying I'll be set free?"

"The legal details are not in my province, however as an end result your freedom is quite possible. There will, of course, be an extensive post-operative program."

"How extensive?"

"We want to be certain the process has achieved our goals. It is, after all, still experimental. That's why I could consider only a volunteer who, shall we say, had little to lose."

"And in case anything goes wrong, there's always the North Annex." As soon as the words were out Matchek knew he had said too much.

Vespa's busy hands stiffened. His bloodless lips turned down in a death's-head snarl. It was the barest fraction of a second, but the impression on Matchek was chilling. Matchek knew he had said too much.

"I'm really sorry you had to see that. The unfortunates housed there can give a wrong impression if a visitor is not prepared."

Matchek glanced over toward the window. they would."

"I can see as how it is really nothing for you to concern yourself with."

The fires subsided in Vespa's deep-socketed eyes and he was in control again. His hands stroked one another. "No, Mr. Matchek, you and I have far more relevant matters to discuss."

Maybe, thought Matchek. *Maybe. But I'm going to be damn careful what I do and say from now on. Before they turn me into a drooler, I'll die trying to get out.*

Dr. Vespa made a notation in a black covered notebook, gave him another of those ghastly smiles, and went out.

That night Matchek lay wide awake, staring at the hairline rectangle of light around door to his room. The decision of when to go had been made when he saw the sudden look of animal fury on Vespa's face. It would have to be tonight.

He reviewed the exits he had mentally charted during his walks with Porter. Silently he recited the schedule he had seen the guards following. The best time to make his move, he decided, would be 3 A.M. Four and a half hours from now. Dark night of the soul.

At 11 o'clock, as Matchek feigned sleep, the door opened.

Through slitted lids he saw Dr. Armand Vespa gesture silently to someone behind him, Before Matchek had a chance to react, a muscular attendant strode to his bedside, seized an arm, and plunged a hypodermic needle into the vein at the crook of his elbow.

Matchek opened his mouth to protest, but a swift paralysis spread through his body and silenced him before he could speak.

As a warm cocoon of silence closed in around him, he heard Dr. Vespa's words.

"Sorry to disturb your rest so abruptly, but considering the events of the day, I've decided to reschedule your surgery for tonight. I hope it doesn't inconvenience you. Sleep well, Mr. Matchek."

Chapter 8

Kristy felt the eyes of the two pool players crawling over her body. She was not unaccustomed to men looking at her, but the men she dealt with in her daily life were, well, cleaner than these two. She moved deeper into the booth.

In the past two years this section of Glenoaks Boulevard had deteriorated. Ernie's, the comfortable neighborhood bar, had been one of the first of the old places to go as the economic and ethnic makeup of the street changed. When the 7-11 store replaced Gilbert's Deli and was robbed almost immediately Kristy stopped walking down here. Her neighborhood four blocks up Lemon Grove was so far unaffected, but she was not unhappy to be moving away.

From the corner of her eye she saw that the pool players had left their game and were sauntering toward her now. One of them still carried his cue, the other hooked his thumbs on either side of his belt buckle, brown fingers directing attention toward his crotch.

Kristy became acutely conscious of the jeans hugging her upper thighs, and the way the soft linen of the shirt lay across her breasts. She wished she had changed into something less provocative when she decided to follow the troubled man from her house.

As soon as the thought arose, Kristy angrily

dismissed it.

It was Sunday, she was packing, and she had dressed for comfort. Damned if she was going to take any of the blame for the prurient minds of a couple of grungy punks.

She looked back toward the men's room. Jay, no, *Jack* had not looked well when he went in. He would probably not offer much physical protection. Still, she wished he would come out before these two started trouble.

The pool players were at the booth now.

"Buy you a beer?" The taller of the two stood with his bony pelvis thrust forward, grinning down at her with macho confidence.

"No thanks."

"Like to buy us one?"

"Sorry."

"You're not very friendly." He turned to the burly one holding the pool cue. "She's not very friendly." And to Kristy again, "Maybe you need an introduction? Okay. This is my buddy Rijo. He don't talk much, but he's okay. And you can call me T.J. How's that?"

Kristy kept her face impassive. She gave the talkative one the coldest look she could muster. "My friend is corning back in a minute."

"Oh, yeah, your *friend.* We saw him. Don't be too sure he's coming back. He barely made it to the john. I think he's one sick puppy."

"He'll be back," Kristy said firmly.

"Okay, fine, we'll wait for him. Meantime we all get acquainted." He slid into the booth next to her. The one called Rijo sat across from them.

"Please go away." Kristy winced at the way her voice quavered when she was trying to project firm, righteous womanhood.

"Hey, that isn't friendly at all."

The one called T.J. rubbed a hand up and down her thigh.

Kristy slapped at it, but he only clamped onto her flesh through the denim.

"Stop it!"

Kristy looked toward the bar. The other patrons and the bartender were studiously ignoring the action in the booth, though she knew they were well aware of what was going on.

The young man next to her followed her glance. "Hey, these are *our* friends, sweetness. You're the one's out of your territory here. Why don't you just be nice and we can all have some fun. There's a little room the other side of the pool tables. Got a nice couch and everything. Me and Rijo can show you a real good time. Can't we, Rijo."

"Oh, yeah," said the muscular one, speaking for the first time. He made kissing sounds at her.

"So you got a choice, sweetness. You can come along with us or you can come along with us."

He grinned across at Rijo, who laughed appreciatively.

Kristy began to feel the cold clutch of physical fear.

* * * * *

Jack Gannon.

He stared at his image in the streaked men's room mirror and tried to relate the face to the name. He still dripped the cold water he had dashed on to ease the lurching nausea.

Jack Gannon.

It would take some getting used to. He still thought of himself as Jay Baysinger, but the evidence was piling up that he was not. So how could he remember all the Baysinger stuff, even if sometimes imperfectly? No answer. And if not Baysinger, who was he, and what was he doing here? Again, no answer.

Jack Gannon.

The bees started up in his head again. The made-up name would have to do for now. The questions he could worry about later, one at a time.

He dried his face, scrubbed his fingers through his cropped hair, and walked back out to the bar.

The pool table was unoccupied. One cue lay across the green felt, the balls were still in place. There was an ominous look to the suspended game.

He started back toward the booth where he had left Kristy.

The pool players were there with her. Trouble. "Don't!" Kristy's voice.

Gannon quickened his step and crossed the floor to the booth. The tall thin pool player was leaning all over Kristy, talking into her ear. The blocky one was sitting on the opposite side, gripping his cue.

"What's going on?"

The pool players looked up at him with arrogant confidence. "Hey, look, Rijo, the sick puppy is back. You feeling better, man?"

Gannon's eyes narrowed. His posture did not change, but under the wrinkled clothing his muscles tensed. "I think you boys better leave."

The thin one erased his sneering smile. "Why don't you fuck off, man. We're having fun here, and you ain't invited."

Kristy looked up at him. "Be careful, Jack."

"You heard her, man. Be careful. Now be a good boy and fuck off."

The bees rose in a swarm. He had the feeling of being drawn up and out of his body by some powerful force. He watched himself play out the scene below, while at the same time he was not a part of it.

"I been nice to you so far," said T.J. "Now I'm giving you one last chance to go before you get hurt."

Gannon seized the younger man by the shoulder. T.J. jerked free, his elbow spilling the beer that remained in Kristy's glass.

"Rijo!"

The muscular youth grunted to his feet, and using the tip of the cue as a prod, forced Gannon back into the other room and up against the pool table. He reversed the cue and jabbed Gannon repeatedly in the stomach with the heavy end. "My friend don't like being touched. We think you better go now."

With Rijo holding her in place, and seeing Gannon in trouble, Kristy called to the men at the bar. "Can't somebody help?"

The drinkers and the bartender were frankly watching the action now, but gave no sign that they hear Kristy's appeal.

Back at the pool table Rijo drew back the cue to drive the butt one more time into Gannon's midsection. This time Gannon's left hand struck like a cobra, grasping the end of the stick.

"That's enough, *maricon!*"

The muscular youth stiffened at the insult. He jerked the stick free of Gannon's grasp. "Now you gonna get hurt, *puto!*"

While he spoke Gannon's right hand reached behind his back over the green felt of the pool table and grasped the first ball it found. Rijo was into his backswing when Gannon slammed the nine ball into the side of his head. There was a muffled bone crack, and Rijo's eyes rolled upward, leaving only the bloodshot whites showing. The cue stick clattered to the floor. Rijo crumpled as though a safe had dropped on his head.

Up at the booth T.J. saw his friend go down and slid quickly out of the booth to face Gannon. His teeth were bared in an ugly grimace. "You gonna pay for that, man."

Gannon walked toward him, hands loose at his sides, eyes bright. In a swift, fluid motion T.J. produced a knife and flipped out a four-inch blade.

"I'll cut your heart out, man," said T.J., but his voice lacked conviction as Gannon continued to advance.

When they were within arm's length of each other T.J. lunged, holding the blade low, going for the belly. Gannon feinted a fraction of an inch to his right. When T.J. went for it, he reversed himself, seized the wrist and elbow of the younger man, and spun him around. The knife clattered to the floor. T.J. screamed like a girl. Gannon slammed his forearm against the edge of the table. The ulna and the radius bones snapped with a report like a double pistol shot. Gannon switched his grip to take T.J.'s chin in one hand with the other clamped behind the youth's head. His teeth showed in a terrible grin as he prepared to snap the boy's neck.

Kristy spoke quickly. "Jack, don't. You've hurt him enough."

Gradually the planes of Gannon's face softened. His separate self floated back from wherever it had gone and slipped into the body. The bees slowly subsided. He threw the whimpering young man aside.

To Kristy he said, "You're right." Looking at the dark faces along the bar, he added, "It's time to go." He took her arm, helped her out of the booth, and led her from the bar.

Behind them the only sound was the moaning of Rijo as he held his ruined arm.

* * * * *

Back at the house on Lemon Grove Kristy sat on the couch and watched the man she called Jack Gannon. He stood at the side of the picture window, peering out at the edge of the drapes.

"Expecting somebody?" she said.

"I hope not. How about you? What happened to you friend?"

"Ross? He gave up on me and went home when I told him I was going after you. He thinks you're crazy."

Gannon turned from the window and faced her. "You're a psychologist, Kristy. Do you think I am crazy?"

"Sit down, Jack."

He hesitated a moment, then walked over and sat in a chair facing her. "I'm still getting used to that name."

"The name's not important. I think we should

talk about what happened in the bar."

He sat down and massaged his forehead. "You scared the hell out of me," she said.

"Sorry."

"No, I'm glad you came back when you did. But I've never seen anybody react so swiftly and so violently. I know for sure Jay Baysinger wouldn't have done it."

He chewed on a knuckle, realized what he was doing, and smiled sheepishly. "To tell the truth, I don't know what got into me. One minute I was feeling sick in the men's room, the next I saw those punks hassling you and something clicked in my head. It was like somebody else took control. I was probably lucky they didn't mangle me."

"No." Kristy shook her head. "They never had a chance. You were so cold and efficient, I really thought you were going to kill the one with the knife. The way you snapped his arm..." she shuddered. "Where did you learn to fight like that?"

"I don't know. Kristy, I honestly don't know what happened to me. Maybe it was the beer. Maybe I can't handle it any more."

"Maybe you, whoever you really are, never could handle it. You've got to remember, you're *not* Jay Baysinger."

"Jack Gannon." He managed an unconvincing grin. "I'm trying."

Kristy leaned forward to touch him on the knee, then quickly withdrew her hand. "I know you are. Don't worry, we'll get it straightened out. Why don't you go clean up while I sort through Jay's clothes to see what I can find for you."

His smile became more relaxed. "A shower sounds good. I am getting a little gamy."

Kristy watched him walk away. He headed unerringly for the bathroom, as though he lived here. The sharp reminders of Jay Baysinger were unsettling, yet she received other disturbing messages from this man. She pushed away the conflicting emotions and busied herself sorting Jay's clothes.

Many of them were laboratory whites—pants, jackets, smocks—not appropriate for Jack Gannon. There were a couple of three piece suits that might serve. While Jay's social attitudes were correctly liberal, his dress was unimaginatively conservative.

On the rare occasions when he dressed casually, he always looked uncomfortable.

Kristy set aside the suits, a tweed jacket, a pair of gray slacks, dress shirts, T-shirts, and boxer shorts. Jay had unusually small feet for a man. He wore a size 7-AA shoe, which surely would not fit Jack Gannon.

At the bottom of the pile she found a wildly flowered Hawaiian shirt. Purchased in Honolulu: Jay had worn it on their honeymoon, then put it away forever. The seven days they spent in the islands had been the one frivolous period of their marriage. And at the end of the week the strain of being away from his work began to show on Jay. Kristy often caught him frowning off at some unseen problem, and his laughter became forced and brittle.

On their return Jay had plunged eagerly into the techno biology experiments that he loved, and that Kristy only vaguely understood. She reflected grimly that their marriage, like the old joke, had started sliding downhill immediately after the honeymoon. There was a time when she thought, foolishly, that having a child might revitalize them. Jay's angry reaction when she told him she was pregnant had been like a knife in her heart.

The abortion had gone off with no complications. No physical complications, anyway. For a long time afterward Kristy could not look at other women's babies without feeling a gnawing emptiness.

Along with the tiny life inside her, the abortion had effectively ended their sex life. She and Jay still slept in the same bed, they still copulated, Jay still reached his quick, silent climaxes. But Kristy, scrupulous now in her ingestion of birth control pills, found that her participation was not really necessary. If Jay detected the change in her response, he never mentioned it.

She vividly remembered the day almost four years ago when he had come home early from the lab, bursting with news.

"You'll never guess who I talked to today."

"Who?" said Kristy, not really caring. "Armand Vespa."

It took her a moment to place the name. "The man who worked with brain-damaged veterans?"

"He's a lot more than that. Dr. Vespa has done pioneering work in the field bioengineering and psycho-technology."

"That's nice." Any interest Kristy once had in Jay's field had long since evaporated. Her own work with troubled children seemed to her much more relevant than exploring the links between technology and the human mind.

Jay was oblivious. "And I can hardly believe this, he wants me to come to work with him at Fairhaven."

"That's up north of here isn't it?"

"Santa Barbara. This is the kind of an opportunity I've dreamed of. Me working with Armand Vespa! I can't believe it!"

Daily commuting would be out of the question, so Jay made immediate arrangements for living quarters at Fairhaven. He and Kristy talked of looking for a place to live in Santa Barbara, but their heart was not in it, and they never got beyond the talking stage.

Kristy remained in the house on Lemon Grove and continued her work at the clinic. Jay came home on weekends at first, but soon stopped coming altogether. Kristy did not protest. In truth, being alone was a relief. The exchange of letters slowed and finally stopped.

Then, a year after he went to work there, came the fateful telephone call from Fairhaven telling Kristy her husband had died in an unfortunate accident.

A polite cough snatched Kristy back to the present. She looked up to see Gannon standing in the archway between the living room and the hallway. He wore a bath towel around his waist. His cropped brown hair glistened wetly against his scalp. His body was lean and long-muscled. Kristy caught herself staring at the bulge in the towel where his legs joined. She looked quickly away.

"I didn't mean to scare you," he said.

"I was daydreaming. Here, I've picked out a few things you should be able to wear. Why don't you go in the bedroom and try them on?"

He took the clothes from her and their fingers touched. A jolt seemed to travel through her nerve endings straight to her vital organs.

Gannon smiled. There was nothing of Jay

Baysinger in that smile. Kristy felt a surge of desire that she had thought was long forgotten.

Embarrassed, she pulled her hands away. "I hope you'll find something that will fit."

"I'm sure I will," he said, and left her.

Kristy listened for a moment to the man moving about in her bedroom, then got very busy with the box of old clothes.

Chapter 9

The Fairhaven Medical Facility does not appear on any road map. No signs along the California coastal byways point out its direction or give its location. Outside the circle of people actively engaged in medical or biological research, the existence of Fairhaven could as well be a rumor.

Only short segments of the old Coast Highway 101 remain alongside the eight-lane interstate that has replaced it. Off one of these segments south of Santa Barbara, a narrow county road angles to the northeast. It climbs ever more steeply into the Sierra Madre Mountains. Nearing the crest an even narrower private road branches off and twists the last two miles up, clinging to the. steep sides of wooded canyons, to the landscaped acreage of the Fairhaven Facility.

The private road ends at a gate of wrought iron scrollwork set in a high masonry wall. A uniformed member of Gunther Tork's security force occupies a wooden gatehouse outside the wall.

Beyond the gate lies a cluster of off-white buildings with roofs of red tile on a rolling, tree-studded lawn. The complex suggests a small college campus more than a government-funded medical facility.

It was to this peaceful mountain scene that Merlin Ryan came on a crisp March morning. After identifying himself at the gate he drove on to the small parking lot in front of the largest building. There he left his rented Ford and produced his FBI identification once more for the guard in the lobby. From there he was directed to Dr. Armand Vespa's office in the rear of the building, where he now sat in the anteroom.

The room was done in a white and pale blue combination that strove for cheerfulness but succeeded only in looking cold. The chair Ryan occupied was unyielding white vinyl that refused to accommodate itself to his bony rear end. The room had half a dozen such chairs and a matching couch. All, save the chair in which Ryan sat, were currently unoccupied. The round, glass topped table in the center of the room was empty and cold as an ice rink. The precisely placed wall prints were geometric pen-and-ink renderings of ugly buildings. With no ashtrays in sight, Ryan kept his cigarettes in his pocket. It was not a room to make a visitor comfortable.

Lacking the opportunity for any other activity, Ryan squirmed in the chair and observed the woman who occupied the white desk outside the door to the inner office. It was, all things considered, not an unpleasant way to pass the time. The young woman had hair the rich color of a horse chestnut, fluffed out from her head in a casual style that must have taken hours to perfect. Her eyes were dark brown, her lips a plump pomegranate. Her chest was a marvel that defied gravity. A nameplate on the desk read: *Victoria Fellows.*

Every few minutes Miss Fellows looked over at Ryan and smiled, displaying a set of beautifully capped teeth.

"I'm sorry there isn't something for you to read, Mr. Ryan. Dr. Vespa doesn't like magazines out here. He thinks they clutter up a room." Victoria Fellow's voice was a contralto purr.

"No problem."

"I can offer you a cup of coffee."

"That sounds good."

"It's de-caf."

"On second thought, never mind."

"I used to drink real coffee too," she confessed. "But it kept me awake half the night."

"That so?"

"Mm-hmm. I live alone, so there wasn't anything to do but watch late-night television. I got to know those love line commercials by heart."

"Love line?"

"You know." She made her voice even huskier and sexier. "*Hi. I'm Taffy. And I'm waiting to talk to you right now. I'll talk about anything you want to. Anything at all. Call me.*"

Then they give you a 976 number and in little tiny letters it tells you it will cost two dollars a minute." She shook her well-coifed head. "What do you suppose they talk about to make it worth the price?"

"I wouldn't want to guess."

"How about a nice glass of ice water?"

"What? Oh, yes, thanks."

Victoria Fellows took a fresh glass from a drawer and poured water from a stainless steel carafe as ice cubes tinkled merrily against the sides. She carried the glass over and leaned down to hand it to Ryan, giving him the full benefit of her matchless breasts. She stood close to his chair while he drank and smiled his approval.

"So you're with the FBI."

"That's right."

"You don't look like an FBI man."

"So I've been told."

"I'd have guessed you for..." She placed two fingers against her cheek and inclined her head. "...a writer, maybe."

"Is that good?"

"It is for me. I like literary men."

"I guess you'll have to keep looking."

"Are you staying in Santa Barbara?"

"For tonight, at least."

"You won't find much to do in town after dark. I know, I live there."

"That's all right. I'm not much of a night clubber."

"Neither am I," she said. "Not since I cut out the caffeine, anyway. I usually just have my little dinner, watch some TV and go to bed. Alone."

"Sounds comfortable."

She looked thoughtful. "You know, I just had an idea... do you like spaghetti? With home-made clam sauce? Fresh clams?"

Ryan held up his left hand and waggled his ring finger. "It sounds delicious, but I'll have to say no thanks."

"Married, huh? Happily?"

"Most of the time. Happy enough so I don't want to mess up."

"She's a lucky woman." Victoria Fellows gave him a more sedate smile and returned to her desk. "Dr. Vespa should be ready for you in about five minutes.

He keeps everybody waiting the same length of time."

"That's all right," Ryan said. "I'm used to waiting." He sat back and tried not to stare at Miss Fellows's breasts. He concentrated instead on the door where neat gold letters spelled out: *Dr. Armand Vespa, Director.*

On the other side of the door Dr. Vespa snapped off the tiny television monitor where he had watched the failure of Victoria Fellows's attempted seduction of Merlin Ryan. It was possible he would have to replace her with a younger girl. Still, she had proved invaluable in extracting information from other visitors. It was possible that Ryan was immune. Certainly, he was not a man to be taken lightly. Dr. Vespa closed the drawer that held the small television monitor. His long, pale fingers tapped a somber rhythm the dark, polished wood of his desk.

Unlike the room where Merlin Ryan sat waiting, Armand Vespa's office was done in dark hues with rich woods and fabrics. His desk was a shade lighter than black. The walls were paneled in solemn oak. A single file cabinet, also oak, stood within his reach. Matched prints of sailing vessels battling stormy seas hung on the wall. Just inside the door a glass fronted case displayed a collection of deadly looking 18th century surgical instruments. The one softening feature of the room was the window directly behind the desk.

Dr. Vespa swiveled in his chair toward the window and allowed himself a moment to enjoy his favorite view—the campus like grounds of Fairhaven. The soft rolling lawns were velvety green, clipped to within a millimeter of his specifications. The gentle brook, specially diverted from Lake Cachuma, wandered among the precisely spaced groves of spruce and aspen.

Fairhaven was more than a place to work for Armand Vespa. It was his home, his kingdom, his life. He had personally laid out the grounds, designed the buildings, supervised every step of the construction.

The facility amounted to a reward from a grateful government for Dr. Vespa's work with Vietnam veterans. He had accepted only those suffering the most severe mental trauma, those who were judged beyond help from more orthodox treatment.

Vespa's innovative methods involved a combination of psychiatric treatment, drugs, hypnosis, and surgery. The results, when successful, were spectacular. The debilitating memories were replaced by pleasant, calming, generic mental pictures. Men who had been written off as hopeless cases were restored to functional lives. When the treatment was unsuccessful, well, the patient was no worse off than when he came in.

With no war to provide traumatized patients, Vespa had taken in selected cases of the deinstitutionalized insane, known charitably as homeless. With their conditions often exacerbated by drugs or alcohol, they seldom made good subjects. Likewise, he had little success with an appeal through the prison system for volunteers. He now had cause to wish he had abandoned that effort before he had ever heard of Louis Matchek.

Dr. Vespa turned back from his window view. Recent events had put his domain in serious jeopardy for the first time. He was ready to fight to save what he had worked for all his life. He would defend Fairhaven in any way, and to any extent necessary.

He thumbed a button in the intercom. "Please send Mr. Ryan in."

Vespa sized up the agent as he entered the office. Not an imposing figure, surely. Unruly shock of red hair, sport jacket that bagged at the elbows, checked shirt that probably came from Sears. A little above average height, long limbed, inclined to a slight stoop. However, the doctor was experienced enough not to judge a potential adversary by his appearance. Something in the mild hazel eyes said *Do not underestimate me.*

"Have a seat, Mr. Ryan. You are my first visitor from the FBI. Have you been shown around the grounds?"

"Afraid I don't have time for the tour, Doctor. From what I saw, it's a nice looking place."

"We try to keep it that way." The doctor's hands folded themselves neatly on the desk before him. He regarded Ryan from the hollows of his eye sockets. "But I don't suppose you came here to discuss the aesthetics of Fairhaven."

"No."

"Shall we get to your business then?"

"Lou Matchek," said the FBI man. "I want to know two things. One, what was done to him here? Two, where is he?"

The skin over Vespa's knuckles whitened. He showed no other reactions. "So you have heard about Mr. Matchek's unscheduled departure. A most unfortunate occurrence. I'm surprised the news reached you so quickly."

"We have our sources," Ryan said. "What we don't know is the exact nature of the experiment you performed on him."

"Actually, there is nothing mysterious about it. It's an extension of my work with dysfunctional memories. We merely severed certain sensory retention loops in the prefrontal lobe and replace them with more benign memory circuits."

"You make it sound as easy as a tonsillectomy."

"Not that simple, perhaps, but neither is it the 'brain transplant' you might read about in the tabloids."

"So what would be Matchek's mental condition now?"

"That is difficult to say. Our intention was to keep him under observation for a period long enough to observe the effects and deal with them as necessary. The severed portions of the cerebral cortex might regenerate, for instance, reviving some of the old instincts. The implanted circuits might decay or malfunction. These are things we could monitor and adjust under controlled conditions."

"Conditions which you no longer have," Ryan said. "Unfortunately." Vespa steepled his fingers, touched them to his pale lips. "I'm not clear on the outside concern over what is essentially an internal matter."

"Maybe I can explain it to you. Warden Getchell is concerned, because a convicted killer is now at large, and he is indirectly responsible. He was, you remember, persuaded to falsify a report of Matchek's death. The Bureau is concerned because it's coming up budget time, and there are those in Congress who would love to involve the FBI in a scandal. And I personally am concerned."

"You personally?"

"Lou Matchek has been kind of a special project of mine. He has information I have been after a long time. If you have any ideas about his whereabouts I'd appreciate your sharing them."

Vespa tried a disarming smile. The effect on his skull face was not pleasant. "At this point in time, I'll have to admit I have nothing to share. I assure you that every effort is being made to locate Mr. Matchek and bring him back safely."

"How, exactly, did he escape?"

"That is not a word we like to use in reference to our patients."

"Doctor, I can't waste time with semantics. Lou Matchek is a coldblooded professional killer. He was here because you specifically asked for him, and you pulled some political strings to get him. You assured everybody that your security system was good enough to keep him here. What happened?"

Two red spots appeared on the tight skin over Vespa's prominent cheekbones. "What can I say? The system misfired. It happens. This was our first unscheduled departure in the twenty years we've been here."

"So what happened?" Ryan said again.

The doctor's hands stroked each other. "I'm afraid I can't supply any details. Mr. Matchek was still under post-operative sedation. It was virtually impossible for him to walk away."

"But that's what he did," Ryan said.

"Yes," Vespa admitted. "I'm afraid that's what he did."

Ryan was silent for a long moment. Then he said, "I don't suppose there has been any public announcement of the escape."

Vespa flinched at the word. "Naturally not. Considering the fact that Louis Matchek is officially dead, it would be embarrassing for many people."

"To say the least," Ryan agreed. "'Coverup' has become a nasty word in Washington."

"It's too early to worry about the news getting out," Vespa said. "I am confident we will have him back in a matter of days."

"Mind telling me how you propose to do that?"

"We have an excellent security force here captained by Gunther Tork."

Ryan looked up quickly.

"You're familiar with him?"

"By reputation. He was with the DEA. Left them rather suddenly after some ugly business in Miami."

"I am aware of that. Whatever his past, Captain Tork has performed most efficiently at Fairhaven. I have full confidence that he will succeed in returning Mr. Matchek." The doctor rubbed his fingertips softly together. "I am wondering, Mr. Ryan, just how the FBI happens to be involved at all in this affair."

"Officially, Doctor, the Bureau is *not* involved. As a Special Projects agent, I am more or less freelancing on this."

"Indeed?"

"That's officially. Unofficially, I can tell you I have been given certain authority, such as the power to subpoena your records."

"That won't be necessary, Mr. Ryan. I'll instruct my staff to cooperate in providing whatever materials you may need."

"Good. I'd like to start with a complete record of

Matchek's activities, everything he did, everything that was done to him from the moment he was transferred here from Folsom."

A bony forefinger traced the line of the doctor's lips. "I think that can be arranged. By, say, the middle of the week I can have the material collated and ready for you."

"Not acceptable."

"I beg your pardon?"

"I need it right away."

"Today? Sunday?"

"You have a problem with that, Doctor? From what I could see the facility seems to be fully staffed."

"No problem, Mr. Ryan. If it is that urgent, I'm sure we can accommodate you. In fact, I'll walk you down to Records myself and instruct the people there to give you whatever you want. Many of our files are on computer, of course. I presume you are conversant with computers."

"I know the fundamentals."

"Then let us get started. After all, we have the same objective—the return of Louis Matchek as quickly and quietly as possible."

"'Quietly' meaning no media involvement."

"I would hope not."

"On that point, Doctor, we definitely agree."

Chapter 10

Dr. Vespa left Merlin Ryan sitting at a small desk in Records with a stack of file folders in front of him and a computer terminal humming at his elbow. Back in his own office he could not find his usual comfort in viewing the Fairhaven Grounds from the broad window.

It would take Ryan several days to work through the complicated paths he had set up, and the essential data, the information that could be damaging to Fairhaven, was effectively concealed. However, Ryan was not a fool, and it would be most unfortunate somehow if he were to locate Matchek before Vespa's people found him.

The intercom sounded its soft warble. "Yes?"

"Captain Tork is here," the modulated voice of Victoria Fellows.

"Send him in."

Gunther Tork filled the doorway with shoulders that looked as wide as his 5 feet 8 inches of height. His black hair was brush cut, his heavy brows pulled together in a perpetual scowl. He marched across the room to stand at near-attention before the director's desk.

"Any progress?" Vespa said without preamble.

"Not so far. Nobody saw him leave. Apparently he scaled the wall and walked down the road to the Coast Highway. There he could have caught a ride."

"*Apparently! Could have!* I expect more from you than suppositions, Captain."

"Yes, sir."

"In which direction might he have traveled on the highway, Captain? North or south?"

"There's no way of telling. I'm working on it."

"Oh? How?"

"My people are questioning anybody with access to the highway for several miles from where the Fairhaven road feeds in. We're asking if they remember a hitchhiker of Matchek's general description."

"You did not, I hope, mention his name."

"No, sir."

"And your results to this point are zero."

"I'm doing my best."

Vespa slammed the desk with the flat of his palm. "Do better! You were, after all, instrumental in bringing him here."

"Yes, sir."

"And you do understand the importance of finding this man and bringing him back?"

"I think I do, Doctor."

"I want to be very sure you do, so I will reiterate. Louis Matchek, depending on his mental condition, may be in a position to destroy Fairhaven and everything I have worked for here. The false story of his death is only one of the problems he could cause. He has undergone the implant process, which we are in no way ready to publicize. Most critically, he has seen the North Annex and its residents."

"I have my man's report on the incident," Tork said. "Security measures at the North Annex will be tightened up."

"Yes, now that the damage may very well have been done."

"Maybe he didn't know what he was seeing."

Vespa spoke with deadly calm. "Lou Matchek is not a stupid man. In our conversation he made it clear that he had guessed the function of the North Annex. That was my reason for the immediate scheduling of his operation. His encounter with the North Annex residents was an incredible oversight on the part of Security, but as long as Matchek was in our control, the damage was correctable. Now, I need hardly point out, he is no longer in our control. He is loose, out there somewhere. If he talks about what he has undergone and what he has seen, it will be calamitous. Never mind that this Matchek person was of no value to society, quite otherwise, as a matter of fact. And never mind that the work we are doing here could be of incalculable benefit to the world. If he talks, misappropriation of government funds will be the least of the charges we will have to face. Add kidnapping, false imprisonment, medical malfeasance, murder. We do not have the luxury of time. There is an FBI agent looking for him too. I have stalled him for the moment, but he is too shrewd to be delayed for long."

Tork's black scowl deepened. "But with the operation and all, how much will Matchek remember?"

"We have no way of knowing. This was the first time the entire operation was performed as I conceived it. The results are not wholly predictable. Our tests were scheduled to begin on Saturday morning. Until then he was supposed to be sedated. And under constant watch. Apparently, he was not as sedated as we thought. Friday night he walked out. Just... walked out." The last words were snapped off like the crack of a whip.

"One of my men should have been assigned to him full time, not that fool Elliot Porter."

"It was important to gain Matchek's confidence. We could never have managed that with one of your uniformed goons shadowing him. Mr. Porter had achieved something of a rapport with Matchek. Or so I believed. He will be dealt with in his turn. I had already planned to discuss with him the blunder of letting Matchek stray too close to the North Annex. And he should have verified the sedation Friday night."

"So Matchek just cold cocks the guy and strolls away." Tork snorted, happy to switch the focus of Vespa's anger. "I hope Matchek at least gave him a good shot."

"Porter's headache is nothing compared to what I have in store for him. But let us not shift all the responsibility onto him. It is Security that should have foreseen and prevented this debacle, and Security, Captain Tork, is your assignment."

Tork stiffened his posture. "I'm aware of that."

"You have one priority now—get Matchek. You were largely responsible for bringing him here. Now you bring him back. Or silence him... but him."

"Yes, sir!" Tork stopped just short of saluting. He spun on a heel and marched out, his shoulders barely clearing the door jamb.

Vespa sat alone for several minutes. His fingers tapped a martial rhythm on the gleaming desk top. Then he rose suddenly and stalked out past Victoria

Fellows. He climbed the stairs to the second floor, walked to the rear of the building, and entered a small room with a couch and two chairs. Elliot Porter reclined on the couch with an ice bag pressed to the back of his neck.

"How are you feeling, Porter?"

The young man got to his feet. "Much better, sir. A grade three concussion is all."

Vespa let him stand, holding the ice bag. "I've read the report of Mr. Matchek's sudden departure. I'd like to hear your version."

"It happened so fast, there isn't much I can tell you."

"Try."

Porter cleared his throat. "Well, it was the regular late check. About three o'clock. I looked into the room through the view screen. Lou... Mr. Matchek was sitting on the bed hunched over. He appeared to be in pain."

"'Appeared to be,'" Vespa repeated with cruel emphasis.

"Yes, sir. I-I could hear him moaning. I knew he was supposed to be sedated, so I unlocked the door and went in."

"Instead of summoning backup personnel, as is clearly spelled out in the procedures, you unlocked the door to Mr. Matchek's room, and you went in. Alone."

Porter's eyes flicked around the sterile office as though searching for an emergency exit. He found none.

"It didn't seem... I mean, he'd never been difficult before... I just didn't think—"

"You just didn't think." Vespa bit off each word

and spat it back at the young man. He let fifteen seconds of silence elapse, then snapped, "Go on."

Porter was now sweating freely. He brought the ice bag to the back of his head and quickly took it away again. "I went into the room, started toward the bed. Suddenly he stood up, and something hit me in the back of the head. I don't remember anything else until I came to, maybe an hour later. My clothes were gone, I was on the floor. I called downstairs and gave the alarm."

"Ah, yes, you gave the alarm. An hour after Matchek had left us. Closer to ninety minutes, according to the report."

"It was hard to judge the time accurately."

"Yes, I suppose it would be. I think, Porter, while you recover from your, er, wound, and until we decide on your future here, you will be relieved of your normal duties."

"I think I'll be all right by tomorrow, Doctor."

"Let's leave that decision up to me, shall we."

"Yes, sir." Porter hesitated. "Uh, one thing, Dr. Vespa." The glittery black eyes stabbed into those of the young man.

"Yes?"

"When he took my clothes he left my wallet behind, but took the cash, about 40 dollars, and my ATM card."

"So?"

"The cash is gone, but I, well, I foolishly wrote my code number on the ATM card. I have several thousand dollars in my savings account. He could draw it all out."

"I see. And are you suggesting that the card be

reported lost or stolen?"

"Well... yes."

Vespa took a step closer to the young man. The shadowed eyes glittered in their deep sockets. "Mister Porter, you are aware of the sensitive nature of the work we do here?"

"Yes, of course."

"And you have been briefed on need for secrecy concerning our operations?"

Porter nodded unhappily.

"Let us assume for a moment that you report this card of yours stolen. Let us further assume that Matchek attempts to use it. The bank computer identifies the card as stolen. Matchek is taken into custody. He is questioned. He talks. An investigation follows. No one at Fairhaven, none of us, Mr. Porter, want that. Am I right?"

"You're right, sir." Porter instinctively leaned back to avoid the black laser glare of Vespa's eyes.

"So I suggest you prepare to write off any amount Matchek may withdraw from your funds. I would hope we will have him back here before he can do too much damage."

Porter could only nod while swallowing to clear his throat.

With no further conversation Dr. Vespa walked out of the room and returned to his office on the first floor.

There he sat stiffly in his high-backed swivel chair and stared down at his long pale hands. He arranged the papers and the single pen on his desk into a strict geometric pattern. He sighed. What was done could not be undone. From now on it was a matter of damage control.

Throughout his life, he reflected, when things were difficult he was always alone. Anytime there was a reward or a prize, plenty of others were around to share. But in times of trouble, he had finally to rely only on Armand Vespa.

He could not recall a time when he had not been isolated.

Possibly he had once been a normal, gregarious child, but he could not remember such a time. All through school he was shunned by his classmates because he looked, and acted, "different." They had names for him—Skull Face, Phantom, Mr. Bones. It was in the darkest years of the Great Depression, his family had more pressing worries than their son's alienation. He retreated to books and solitude.

By the time he had earned a medical degree at the age of 21, Armand Vespa was known more for his brilliance than his abysmal ugliness. Except, of course, in the snickering remarks behind his back that people thought he didn't hear. He knew what they called him, but now he didn't care. He was clearly their superior.

Dr. Vespa spent little time speculating about the direction his life might have taken, had he been more of a normal child.

He preferred to look on his ugliness as a challenge that led him to his considerable accomplishments. By age 24 he had earned several advanced medical degrees and had published in the most prestigious journals. Before his thirtieth birthday he was recognized as a top authority on the brain, and was prominent in the study of electro-biological response mechanism.

One entire room in his living quarters was full of

awards and citations. It gave Vespa a sensual pleasure to walk through that room positioning and stroking the mounted plaques and certificates of honor. Still missing was The Big One—the Nobel. And it was not out of reach, could the current project be salvaged. It was his Dream.

With Lou Matchek at large, the Dream was in jeopardy. The doctor's eyes burned in their deep sockets. The Dream must be saved, no matter what the cost.

Chapter 11

"Well? What do you think?"

The newly christened Jack Gannon stood in the doorway with his arms spread wide. He was wearing one of Jay Baysinger's gray three-piece suits and a white shirt, open at the collar. He shifted his weight, and the pants started to slide down his hips. He grabbed them with one hand.

Kristy stifled a laugh. "A bit loose around the middle, but if you cinch up a belt they'll stay on. Anyway, they'll do until you can get some new things."

His eyes grew serious. "Does it bother you seeing me in these clothes?"

"Not really. Does it bother you wearing them?"

"Why would it? As far as I'm concerned they're mine. I thought they might stir up old feelings in you."

She shook her head. "I lost any real feeling I had for Jay a long time ago. His clothes are just... old clothes."

"You sure?"

"I'm sure." She was thoughtful for a moment. "There are things about you that remind me of him, or there were at first. Not so much now. You seem to be changing little by little. It's like there's another personality trying to get through."

"Maybe something like that is going on."

Gannon frowned. "My brain keeps flashing pictures and names I seem to know, but don't understand. The thing is, I'm still carrying around a lot of Jay Baysinger." He unbuttoned the shirt and peeled it off. "You put too much starch in these."

"Jay liked a lot of starch."

"He did? Now why didn't I know that?"

"There are big gaps in what you know about Jay."

"So it seems. For instance, I know I... *he* had an appendectomy at age 15. I can remember the pain in my right side, the ride to the hospital, the anesthetist telling me to count backwards. I remember it all distinctly." He rubbed his flat stomach. "But I don't have a scar."

"So I see."

"And when I was taking a shower I found some other scars that shouldn't be there."

"Really?"

"Really. Want me to show you?"

The conversation was getting uncomfortably close to flirtation. Kristy tried to deflect the growing excitement she felt.

"I'm not into scars."

"What does turn you on, Kristy? I remember where you really liked to be touched."

She moved close and stopped him with a hand on his lips. "You're Jack Gannon, remember? I don't want to hear another man's memories of me coming from you."

Without warning his arms went around her. She found him surprisingly strong as he pulled her against him. His chest was hard and hot against her. She took her hand away from his mouth, and he kissed her fiercely. She pushed against his bare shoulders, trying vainly to force him away from her. She tightened her mouth against his probing tongue.

For a fractional moment she yielded, molding her body to his, taking his tongue. Then instantly she tensed, pulling back.

"No, Jack. I'm not ready for this."

His hands gripped her shoulders, then slowly relaxed. "Right. I forgot for a minute there that you aren't really my wife."

"I forgot some things too. For a minute. Like I don't leap into bed with a man on the first date. Hell, this isn't even a date, is it." She laughed self-consciously. "Let's try to keep it platonic, okay? For now, at least."

"For now," he said. "It's not going to be easy."

"Nothing is easy that's worth waiting for."

He showed her a grin. "If you'll excuse me, I think I'll just step back into the shower."

* * * * *

Half an hour later they sat in the living room, she on the couch, he in a chair placed at a careful distance. There was no touching, no exchange of cozy glances. It was all business now. And yet the atmosphere between them was changed. Their words came more freely, their gestures were more natural. And their eyes were bright with the promise of intimacy to come.

"The first thing for us to do," she said, "the most obvious, is to call the police."

He froze. "No!"

The violence of his reply made her jump. "Why not?" Gannon looked down at his clenched fists. Slowly he straightened his fingers.

"I don't know. The same thing happened when I was here before. When somebody says *police* it's like I'm grabbed by the throat. I don't know why, but I can't talk to them."

Kristy studied him. "I don't understand. Are you wanted for anything?"

"You're kidding. I've never had more than a parking ticket in my life, and I always paid those instantly. You can't find a more law-abiding citizen than Jay ..." His voice faded to a murmur, "...Baysinger."

"That's right," she said. "Jay Baysinger would have no reason to be afraid of the police."

"I keep forgetting," he said.

"Exactly. What crime might Jack Gannon be wanted for? Or whoever it is behind the Jack Gannon mask?"

"It's a blank," he said. "Or close enough. I can't tell you why, Kristy, but I will not... I will not go to the police. I won't stop you from calling them if you feel you have to. But if you do, I'm outta here. I wish I could explain it. I wish I understood it myself, but I can't and I don't. So there it is."

Kristy looked at him for a long time with her head cocked to one side. Then she nodded as though making up her mind about something.

"Okay, Jack. No police. For now. But we have to start somewhere. We've already made progress."

"We have?"

"Well, we've got a name for you. And there seems to be another personality peeking through sometimes. That's got to be an improvement. You walked in here this morning thoroughly convinced you were Jay Baysinger."

"That sounds so... foolish now. But it's true.

There was no doubt in my mind, No pretense. When I walked in here I *was* Jay Baysinger. And even with all this Jack Gannon stuff, I still feel like Jay Baysinger." He caught her look. "Most of the time."

"All right," she said, "Something had to happen to you to bring on this delusion. Let's try to figure out what it was. What facts do we have to work with?"

"You tell me," he said.

"Not a lot," she admitted. "Fact one, you are *not* Jay Baysinger. Two, you do know a lot about Jay, including some intimate details you could not have picked up casually. Three, you're three years behind."

"I don't see how this is helping."

"Stay with me. Let's try a hypothesis. Somewhere, at some time you knew Jay Baysinger. You probably knew him quite well.

The big question is how could so much of another man have gotten so deep into your consciousness?"

"I give up," he said.

Kristy sagged back against the cushion. "I don't know either. Just guessing, maybe there was some traumatic experience that affected you strongly enough to make you assume his identity."

Gannon shook his head helplessly.

"Work with me on this, Jack. From what you've told me, you seem to be stuck in time three years ago with Jay. Let's start there." She closed her eyes and massaged them with her fingertips. "It was just about three years ago that Jay left his job here at International Biotech and went to work up at Fairhaven."

"Wait a minute." Gannon frowned, chewing at a knuckle.

"What was that name?"

"Biotech?"

"No, the other one."

"The Fairhaven Medical Facility. It's kind of a hush-hush place funded by government money. It's up the coast by Santa Barbara. Does the name mean anything to you?"

"Yeah. Something... something, but I haven't quite got it. Go on."

She continued cautiously. "We were going to look for a place to live up there, but Jay—" She broke off and peered at Gannon. "Are you all right?"

His head was down. He scrubbed his fingers through the cropped brown hair. "I don't feel so good. Give me a minute."

Gannon breathed deeply in and out. He leaned back in the chair with his eyes closed. Kristy sat silently watching him.

* * * * *

The soft buzzing of the bees that had lurked in his head since this morning swelled into a sound like rushing wind. He put his hands to his head and drifted with the sound.

Jay Baysinger walked along the curving path through the grounds of Fairhaven with Dr. Armand Vespa. Although they walked side by side, the younger man gave the impression of holding himself a deferential half-step behind Vespa. He glanced up often at the gaunt doctor. Vespa kept his eyes to the front.

"I want you to be absolutely sure you want to do this," Vespa said.

"I have no doubts," Baysinger said. "I've been thinking about it since you first described the process to me. And you agreed that I would be an excellent subject."

"That is true. In the past I've come up with useless, jumbled results. They were reflective, I now realize, of the donors' minds. I was forced to use subjects whose mental processes were skewed or damaged. Your mind, on the other hand, is healthy, highly trained, thoroughly organized. It should provide exactly the kind of memory pattern that will transfer readily to a silicon microchip."

"I'm eager to get started," Baysinger said.

"I don't deny that this would be a leap forward for my process. In my early work, without using human donors, I was able to inscribe only bland, generic memories generated by a computer. The resulting implants were... less than satisfactory."

"It was pioneering work, Doctor, not your fault."

"Yes, yes, and then there were the attempts to use faulty human donors, with even more discouraging results. You have seen the North Annex."

"Yes, sir, I have. There is always a price to be paid for the advancement of medicine."

"You do understand that even at the stage I am now there may be side effects. The procedure does, after all, involve minor cranial surgery and physical contact of the electrodes to the frontal lobe of the brain. I would expect only a slight temporary discomfort afterward, but we can never be 100 percent sure."

When Baysinger did not respond immediately, Vespa looked over and saw him staring off through the grove of aspen trees to the blockhouse beyond the stream.

"You're having doubts, Mr. Baysinger?"

"No, no. Well, maybe, just for a moment..."

Vespa gave a short barking laugh. "I think I can assure you the mild side effects we might expect are hardly likely to put you in the North Annex. I have made considerable progress in my techniques, and those unfortunate souls were flawed to begin with."

"I understand that, Doctor, and I'm ready to get on with it."

Vespa sobered. "I'm proud of you. It's quite possible your contribution will produce a microchip that will eventually benefit those poor people. To say nothing of the rest of mankind."

"I'm willing to take any risk it might entail," said Baysinger.

Armand Vespa patted him lightly on the shoulder, a rare gesture for a man who was not given to touching.

* * * * *

The rushing wind in Gannon's head subsided to a murmur. The bees settled down. There was a crack like static electricity. Gannon pushed the heels of his hands against his temples, and abruptly the buzzing stopped. His eyes snapped open and he stared at Kristy.

"Armand Vespa," he said.

"Yes?" She leaned forward eagerly. "What about him?"

"The name... gives me chills. I don't know why. Who is he?"

"He's the chief of the Fairhaven Facility where Jay went to work. A genius, I guess, in his field. Jay worshipped the man."

"What , exactly is his field?"

"You don't know?"

"The memory gets foggy. I know and yet I don It know, if that makes any sense."

"Not really, except that it moves you a little further away from Jay Baysinger. Armand Vespa has won all kinds of prizes in techno-biology. His specialty is sort of marrying computer technology to the human brain."

Kristy stopped talking suddenly and stared at Gannon. "What's the matter?" he asked.

"I was just wondering how you're mixed-up memory ties in with Armand Vespa and what he was doing up at Fairhaven. Maybe we ought to take a run up there."

Darkness. Running across a spongy lawn, scaling a wall, running, stumbling down a narrow road. The highway. Headlights. Whoosh of cars and trucks passing him up, ignoring his outstretched hand. Then a truck door opens. He sits on a tall leather seat beside a sweat-smelling driver.

"No!"

"What is it?"

"I can't go back there."

"Back?"

His eyes widened. "I did say *back there*, didn't I. But was that Jay Baysinger talking? Or... or Jack Gannon? I don't have any clear memory of it. Just a feeling. But it's a powerful feeling. Running away. I can't explain it. I can't tell you why."

Kristy frowned. "You're really cutting down on our options, you know. No police, and no Fairhaven. Where do *you* want to start, Jack?"

He rubbed his head. "I'm sorry. I can't think

right now. I'm tired and I'm confused."

"Well, I guess you're entitled," she said more gently. "Why don't you get some sleep? Maybe it will help clear your thoughts."

"I suppose it couldn't hurt," he said.

She saw his eyes flick toward the bedroom. "I'll make a bed for you here on the couch."

He gave her a tired smile. "That'll do nicely." In a lower tone he added, "...for now."

Chapter 12

The Sea View Motor Hotel on Highway 192 northwest of Santa Barbara had no view of the ocean. It had no view of anything, unless you wanted to count the Exxon station across the highway and the scrubby hillside beyond. What it did have was a dry swimming pool, a broken soft drink machine, and a malfunctioning neon sign that blinked: *VACA CY*. There was no cable television, no coffee shop, and no overemphasis on cleanliness.

Room 9 in The Sea View did include, however, everything agent Merlin Ryan required. There was a serviceable bed, a telephone, a table to work at, a chair to sit on, and a functional bathroom. He was not, after all, planning to spend a significant portion of his life here.

At eleven o'clock Sunday night Ryan sat at the table in his T-shirt, shuffling repeatedly through the stack of records and computer printouts he had brought with him from Fairhaven. He frowned in frustration.

One thick folder contained an extensive biography of Lou Matchek. It told him little he did not already know. There was the standard deprived childhood. Maybe more deprived than most. No father of record. Mother a prostitute and heroin addict, regular customer at Los Angeles County Jail, present whereabouts unknown.

There was a series of foster homes where a hair-trigger temper repeatedly got the boy ejected. There were numerous early brushes with the law, none seemingly serious at the time.

Finally came the manslaughter charge that put him in a so-called "correctional institution" for a year. If young Lou Matchek by then retained any good qualities, they were beaten out of him at Valleydale Youth Institute. Matchek had come out with his anger intact, but his temper under tight control. There were no more arrests recorded until the Niedenfuer killing, but there was no shortage of suspicions.

And no shortage of rumors. Hardly a top-level hit went down that was not attributed to Lou Matchek. As his reputation grew, his visibility decreased. Before his arrest on the Niedenfuer matter, no photos were known to exist. He changed his address three or four times a year. He always rented furnished, always paid several months in advance. Of his association with Nick Tenzi, little was known, nothing was proven.

The folder ended with the spurious press release announcing Matchek's death in a fight at Folsom. The body, the story said, had been cremated.

As for his experiences at Fairhaven, there was the notation of his admittance, a chart of his recovery from the knife wound, brief mention of an operation, and little else. A big chunk of information seemed to be missing.

What had happened to Lou Matchek in the three months he had spent here? More important, where was he now? Dr. Vespa had provided him with stacks of data, but none of it led in the direction he wanted to go.

He set aside the Matchek folder and pulled in the one concerned with Dr. Vespa and the operation of the Fairhaven Medical Facility. The doctor had impressive credentials all the way back to his graduation from the University of Chicago Medical School at the age of 21. Fairhaven was a pet project, funded by congressional grant, as a reward for his work with Vietnam veterans.

There was no denying that Armand Vespa had done some valuable work. He took in some of the least promising cases from homeless shelters, welfare wards, and overcrowded public institutions. The authorities were glad to be relieved of these people, who could not be legally locked up yet were unsafe to leave at liberty. Vespa promised and, as far as anybody could tell, delivered first class care for these hopeless cases, each of which he personally approved for acceptance. His work, only sketchily defined, markedly improved the mental condition of a number of his subjects. Some actually returned as functioning members of society. And the others, those who did not respond to Vespa's specialized therapy, they were guaranteed perpetual care, relieving society of the burden.

Again there were significant gaps in the data. Armand Vespa, patriot and benefactor of the downtrodden. Ryan couldn't buy it.

He closed the Vespa folder and stacked it atop the one on Lou Matchek's history. The shadowy operations at Fairhaven might bear looking into, but that would have to be another time. The focus of Ryan's investigation was Lou Matchek, his whereabouts and his present activities. No diversions could be allowed. He read again the brusque report he had called up from the computer detailing Matchek's stay at the facility.

Admitted to Fairhaven in January in critical condition from knife wound. Responded slowly to physical therapy. Judged strong enough in March to undergo minor cranial surgery.

Minor cranial surgery? Ryan underlined the term in heavy black.

Implantation, code 137596, performed March 3. Post-op recovery slow, but not unduly so. Then patient Matchek, presumably sedated, disappears from the facility Friday, March 9.

Code 137596.

Time and again Ryan's research butted up against that cryptic number. He had been unable to uncover its meaning. Typing it into the computer brought no response.

Armand Vespa made himself unavailable after opening the files to him. Code 137596. What the devil did it mean?

With a sweep of his arm Ryan pushed all the files to the far side of the table. He stretched, leaned back in the chair, yawned mightily. He was tired and he was frustrated. He needed rejuvenation.

His digital watch read 12:45. Linda would be in bed. Asleep, probably. Or maybe reading one of those goofy romance novels she liked. He could visualize her blue-black hair spread out on the pillow. Her coffee brown eyes serious as she read the amorous adventures of her latest spunky heroine. He smiled softly, picturing the way Linda took her plump lower lip between her teeth when she concentrated.

He picked up the telephone from the floor where he had put it out of the way and dialed the motel office. The manager connected him for a long distance call and he dialed his home number in Seattle.

The phone was picked up after the first ring.

"Hello?" Linda's voice was soft and musical, with the barest trace of accent.

"Hi, honey."

"Merl, you all right?"

"Fine. Just tired and lonesome."

"That's good. The lonesome part, I mean."

"How's Adrienne?"

"Excited. They had an airline pilot come in and talk to the second graders today about his work. Guess what she wants to be now."

"A stewardess?"

"Hah, not likely. She's going to be the next century's Amelia Rhinehart."

"Earhart."

"Whatever. When you coming home, Merl?"

"I don't know. Soon, I hope."

"Your case not going so good, huh?"

"Slow." Ryan never discussed specifics of his work with Linda. She never asked questions beyond the generalities he offered. The arrangement worked for both of them.

Linda knew her husband's work was mostly secret and sometimes dangerous. She also knew he loved his work, so she would never complain. She never told him about the chills she sometimes felt when he was away. But he knew. That was one reason he called often to reassure her.

"Well, take care of yourself."

"You too. I love you."

"You better. We miss you."

Ryan hung up the phone gently. It took a very

special woman to stay married to a man in his line of work. Divorces among law enforcement personnel, like the suicide rate, were well above the national average. In Linda Carasquel he had found all the woman he would ever want. He gave himself a couple of minutes to anticipate the coming reunion, then he shifted mental gears and went back to work.

An hour later he was still running into the same dead end when a soft knock at the door roused him. Looking out from the edge of the curtained window he saw a pale, balding young man glancing furtively in both directions. Ryan retrieved his Chief's Special from the bedside table and held it out of sight in his right hand as he opened the door to the limit of its chain.

"Mr. Ryan?"

"Yes."

"My name is Elliot Porter. I work as a medical aide up at Fairhaven. I understand you're looking for Lou Matchek."

"That so?"

"I have some information that might help you."

Ryan released the door chain and admitted the perspiring young man. Unobtrusively he slipped the revolver into his hip holster.

Ryan motioned Porter into a chair and sat down on the bed. Porter leaned forward nervously as he outlined his normal duties at Fairhaven.

"What was your connection with Lou Matchek?" Ryan prompted.

"I was assigned to stick with him when he was first brought here. He didn't seem like much of a threat in his condition, but Dr. Vespa didn't want him left alone at any time."

"That was before the operation?"

"Yes, while he recuperated from the stab wound. For the first week after the operation he would be incapacitated, so there was no need for full time surveillance. Or so we thought. I was just supposed to look in on him from time to time in case he became suddenly lucid."

"You looked in on him last Friday night?"

"Yes. He was supposed to be sedated, but they found out the next day he'd been holding the pills under his tongue or something, pretending to swallow, then stashing them in the mattress. When I came around at 3 A.M. he was sitting up, and I thought something was wrong. I went in and he clipped me." Porter touched his fingers gingerly to the base of his skull. "Right here. The next thing I knew, it was dawn. I had a terrible headache and my clothes, my cash, and my ATM card were gone."

"I got all that from Dr. Vespa," Ryan said.

"I figured you did. He blames me for the whole mess. If we don't get Matchek back, I'll be in deep trouble. Dr. Vespa is big on discipline."

"Sounds like the military," Ryan said.

"Except you have the right of appeal in the military. At Fairhaven Dr. Vespa is the absolute master. He wouldn't even let me report the stolen ATM card."

"That's interesting," Ryan said, "but not a whole lot of help."

"Maybe this will be. I saw him take you down to Records." He nodded at the file folders and accordioned computer printouts stacked on the table. "And I see you brought a lot of data out with you."

"So?"

"Did you run into a computer code you couldn't break? A number code?"

"One-three-seven-five-nine-six." Ryan knew it by heart.

"It's half of a double code. You need a second key to open it up."

"And you have the second key?"

"Unless they've changed it in the last couple of days. I doubt that they've thought of it yet, what with all the excitement."

"Why would you give it to me?" Ryan asked.

"Something bad is going on at Fairhaven. I guess I knew it from the time I started there, but I was blinded by the brilliance of Dr. Vespa. I've stayed with him almost two years because I believed in what he was doing. Some of his results were almost miraculous. Others, well, he had some failures too. His methods weren't always orthodox. But I reasoned he wouldn't be the first great man to bend a few rules to achieve a breakthrough. I wanted to be a part of it. I wanted to be on the team. I have a degree in microbiology, but at Fairhaven I'm nothing more than a flunky. I hoped that one day I'd be moved into the inner circle, but it didn't happen. Now I know it was never going to happen. Dr. Vespa used me, the way he uses everybody."

"How did he use Lou Matchek?" Ryan asked.

"I don' t know, but I have a sense that whatever it was, it will sink Fairhaven if the news gets out. And if that happens, a lot of people are going down with the ship. I don't want to be one of them."

Ryan sat quietly and let Porter get the speech off his chest. He was convinced the man was telling the truth.

"So you have the second half of the key?" he said when Porter wound down.

"I have it."

Ryan waited.

"My savings could be wiped out if Matchek uses my ATM card. I told you Vespa wouldn't let me report it stolen."

So much for noble motives. Ryan was on familiar ground now. "How much do you stand to lose?"

"I have more than five thousand dollars in the account."

"If your information is good the bureau will make it up."

Ryan had no authority to make a deal, but such details had long since ceased to bother him.

"Kaposvar." Porter pronounced the word, then spelled it slowly.

Ryan repeated it. "Does it mean anything?"

"It's the town in Hungary where Vespa's father was born. Type it into the computer along with the number code and you'll unlock the files he doesn't want you to see."

"I'll try it," Ryan said.

Porter peered uneasily at the curtained window. "I'd better get back up there. I made sure I wasn't followed here, but they may have someone checking my room."

Ryan let the nervous young man out and returned to the table. On a scratch pad he penciled *137596 KAPOSVAR.* He stared at it for a moment, then tore off the sheet, shredded it, and flushed the bits down the toilet. He would sleep now, then hit Vespa's computer tomorrow with the double code. It was gratifying when loose ends began to come together.

He went to bed, closed his eyes, and dozed. He dreamed of Fenway Park. He was sitting behind first base, flanked by his wife and his little daughter. The Red Sox were winning big. A happy dream. Merlin Ryan slept with a smile on his face.

Chapter 13

About the time Merlin Ryan was settling in with his file folders and printouts in the Santa Barbara motel, Nicholas Tenzi was sampling a glass of wine as an anxious waiter stood by holding the bottle. Tenzi swished the wine from one cheek to the other, sluiced it under his tongue, chewed it, swallowed it, rolled his eyes.

This performance was taking place at a secluded table in Le Coutil on Wilshire Boulevard at the edge of Beverly Hills. Le Coutil was a restaurant with pretensions to elegance, but which was dismissed by important people for those very pretensions.

Not that the owners, an Iranian corporation, were hurting for business. Attorneys, television producers, brokers, real estate developers, car dealers who did their own commercials, tourists from Texas, a few vaguely familiar actors, and people like Nick Tenzi patronized Le Coutil and thought it was the last word in refinement. After all, the place was identified only by a tasteful black and silver plaque next to the solid oak door, and no prices were printed on the menu.

Nick Tenzi dabbed at his lips with a napkin and frowned. "You got anything better than this?"

The waiter snapped to attention. "That is Chateau Monbouquet, our very best, m'sieu."

"Well, bring me something with a little more bite to it, know what I mean?"

"Yes, sir. Right away, sir." The waiter clutched the offending bottle to his chest and fled.

Nick Tenzi was a neat little man with small, delicate features. He patted his smooth black hair, combed fashionably straight back from his pale forehead. He brushed invisible flecks of lint from his silk lapels.

"You don't speak up, they'll dump their leftovers on you," he said. "At a couple hundred bucks a bottle."

The other two men at the table, Drummer Cahane and Roy Kilgore nodded to show they had absorbed the lesson in wine appreciation.

Drummer Cahane was uncomfortable with his bulky frame squeezed into an Italian-cut suit. It pinched him under the arms, and the unaccustomed necktie felt like a noose. In the gym, wearing shorts and a muscle shirt, Drummer drew awed glances from the less muscular members. But in a suit he was just another bulky clod. He was thinking now that he did not know Chateau whateveritwas from chicken piss, but he did know who paid him, so whatever Nick Tenzi wanted to drink was just fine.

Roy Kilgore, long faced and dour, recognized all this wine tasting for the pretentious crap it was. Personally, he would rather have had a nice Jack Daniel's Black, but like Drummer he understood his place and was careful not to contradict the little chief.

A new waiter floated over to the table carrying a cordless telephone. "A call for you, Mr. Tenzi."

"You know I don't take phone calls here."

"The caller assured me it was urgent. She said to tell you it was from Fairhaven."

Tenzi flicked his eyes around the room to assure himself no one was paying undue attention.

"Okay, okay, let's have it."

The waiter proffered the instrument.

Tenzi spoke low into the mouthpiece. "Yeah?"

As he listened to the voice on the other end his thin eyebrows drew together in a frown. He licked his lips and swallowed.

Drummer Cahane and Roy Kilgore listened intently to Tenzi's half of the conversation while trying to appear uninterested.

"When?... Why didn't you call me before?... Any word on where he headed?... Do the cops know?... Okay. Anything happens call me right away."

He pushed the telephone back at the waiter without looking at him. The man vanished with the instrument. Tenzi flicked his eyes across the other two men at the table.

"Trouble," he said.

The others leaned forward, their eyes hard. "Matchek's out."

"Oh, shit," said Drummer Cahane.

"Son of a bitch," said Roy Kilgore.

Their concern was genuine. The Matchek name triggered memories of the night they had paid a visit to Ira Niedenfuer, a one-time associate of their boss. Niedenfuer was in deep trouble with the Justice Department, and was rumored to be ready to try to talk his way out of some of it.

It was not the first such assignment for Kilgore and Cahane, but it was the most important. Their targets were usually the small fry who were holding out or trying to quit the organization. Sometimes their job was merely to break a couple of feet, or mark up a man's face. Sometimes it was a more permanent message. Niedenfuer was an important hit, the kind that usually went to Lou Matchek. In fact, this one did go to Matchek, only Cahane and Kilgore were going to be there first and be gone by the time Matchek, and the police, arrived.

The job was done swiftly and without a hitch. Niedenfuer was so surprised when Kilgore pulled a gun that he had no time to react before the .38 slug blew a hole through his right eye and out the back of his head.

When Matchek showed up an hour later prepared to deal his own punishment to Niedenfuer, imagine his surprise to find the man already dead and the police waiting as he left the house.

Cahane and Kilgore now looked to Tenzi for a plan to keep Matchek from exacting his price for their part in sending him to Folsom.

Tenzi's lips peeled back from his small, sharp teeth. "Goddammit, I knew something like this would happen. I fucking knew it. The minute Vin Faccio screwed up and they put out that phony death story I fucking knew we were gonna have trouble. Motherfucker!"

"What happened?" said Roy Kilgore. "I don't want to talk here."

Tenzi stood up and tossed his napkin onto the table. The other two hastily followed, looking anxiously toward the door as though they expected the avenging Matchek to come stalking through it, a gun in each hand.

Magically the maître d' was at the table. "Is there a problem here, Mr. Tenzi?"

"Scrub the dinner tonight. I got business."

Followed by his lieutenants, Tenzi marched out of the restaurant, the curious eyes of other diners marking his departure. Those in the know whispered to their table mates that the little man was Los Angeles' leading gangster.

And indeed, since the free-wheeling days of Mickey Cohen and Bugsy Siegel, the local organization had decayed to the point where Nicholas Tenzi was it. With Mexicans and Colombians and blacks, and now even Vietnamese gangs staking out big chunks of the Los Angeles turf, there was not much left for the old traditional racketeers.

Outside the restaurant a red-jacketed attendant leaped to retrieve Tenzi's midnight blue Mercedes. Drummer Cahane tucked a bill into the man's palm and slid in behind the wheel. Tenzi and Kilgore climbed into the back seat as the attendant held the door.

When they were out on Wilshire Boulevard heading west Tenzi said, "That phone call was from the broad I got feeding me information from that government nut house up by Santa Barbara. The one where they took Matchek. I knew we had trouble when that bastard angled his way in there."

"How did he crash out?" asked Cahane from the front seat.

"Who knows? The sons of bitches got careless. Friday night they had him, Saturday morning he was gone."

"He was out Saturday?" Kilgore said. "This is

Sunday."

"I know what day it is," Tenzi snapped. "The broad didn't find out about it until today. They are naturally not making a big deal out if it, since they already put out the news that the son of a bitch was dead."

"So the cops aren't looking for him?" said Drummer.

"Why would they? As far as they're concerned, he's a corpse. There is some FBI guy sniffing around, though. She couldn't find out what his angle is."

"What were they doing with Matchek up there, anyway?" Kilgore asked.

"Some new kind of treatment where they cut out a chunk of his brain or something." said Tenzi.

"Maybe it turned him into a vegetable," Drummer suggested. "That can happen."

"We should be so lucky," Tenzi said gloomily.

"Why didn't we have somebody ice him up there?" Kilgore asked.

"Security was too tight. I already had Faccio in place at Folsom. I got the babe at Fairhaven to feed me information, but she's not going to ice anybody for us."

"They shoulda for Chrissake held onto him." Drummer said.

"Shoulda, shoulda," Tenzi mocked. "Vinnie Faccio shoulda done his job right at Folsom and we wouldn't have Matchek to worry about now."

"Do you think he knows you sent Faccio?" asked Drummer.

"Sure he knows. Matchek ain't stupid."

"So he'll come here?"

Tenzi met Drummer Cahane's eyes in the

rearview mirror. "What do you think?"

"Jesus, he probably figured out who really did Niedenfuer."

"You're getting the picture," Tenzi said.

They drove on silently for several blocks through the evening traffic.

"So... where to?" Drummer asked.

"Go on up to my place. If Lou Matchek's back on the street, we got to make plans."

Drummer turned up Westwood Boulevard, past the UCLA campus to Sunset, then into Beverly Hills to Benedict Canyon. They followed the twisting road up through the cleft in the Santa Monica mountains, and off into a narrow cul-de-sac where Nick Tenzi's fieldstone and redwood house stood all alone at the keyhole end.

The Mercedes rolled up the driveway and Drummer parked in front of the three-car garage next to Kilgore's Caddy. As they stepped out of the car they were met by a lean, mean looking Doberman. The dog growled menacingly at Tenzi, then trotted over to Drummer Cahane grinning and fanning its stump of a tail.

"Stupid mutt," Tenzi grumbled. "A thousand dollars to make an attack dog out of him and the only one he growls at is me."

Drummer scratched the Doberman's head, then nudged him aside and followed his chief to the front door. Tenzi tried the latch, found the door unlocked, and let the breath hiss out through his teeth in exasperation.

In the big, over-furnished living room Helene Tenzi sat in a deep chair with her legs tucked under, watching an old romantic movie on the nostalgia channel.

A tall glass of vodka mixed half and half with Diet Pepsi sat on a table within easy reach.

Helene's white-blond hair was carefully moussed into place. She wore a black satin robe that was open over a lacy black teddy.

"Hi Hon," she said. "Back already?"

"For Christ sake put something on," Tenzi said.

Cahane and Kilgore looked off in other directions as Helene got out of the chair and pulled the robe together.

"What was the door doing unlocked?" Tenzi demanded.

"Gee, was it? I guess Ahmed forgot to push the button when he left."

"What was that Hindu doing here? Isn't your yogi lesson on Saturday?"

"Yoga," Helene corrected. "Ahmed had a schedule conflict so he asked if tonight would be all right and I told him sure."

Drummer and Kilgore stole a glance at each other and quickly looked away.

"We'll talk about Ahmed later," Tenzi said. "Find something to do. We want to talk."

"Could you and me talk for a minute first?" Helene said. "It's kind of important."

"It'll keep," Tenzi said. "Take a hike."

Helene looked at him for a moment, then used the remote control to kill the television. She picked up her drink, skated her eyes over Cahane and Kilgore, and walked out of the room.

Her figure had softened a little since her dancing days, but she could still draw long appreciative looks, which the two men not married to her were now at pains to suppress.

When they were alone Tenzi said, "The first thing we got to find out is where he is."

Nobody had to be reminded who he was.

"We don't know where to start looking," Cahane pointed out.

"Of course we don't, but we've got contacts on the street. People who know Matchek on sight."

Drummer Cahane pulled on his lower lip. "But if everybody thinks he's dead, who's gonna look for him?"

"We are going to inform the people that Matchek is not dead, and that he's out there, and that I want him," Tenzi explained patiently. "Do you think you two can handle that?"

"We can get the word out," Kilgore said, "but nobody who knows Lou Matchek is going to be in a hurry to finger him."

"They will if there's something in it for them."

"How much?" Drummer asked. He was already feeling edgy, as though Lou Matchek were even now listening to their conversation, planning to pick them off one by one.

"It will depend on how good the information is. Let them know it will be worth their while. You know the people who will get the word spread around."

"When do you want us to start?" Kilgore asked.

"Right now, unless you got something better to do."

Cahane and Kilgore hitched their jackets into place and marched out together. A minute later a car engine fired and tires squeaked on the asphalt as they wheeled out of the cul-de- sac.

Helene came back into the living room. "Can we talk now, Nick?"

"Later, okay?. I got a lot to think about."

"Can I get you a drink or anything?"

"Just give me some space. Go take a bath or something."

A cloud crossed Helene's face, but Nick Tenzi did not see it. After a moment she turned away from him and walked out.

When he was alone Tenzi went back and double-locked the front door. He walked through the house making sure the ground floor windows, the sliding door onto the patio, and the back entrance were secure. Then he went to the bar, poured himself a balloon glass of Hennessey, and sagged into the chair Helene had vacated.

Self-doubt was not a failing of Nick Tenzi. A man in his position, fighting to hold together a collapsing organization, dealing with the people he couldn't turn his back on, could not afford even a slight slippage in confidence. He had schooled himself over the years to speak with a powerful voice that would brook no contradiction. As a smaller than average kid on the streets of Cleveland he had developed a swagger and practiced a sneer to compensate for his lack of size. Only in rare moments, when he was alone and the old fears crept back into his mind, did Nick Tenzi allow himself to admit that he might not be as tough as he pretended.

"Lou Matcbek."

The sound of the name spoken aloud grated like claws on a chalk board. Tenzi could close his eyes and see the tall, lean killer standing before him in his careless slouch, lips in a grim line, icy gray eyes looking right into his brain. One of the biggest mistakes he ever made was contracting with Matchek in the first place to eliminate some troublesome rivals. Oh, he was good at his trade, all right. Too fucking good.

Nick would concede now that another huge mistake was setting Matchek up for the bust. His only defense was the loser's wail: It seemed like the thing to do at the time. Rationally he had to admit that the man had never showed any inclination to move in on Tenzi's operation. As far as anybody knew, Lou Matchek was perfectly content doing what he was doing. Why shouldn't he be? He was paid more for a single job than most people in honest professions earned in a year. He was feared and respected by everybody who knew his name. That was part of the problem. Nick Tenzi always had a sneaking suspicion that people laughed at him behind his back. Nobody laughed at Lou Matchek. If he had snapped his fingers the men who were in Tenzi's pay would desert and go over to his side in a flash. Tenzi was sure of it. He began to look for a chance to eliminate the potential rival.

The opportunity presented itself with the Ira Niedenfuer problem. Niedenfuer was a sleaze bag who had foolishly appropriated more than his share of his union's pension fund, and had come under the scrutiny of the Justice Department. The asshole was gutless, and word reached Tenzi that he was ready to spill, supplying the feds with information that could seriously hurt the organization. Obviously this could not be allowed to happen, so Lou Matchek was called in.

Matchek always insisted on picking the time and place for his work. This time Tenzi manipulated events to place Niedenfuer in a location that would look perfect for his elimination at a time chosen by Tenzi. Cahane and Kilgore were then sent out to do the job an hour earlier. An anonymous call had the police waiting for Matchek when he walked away from the corpse.

To Nick's considerable disappointment, the police had collared Matchek without violence, leaving him dangerously alive. At least they were happy enough to nail the notorious hitman so they did not look too hard for additional evidence.

For that trial Tenzi had provided the best legal help, not without a nagging fear that they might actually get him off.

Luckily, the planted evidence was convincing, and Matchek was convicted after only two hours deliberation by the jury.

Tenzi suffered another setback when the same jury failed to recommend the death penalty, opting instead for a life sentence without the possibility of parole. Like everyone else in California, Tenzi knew that there was no such thing. Some procedural loophole could always be found. A new governor could commute the sentence. A new legislature could change the law. A bleeding heart appeals court could throw the whole thing out.

And no matter what anybody said, no prison was escape proof. If Lou Matchek ever found out who set him up, somehow he would get out and come to even the score.

Since he would be denied the pleasure of watching Matchek die with a lungful of chlorine gas, Tenzi had commissioned one of his men already at Folsom to do the job up there. It would not be the first assassination in the prison system. With witnesses reluctant to speak up, such killings had a good chance of going unpunished. And even if Vin Faccio were nailed, he was in for life, and there was little more they could do to him. And there were ways of rewarding a man, even locked in the forbidding Folsom. Tragically, Faccio had botched it. He was dead and Matchek was alive. And now the nightmare had begun. Lou Matchek was loose.

Tenzi jerked upright in the chair. Was that a noise at the door? He moved silently into the entrance hall, took out the 9-millimeter Browning he kept in a drawer in the hall table.

Holding the pistol he peered through the fisheye lens in the door.

Nothing out in front but the empty floodlit expanse of lawn.

Something soft hit the door panel. Tenzi jumped back with a gasp, almost dropping the pistol. Then he heard a low growl.

His nerves twanged as he made his muscles relax.

Some fucking guard dog the Doberman had turned out to be. Loved everybody except the man he was supposed to guard. If it hadn't been for his wife's affection for the hound, Tenzi would have had it gassed long ago. Well, to hell with her. That dog was going to die. He'd get himself a pit bull. One he could trust to rip apart anybody who didn't belong there.

Tenzi walked once more around the house, checking all the locks again. Satisfied at last, he swallowed what was left of the brandy and went to bed. Helene, curled on the far side of the super-king, appeared to be asleep. Good enough. Tenzi was in no mood for fooling around tonight.

He lay for several hours in the dark, staring at the ceiling, listening to Helene's gentle snore. In his mind the lean menacing figure of Lou Matchek stalked through the night coming closer, ever closer.

It was after three o'clock when he dropped off at last into a troubled sleep.

Chapter 14

The immediate, instantaneous emotion was terror.

Where the fuck am I?

In a bed, no, not a bed, a couch. A living room. Strange living room, yet not strange. Buzzing in head. Dream. Bad dream. Got to wake up. Got... to... wake... up...

Then reality came spilling back in wild disarray.

Baysinger. Gannon. Baysinger. Gannon. Baysingergannon. And... Something else. Something dark. Something hidden.

He sat straight up, his eyes wide and staring as he swiveled his head, looking around the strange, yet familiar room.

The smell of fresh coffee pulled together the kaleidoscopic images tumbling through his head. He breathed deeply, feeling the pulse pound in his temples.

Kristy came into the room. She wore lime green pants of some stretchy material and a UCLA T-shirt.

"You're awake."

He stared at her, putting a name to the face. "How do you feel?" she asked.

"How do I look?"

"Like you saw a ghost."

"You're close."

"Sleep poorly?"

"Woke up poorly."

"Want some coffee?"

"That sounds good." He rubbed his chin. The growth of beard was heavier than it should have been. "What time is it?"

"Quarter to three." She followed his eyes to the curtained window. "That's right, three in the afternoon."

"Why didn't you wake me?"

"You seemed to need the sleep."

He started to chew a knuckle, changed the gesture to rub his bristly jaw.

"There's a razor in the bathroom you can use," she said.

"Thanks. I'll take a cup of coffee with me."

"How do you like it?"

"Same way as always—black with sugar." She gave him a look.

"Sorry That was Jay Baysinger talking."

"It's all right," she said. "We'll work it out."

He followed her into the kitchen where she poured him strong coffee in a heavy mug, added a heaping teaspoon of sugar. He carried into the bathroom.

The sink and counter were cluttered with woman things. Skin softener, styling gel, shower cap, glycerine soap, curlers, cosmetics. A new Bic disposable razor and a fresh aerosol can of shave cream were set apart from the rest. Kristy must have gone out this morning and bought them.

Gannon washed and shaved deliberately, looking deep into the face of his mirror image, wondering what things those gray eyes had seen that he did not remember. Whose eyes were they, really?

He still carried a lot of Jay Baysinger with him. The spicy smells of Kristy's bathroom were familiar. He knew the royal blue velour robe that hung from a hook on the inside of the door. He had given it to her a year ago. No, it would not have been a year ago. But hell, he hadn't given it to her at all. He was not, repeat *not* Jay Baysinger. Then how did he know all this? How, damn it?!

He concentrated on the shave, pushing away memories and feelings that were not rightfully his. Unless he found the answer to these questions soon, he could slip over the edge into madness. A bad, bad thought. He rinsed and dried his face, inspecting the tiny scars around the chin and in one eyebrow.

Then there was the still tender scar on his lower back and the odd little diamond at his hairline. How did he get those? When? Too many questions, too few answers.

He replaced the razor, and carried the empty coffee mug out to the kitchen.

Kristy sat at the table waiting for him. He put on a smile for her.

"Feeling better?"

"Some. You make good coffee."

"You hungry?"

"Starved."

Kristy started to rise.

"Don't get up. I know where everything is."

"Maybe not," she said. "I've made some changes."

He peered into the refrigerator and turned back, frowning. "Where are the eggs?"

"No eggs," she said. "Too much cholesterol."

"Ah. No bacon either, I suppose."

"That's right. Too much fat. There are plenty of fresh fruits and veggies. And some oat bran."

"Oat bran?"

"It's good for you. Lots of fiber."

"When did you become a health food freak?"

"I've always been concerned with what I ate. Since I don't have anyone else to feed now, I keep the food around that I like."

"Fair enough."

While Kristy watched, Gannon prowled through the refrigerator and cupboards. He came up with rye bread, Jarlsberg cheese, an avocado, lettuce, tomato, lo-cal mayonnaise. Moving efficiently, he built a thick sandwich, put it on a plate, sliced it diagonally, and joined her at the table.

"Where did you learn to make a sandwich like that?"

"Damned if I know. Want one?"

"No thanks, but it does look good."

"When a man lives alone he picks up a few survival skills." Kristy stared at him. "Did you hear what you just said?"

"Huh?"

"*When a man lives alone.* That's not Jay talking." He frowned. "No, I guess it isn't. But who is it?"

"Jack Gannon. That's good enough for now. The more you lose of Jay, the closer you'll get to whoever's inside. There's no need to push it."

He took a bite of the sandwich and chewed thoughtfully. "I hope we're not going to be sorry."

"About what?"

He tapped his head. "About meeting the guy whose hiding in here when he finally decides to come out. The guy with all the scars. Sometimes I get pictures, barely a flash and gone, that leave me feeling like a cold wind just blew past. The guy inside may not be somebody you'll want to know."

"Let's not worry about it now. You and I have work to do."

"Don't you have to go to the clinic?"

"I've got time off coming. I called in this morning and took it."

Gannon looked at her gravely. "Kristy, are you sure you want to go on with this? We don't know where it's going to lead. You might be getting yourself involved in something you're not going to like."

"Hey, I'm already in. And don't think I'm being charitable. Call it professional curiosity if you want to. I'm dying to know how this is going to come out. It could make a damned interesting article for some professional journal. You get points for those in my profession."

He gave her a long look. "There's more, isn't there."

"All right. I told you I was never quite satisfied with the story I got of what happened to Jay. You're a key to finding out."

"It might be something you're better off not knowing."

"Let me worry about that, okay?

"Okay, sure, if that's what you want."

"To get started I thought we might—"

He held up a hand to silence her. "I want to get some air before we start making big plans. Let me walk around a little, sort out my thoughts, then we'll talk."

"You want company?"

"No." He saw her look and softened his tone. "I really need a little time alone."

"I understand. We'll talk when you come back."

Once he was outside, walking down Lemon Grove Avenue away from the little ranch house, Gannon was aware of an unfamiliar ache in the area of the diaphragm. It took a moment for him to realize with a start what it was. The pain of loss. It was more than the Jay Baysinger memories of tender times together. In the past two days Kristy's sincerity and her willingness to help him without considering the risk to herself had touched something deep inside. Now that he had made his decision to leave, he missed her.

Gannon exhaled sharply through clenched teeth. He had no time for juvenile sentimentality. From somewhere he was getting a sense of urgency. A message that there were things to do. And he had to do them alone. The woman would just slow him down.

And a dark, formless fear tugged at him, a fear that he would hurt Kristy by staying with her. Any way he looked at it, it was better that he leave her now. He resisted an impulse to look back, and quickened his stride down the hill.

At Glenoaks Boulevard he stopped and looked across the way at the front of El Gato. He remembered the sudden violence of the day before and wondered that he was not more shaken by it.

A dark youth with a Zapata moustache slouched against the stucco wall cleaning his fingernails with a knife. Another, wearing a black hairnet, squatted beside him. They watched Gannon with hooded eyes. It was a different pair, but they were out of the same mold as the pool players of yesterday. Gannon stared back at them until they looked away.

As he continued down the street he pulled out Elliot Porter's automatic teller card and checked the number penciled on the back. *6256.* There was a better than even chance that the number was Porter's personal code for the ATM. What a jackass, Gannon thought. In spite of the ubiquitous warnings not to do so, some dipshits would still write the code number on the card, making it easy for a thief.

It struck Gannon that he had fallen easily into the role of thief. Jay Baysinger could never have done it. He was gradually learning more about the shadowy figure still hiding behind the Gannon mask. What he had learned so far he did like very much.

There was really not much risk involved. If Elliot Porter had not reported his card missing, he was soon going to have his bank account lightened. And if the card was on a missing list, the machine would eat it, and Gannon would simply walk away.

After several blocks he saw a small branch of the Farmers & Merchants Bank on the other side of the street between a flower shop and a dry cleaner. The ATM in its little alcove bore the same star symbol as Elliot Porter's card. Gannon started across the street.

* * * * *

The young man with the hairnet plucked at the sleeve of the one with the moustache. "You sure that's him? The one who done T.J. and Rijo?"

"It's him. You saw the way he looked at us. T.J. figured he might be back." Zapata hesitated, frowning.

"What's the matter?"

"I don't know. There's something familiar about him. Like I seen him before. Or a picture of him."

"We gonna take him or what?"

Moustache looked up and down the street. Afternoon traffic was light. Only a few pedestrians wandered the sidewalks. "We take him. But don't get careless. You know what he did to those guys."

"He must've sucker punched Rijo. Hey, he's crossing the street. What's he doing?"

The moustache spread in a grin. "Oh, man, this gets better and better. He's taking some money outta the bank machine. I love it."

Staying close to the front of the building, the two young men moved swiftly toward the bank.

Gannon eased Elliot Porter's card into the slot in the front of the ATM and watched as it was sucked from his fingers into the bowels of the machine. An 8-inch screen spelled out in pale green letters the steps to follow. The first was to punch in his code number. Gannon obliged: 6-2-5-6. Next he was directed to choose the function he wanted, deposit or withdrawal, and from what type of account. He punched withdrawal and took a chance by hitting the button for Checking. The machine clicked and asked him the amount. The usual maximum on these things was $200. If Porter didn't have that much, he would try for less. He keyed in the figures.

The ATM whirred and clicked. It regurgitated the plastic card along with a record of the transaction. With a soft clank, metal fingers offered a sheaf of 20-dollar bills. Gannon scooped out card, note, and money and stuffed them into a pocket.

"Thank you, Elliot Porter," he muttered.

He turned in time to see the two idlers from El Gato moving purposefully toward him. A warning bell clanged in his head.

His muscles tensed reflexively. He shifted his feet for balance.

The one with the moustache shot out an arm and stopped his companion cold.

"Hey, whassamatter?"

"We made a mistake, man. Let's get outta here."

With Hairnet still protesting, Zapata pulled him away down the street while the man at the ATM watched with ice cold eyes.

"Whattayou doin'?"

"Shut up. You know who that was?"

"No."

"Lou Matchek."

"So?"

"Man, don't you know anything? Lou Matchek was just about the hardest thing going in this town before they nailed him for a hit last year and locked him up. Word was he got wasted up at Folsom, but that was bullshit. He's on the street, and Nick Tenzi's put out a reward for anybody who spots him. Which is what we just did."

Hairnet was impressed. "Nick Tenzi?"

"Well, Jesus, at least you know who somebody is."

"Fucking right I know. You said reward?"

"Yeah." Zapata pulled his friend into an alley. "He must be staying around here somewhere. Let's follow and see where he goes."

* * * * *

Gannon watched the two young men disappear into an alley.

Gradually his body relaxed, but his mind stayed alert. They had been planning to mug him. Then they changed their mind. Why?

His reactions had been instinctive, unrelated to anything Jay Baysinger would have felt. He could sense the Baysinger persona flaking away bit by bit, like an imperfect skin graft.

Underneath was... what?

He had money now, a little. He could get away from here and go... where? And why?

Impulsively he walked into the flower shop next to the bank.

* * * * *

Kristy opened the door instantly at his knock. Her cheeks were lightly flushed, her eyes bright. "You're back."

"Uh-huh."

"You were gone so long, I thought maybe you weren't coming back."

"I did have something like that in mind."

"And?"

"And I couldn't do it." He brought his right hand into view from beyond the edge of the door. "Here."

She took the flowers, long-stemmed white roses, and inhaled their fragrance. "They're my favorite."

"Yeah, I know."

She lay the flowers gently on a table just inside

the door.

Together they walked into the living room. Gannon kicked the front door shut behind him and pulled Kristy into his arms. He kissed her hard and long. She responded with her entire body. This time there was no holding back.

Their mouths pulled apart for a moment, and they looked into each other's eyes. Kristy's breasts rose and fell with her breathing. She nodded yes to his unspoken question. They walked, fingers laced together, into the bedroom.

For the first time in years Kristy gave herself completely to passion. She bucked and bit and cried out and held no emotion back. And he touched her, tasted her, took her in a reckless, yet strangely tender way. His thumping climax came just seconds before her own.

They lay afterward, their sweat-slick bodies still touching. Gradually their breathing returned to normal. He picked up the towel from his shower that still lay beside the bed and offered it to her. She pushed the towel away and turned to look at him.

"Tell me something," she said.

"If I can."

"Who am I in bed with?"

"Say again?"

"You know what I mean." She lay a hand flat on his damp stomach. "Who is this man I've just fucked?"

"Gannon's the name," he said. "Jack Gannon."

Kristy sighed and kissed him lightly on the shoulder. "Thank God. I know Jay Baysinger could never do some of the things to me that you just did, but I wanted to be sure."

"He'll never know what he missed." Gannon

grinned at her and felt his body easing slowly into blessed relaxation.

* * * * *

A block down Lemon Grove Street the two young men from El Gato squinted at the yellow bungalow.

"You get the number?" asked the one with the Zapata moustache.

"One-four-three-six," said the one with the hairnet.

"*All right*! Let's get to a phone."

Chapter 15

Kristy awoke slowly and luxuriously. The sheets were cool against her nude body. She tingled with an overall sensation of good health and completeness. She smiled, eyes still closed, floating in the good feeling as in a warm, bubbly pool.

Gradually the real world eased into her mind. She did not stop smiling.

From her customary S-curved sleeping position on her side, she rolled onto her back and stretched out a hand to the other half of the bed. Her fingers found rumpled sheets and a dented pillow, but no warm body.

Kristy opened her eyes and sat up in bed. In an instant of panic she thought, *He's gone!* Just when, for the first time in oh-how-many-years a man had come into her life who made her feel wholly alive and vital, he leaves in the morning.

She shook off the irrational panic, swung her legs out of bed. Her feet found the furry slippers next to the night stand. She crossed to the closet, took down a quilted satin robe, and walked out to the living room.

Jack Gannon, wearing a pair of Jay Baysinger's pants that fell just to his ankles, stood barefoot and bare-chested at the side of the wide picture window. He peered out through the gap at the edge of the curtain. Kristy walked up beside him and touched his shoulder.

He turned, grinned down at her, then took her in his arms and kissed her. It was a long, intimate morning kiss, as natural as though they'd been doing it for years.

"I didn't hear you get up," she said.

"I thought about waking you, but you looked so cute I decided to let you sleep."

"Next time wake me."

"I will." He frowned slightly as he looked back toward the curtained window.

"Something wrong?"

"The same dark blue Cadillac has driven past the front of the house three times in the last half hour."

"There are a lot of blue Cadillac."

"This was the same car."

"Did you see who was driving?"

"The windows were tinted too dark."

"So what's the problem?"

"I think they were checking this house."

"It could be somebody in the neighborhood. Left home, remembered something, went back for it, and left again."

"I don't think so."

"Jack, aren't you being a touch paranoid?"

"Just because I'm paranoid doesn't mean they aren't after me."

She did not smile at the old joke.

"Maybe you're right," he said, with an unconvincing grin.

"I hope so." His unease began to infect her.

"I made some coffee," he said. "Tried to, anyway, with your machine. What happened to the old electric percolator we you used to have?"

"I junked it. Let's go out and see how you did

with Mr. Coffee."

Kristy poured out two cups, made a wry face when she tasted hers.

"Too strong?"

"Just a touch. I think you can use a lesson in coffee making."

They sat across from each other, sipping at the bitter coffee, making small talk about things that did not matter to either of them. Soon they fell silent.

Kristy touched his hand. "Jack, we've got to do something about you."

"I promise I'll learn to make better coffee."

"I'm serious. I know you've got this hangup about going to the police, but that's the only move that makes any sense. If there really is somebody watching the house, you could be in some kind of trouble we don't know about. If you and I keep plunging ahead blindly without help, we're only going to get in deeper."

He opened his mouth to protest, closed it again. "All I can tell you is some inner voice says. *Do not go to the police.* The voice isn't explaining why."

"That's not rational."

"I know." He was silent for a moment. "And since I can't come up with a better suggestion... let's do it."

She smiled at him in relief. "At least if you're not wanted for anything, we can find that out. That will be one problem we won't have to worry about."

"What if I'm still wanted?"

"I guess we'll find that out too. There aren't any guarantees in life."

They dressed, Gannon making himself as presentable as he could in one of Jay Baysinger's jackets, a white shirt, and a conservative necktie. They went outside and Gannon checked the street in both directions. He hoisted the garage door and stood back, looking at the husky 4-wheel-drive vehicle inside.

"This is what you traded the Pinto for?"

"Why not?"

"It's a truck."

"Multi-purpose vehicle," she corrected. "A Dodge Raider."

"It looks like a truck to me. You do a lot of off-road driving?"

"I like it, that's all. Driving this I get more respect on the road than I did with the Pinto. You got a problem with that?"

He spread his hands. "Hey, not me. I like it."

"Would you like to drive it?"

"Yes, I would. If it's all right."

She handed over the keys. "Be my guest. Do you know... or do you remember where the Glendale police station is?"

His expression tightened for a moment. "Somewhere downtown."

"It's on Isabel near Broadway. We can take the freeway, or you can drive along Cumberland at the edge of the park."

"Let's go by the park. Then if they lock me up I'll have the memory of a last scenic drive."

"I don't like jokes like that."

"Sorry." He keyed the Dodge to life and backed out of the driveway onto Lemon Grove Street.

Brand park lay at the high end of Lemon Grove Street. It was a broad expanse of green that stretched along the northern limit of Glendale and sloped up to the base of the Verdugo Mountains. It's centerpiece was the Grecian Brand Music and Art Library in white stone. Spread over the length if the park were softball fields, picnic grounds, and nature trails that snaked up into the hills. The shades of green were so intense they hurt the eyes.

Gannon, however, was not looking at the park. His eyes flicked back and forth between the street ahead and the rearview mirror.

"There they are," he said. "There who are?"

"The guys in the blue Cadillac. Two of them. Following us."

"Are you sure?" Kristy started to turn.

Gannon put a restraining hand on her shoulder. "I'm sure. Don't turn around."

Mid-morning traffic was scattered along Cumberland. Gannon increased his foot pressure on the accelerator. Gradually the Raider gained speed. Behind them the Cadillac kept pace, steadily closing the gap between them.

Gannon's mouth compressed to a thin, tight line as he watched the pursuing car gain. He saw the occupant of the passenger seat lean to his right and hold something out the window. As he watched, the Cadillac suddenly leapt forward, eating the pavement between it and the Dodge.

"Hold on," Gannon said.

As the Cadillac slid over to the left and came up almost abreast of them he cranked the steering wheel hard in that direction, cutting them off. He tromped on the accelerator and the Raider surged forward. The Cadillac slewed sideways with a scream of rubber on asphalt. The Dodge jounced over the curb and fishtailed up a narrow roadway leading to the picnic grounds.

Behind him Gannon saw the pursuers right their car and dig into the road after them. He could see now what the passenger was holding out the window. A gun.

He clamped his right hand on the back of Kristy's head and pushed.

"Hey!"

"Get down!"

"What's going on? Who's in that car?"

"Get down, damn it! I don't know who they are, but they're not friendly."

A muffled sounded over the roar of the two engines.

Another. Something thunked into the backside of the Raider and the rear-mounted spare tire deflated with a loud hiss.

"My God, they're shooting at us."

"Now will you get down?"

Kristy unbuckled the restraining seat belt and scrunched down into the leg space in front of the seat and under the glove box. She looked up past the shift lever at Gannon. "What are you going to do?"

"Try to lose them. Brace yourself."

He jerked the wheel back and forth, skidding from one shoulder of the narrow road to the other. Behind them the gunman pulled his weapon back inside as the driver kept them a few yards behind.

* * * * *

"Dammit, Drummer, can't you keep the car steady?"

"I *am* keeping it steady. Can't you shoot straight?"

"Get closer. That fucking spare tire blocks my line of fire."

Gannon spun the truck around a dogleg curve. His eyes widened at the sight of a yellow wooden barrier in the road ahead. Beyond it the asphalt and base were cut away leaving a three-foot vertical ditch. Piled on both sides were lengths of concrete sewer pipe.

"Shit!"

As the Cadillac skidded around the dogleg, Roy Kilgore smiled. "Now we've got the sonofabitch." He leaned out the side window and braced the pistol in a two-handed grip.

* * * * *

While Jack Gannon fought to stay out of the ditch and Roy Kilgore tried to steady his aim, Merlin Ryan was easing his rented Ford to the curb in front of Kristy Baysinger's house on Lemon Grove.

It had taken him most of yesterday and into the night to break the Fairhaven computer code, even with the second key given to him by Elliot Porter. When he finally did hit the correct keys, the information poured out as though from a suddenly unstoppered jug.

He did not stop to enumerate the various laws being broken at Fairhaven Medical Facility. A full-scale investigation could follow. Right now Ryan's only purpose was to find and neutralize Lou Matchek. Oddly, he felt a growing kinship to the convicted killer. That was something he would have to explore later.

The relevant information he uncovered concerned a young researcher who came to work at

Fairhaven some three years ago. The researcher's name was Jay Baysinger. In a signed and witnessed document, Baysinger had volunteered for an experiment that would imprint his memory on a micro-miniature computer chip.

The memory circuit replacement of which Vespa had spoken so casually was described as an implantation of the tiny chip directly into the subject's brain. The theory was that traumatic and destructive memories would thus be replaced by good thoughts. It was an expansion of the methods Vespa had used to cleanse the memories of Vietnam veterans by erasing the ugly pictures. The implantation of Baysinger's memory was to be the first in which a healthy human donor had been used.

Apparently the experiment was interrupted as unfortunate side effects were noted in Baysinger. The nature of the side effects was obscured to Ryan by the arcane medical terminology, but he got the impression that Baysinger never recovered from the transfer of his memory circuits to the microchip.

The file closed with conflicting records. One reported Baysinger's death in a laboratory accident, the other detailed the mental deterioration of a patient identified by the code number 137596.

Ryan made careful notes on questions to be pursued later, then, reasoning that the Baysinger memory chip was the one now implanted in Lou Matchek, he set out backtracking the missing researcher.

The personnel records at Fairhaven *gave* him the last recorded address for Jay Baysinger on Lemon Grove Avenue in Glendale. A telephone book confirmed that a K. Baysinger now resided at that address. That, Ryan assumed, would be the wife, Kristiana.

He rang the doorbell now and waited, glancing around the neighborhood for any hint that his quarry might *have* come this way. Everything seemed blatantly ordinary.

There was no answer to his ring, no sounds from inside the house. The neighborhood was peaceful.

Ryan scribbled a note on one of his cards and slipped it between the door and the jamb. He popped open a leather-bound notebook and ran a finger over the address printed under the next name on his list. Nick Tenzi.

Chapter 16

The trench directly in front of him was deep enough to disable Kristy's truck, even if Gannon did somehow bounce it over the pile of pipes. He cranked the steering wheel hard to the right. The truck slewed, tipped, swayed, and at the moment when it seemed the vehicle must roll, righted itself as they bounced over the rounded berm at the side of the road and dove down the grassy bank onto the picnic grounds.

Behind them Drummer Cahane jammed his foot down on the brake pedal. The Cadillac slid, leaving greasy black rubber tracks.

"You missed the son of a bitch," said Cahane.

"If you'd kept the fucking car steady I'd have blown his fucking head off."

"Yeah, right. What do we do now?"

"Follow them!" Kilgore snapped. "What the fuck do you think?!"

Cahane shot him a dark look, then steered the Caddy over the edge of the road and down the bank, wincing as the car bottomed on the lumpy slope.

"We're going to fuck up your car."

"I can get another car. Drive this mother and see if you can get me a clear shot."

A picnicking family from Vermont looked up in alarm from their potato salad and Kool-Aid as the

Dodge careered toward them across the grass. It blasted by scant yards from their blanket covered table. Father, mother, son, and daughter stared open mouthed, then spun back to see a wildly bouncing Cadillac following the truck. As the second car roared past they could see the passenger leaning out of the side window, trying to steady a semi-automatic pistol.

"That man had a gun!" the woman said as they stood watching the receding vehicles.

"They're probably making a movie," the man said.

"Oh, wow!" said the little boy.

The man in the Cadillac fired. The gunshot might have been a movie effect, but it sounded real. The man looked back for a following camera truck. All he saw were other astonished picnickers.

He turned to his family. "Let's go, Mother. Kids, pick up your things and get to the car."

The family swiftly collected their uneaten food, blankets, Frisbee, transistor radio, and Guide to Greater Los Angeles, and scrambled to their automobile. They cast fearful glances back to see if the two wild drivers were returning. The parents were already framing the story they would tell friends back in Underhill Center. It didn't really matter whether it was a movie or people were really shooting at each other. Things like this did not happen in Vermont.

Gannon kept the Dodge on a slalom course between trees, barbecue pits, swing sets, children, dogs, and startled adults. Part of his mind seemed to look on as an observer, wondering at the icy calm he displayed during the frenzied ride.

Behind him the Cadillac, without the bite of

a four-wheel- drive, still managed to hang on grimly. Kilgore braced one shoulder against the window and leveled the .45 at the back of Gannon's head. In his mind he saw the skull exploding, blood and brains spraying the cab, the Dodge spinning out of control, going down in flames. He squeezed the trigger. At the crucial instant the front wheel of the Cadillac hit a metal sprinkler head, jouncing the car just enough to throw off his aim.

The windshield to the right of Gannon's sight line spidered suddenly as the slug passed completely through the cab of the Dodge. Kristy looked up at Gannon from her cramped space on the floorboards.

"What's happening?"

"Stay down," he said.

They rumbled out of the picnic area and Gannon steered toward a softball game in progress up ahead.

The roar of the oncoming vehicles halted the game, and the team in the field turned to watch the four-by-four and the Cadillac leap and bounce over the lawn toward them. Gannon sent the Dodge into a sideways skid, then gunned it to loop inside the center fielder. Picking up speed, he headed off and away from the game.

Drummer Cahane was closing in slowly with Kilgore readying for another shot when Gannon went into his maneuver. Cahane braked suddenly, sending the Cadillac sliding over the grass for a dozen car lengths before it came to a stop.

Kilgore pulled himself back inside. "What the fuck you doing?"

Cahane jerked his head in the direction of the softball players, who were starting to walk toward them. "Take a look at the shirts on those guys."

As Cahane wheeled the car back in the other direction Kilgore peered out at the fielders now trotting in their direction. Their green and gray sweat shirts bore a gold six pointed star and the legend *Los Angeles County Sheriff's Department.*

The softballers jogged to a stop as the Cadillac roared away over the grass opposite the direction the Dodge had taken. "What's with those crazies?" the pitcher asked the second baseman.

"Who knows?" The second baseman pounded the ball into the pitcher's glove. "They're Glendale's problem. Come on, let's get these guys out."

The pitcher shrugged and returned to the mound. It was the last of the seventh and he was protecting a one-run lead for the Sheriffs over the Public Defenders. He could not let a couple of goofy drivers distract him from blowing down these bleeding heart lawyers.

Gannon steered up from the grass onto another of the roads that snaked through the park. "Okay," he said, "come on up."

Kristy eased awkwardly back into the seat and rubbed a bruise on her shoulder. She touched the hole in the windshield, then looked back through the shattered rear window.

"Did you lose them?"

"With the help of the L.A. County Sheriffs."

"What?!"

He explained about the softball game.

"If they were sheriffs, why didn't you stop? They could have helped us."

"Hunh-uh. No sheriffs. No police. My first instinct was right. I knew it as soon as I saw those stars on their shirts."

"But I thought we agreed—"

He raised a hand to silence her. "Forget it. I know now what I've got to do."

She sat back and looked at his face, grim and implacable in profile. She wondered seriously who this man was. There was no sign now of her mild, self-involved husband, Jay Baysinger. Nor was this the warm and passionate Jack Gannon she had slept with last night. A stranger had somehow gotten into the cab and taken the wheel. She rubbed away the gooseflesh on her upper arms as he drove out of the park and headed back toward Lemon Grove Avenue.

At the end of her block, when he had assured himself the Cadillac was nowhere in sight, Gannon pulled to the curb. He inclined his head toward the door on her side. "I'll drop you here."

"What do you mean drop me? Aren't you coming in?"

"No."

"Jack, what's the matter?"

"I have things to do."

"What things?"

"You don't want to know."

She sat staring at him. His face, his voice, his body language all were different. Somehow on the frightful ride through the park *he* had changed into... into what?

When she did not move he reached across her and opened the door. She climbed out and stood in the street for a moment, holding the door open.

"Are you coming back?"

"I don't know."

"Will I hear from you?"

"Don't worry, I'll take care of your truck." Gannon and grasped handle and pulled the door shut.

He felt as much a spectator to the scene as was Kristy, standing there at the curb. Somebody else was directing his life now, and he was powerless to stop.

Kristy watched the Dodge wheel away from the curb and roar off toward the freeway. She was torn by conflicting emotions. A few days ago her life had been well ordered, her future predictable. Then this man came into her life and turned everything upside down. She stepped back from the curb and forced herself to breathe slowly and deeply until she felt she had regained control.

What to do now? Call the police? And tell them what? Surely the shooting in the park constituted a crime, but she never got a look at the men who were chasing them. All she was likely to accomplish was to get Jack Gannon in more trouble than he already had. She was not ready to do that.

Would she ever see him again? she wondered. He hadn't said he would return, hadn't given her any reason to think so. All the same, she had a gut feeling that he would be back. At least, she would give him the chance. She turned and walked slowly down the street toward her house.

As she approached the front door she saw the white business card, tucked in the crack at the jamb.

Chapter 17

The Dodge seemed almost to steer itself over the freeway and into the seedy eastern section of Hollywood. As Jack Gannon continued his weird observer-like experience, another part of his mind drove on with grim determination toward a fixed destination. The traffic sounds outside were muted by the buzzing-rushing inside his head.

He pulled to a stop on Santa Monica Boulevard just east of the freeway and got out of the truck. Still feeling like an astral watcher, Gannon saw himself walk half a block down the street to stop before a lot enclosed by a chain link fence. A rusted gate hung open. A low, soot-stained building squatted well back from the street. A dented metal sign on the building identified it as *X-L Auto Body*.

The yard in front of the building was grown over with weeds and littered with the decaying corpses of automobiles.

Salvageable parts—wheels, doors, headlights, bumpers—were thrown into haphazard piles. Gannon walked in through the open gate and headed for the building.

A man with long greasy hair and a belly that bulged out from under his T-shirt appeared from behind the husk of a crumpled Oldsmobile.

"Looking for something special?"

"Marty Paich." The name came out automatically. It meant nothing to Gannon the observer, but the man using his body knew it. The voice that spoke through his mouth was hard-edged and cold.

The fat man looked him over cautiously. "Who wants him?"

"I want him. Now."

The expression in the icy gray eyes convinced the other man not to argue. "He's in the back."

Gannon brushed past him and walked through the dim, grease smelling building and out the rear door. The back lot was screened from outside view by an 8-foot wall on three sides. The cars back here were new and expensive. BMWs, Porsches, top-of-the-line Nissans and Toyotas. Several had windows masked for painting. A lean man with thin yellow hair worked with a grinder on the engine serial number of a Mazda RX-7. Gannon stood behind him until he looked up. The man started in surprise, nearly dropping the electric grinder. He shut it off immediately.

"Hello, Marty."

"Matchek!"

Memory currents jumped across gaps in his mind. Faulty relays clicked in.

"What did you call me?"

Paich looked around the lot, saw no one else there. "It was just the surprise. I wasn't expecting you. I mean, I didn't know you were out. I mean, we heard you was dead."

"What *do* you mean, Marty?"

"Nothin'! Hey, don't worry, I don't know you, I ain't seen you. You know you can rely on me, Lou."

"I hope so. I need a piece."

"Uh, right, Lou. Maybe tonight we could meet."

"I need it now."

"I'd really like to help you out, but I keep most of the merchandise at my place. All I've got here is a couple of samples."

"Show me."

Paich started to protest, thought better of it. "Right. Just let me wash my hands."

"I'll go with you."

He followed Paich to a foul smelling bathroom inside the building. He waited while the mechanic scrubbed his hands with rough pumice soap and dried them on a greasy roller towel. From time to time Paich would glance over at him with a tentative smile. He got no smile in return.

"Were you looking for anything special?" Paich said when they left the lavatory. "Like I said, the best hardware is back at my place."

"Just show me what you've got."

"Sure, Lou. Glad to."

Paich led the way to a heavy wooden cabinet in a corner of the building. The drawers secured by heavy padlocks. He keyed open the lock on the bottom drawer and pulled it out. Inside were more than a dozen guns ranging from a tiny .25-caliber purse pistol to Mark V Weatherby Magnum rifle that could blast through a car door.

"Just a few samples, huh?"

Paich giggled nervously. "Guess I had more here than I thought."

"I guess you did." He hefted several of the weapons and sighted along the barrels.

Paich stood by, his eyes jittering around the room. "Nobody saw you come in did they?"

"What do you think?"

"No, 'course they didn't. I'm just jumpy, the surprise of seein' you and all."

"I'll bet." He balanced a blue steel Colt Trooper with a 4-inch barrel. "How much?"

"That one? I'm asking four-fifty."

Gannon dug through the wadded bills in his pocket. "I'll give you a hundred."

"Hell, Lou, I can't take that."

"Yes, you can."

"Jesus, I'm losing money."

"Put the rest on my tab."

Paich looked pleadingly into the ice gray eyes, saw no compromise there.

"You got ammunition for this?"

"No three-fifty-seven, but I can let you have a box of .38 special."

"That'll do."

Paich retrieved the box of shells from another drawer and handed it over.

Jack Gannon, watching as though in a drugged out dream, saw Lou Matchek take the revolver. He knew now beyond a doubt who was in charge. Like it or not, there wasn't a damn thing he could do about it.

Matchek loaded the revolver, tucked it into his belt, adjusted Jay Baysinger's jacket to cover the butt. He gave Paich the bills from his pocket, keeping only a twenty and some change.

"See you, Marty."

"Yeah, right. Hang loose, Lou."

Matchek walked out the front of the building.

As soon as Paich stopped watching him, he ducked behind the corpse of an old Chevy. The fat man with the greasy hair eyed him suspiciously, but turned quickly away when the gray eyes met his.

At the wall phone just inside the building Marty Paich nervously punched out a number. He chewed his wispy moustache while he waited for someone to pick up on the other end.

"Granite Enterprises." The voice was cool, competent, and feminine.

"I gotta talk to Nick Tenzi."

"May I tell him who's calling?"

"Marty Paich. From X-L Auto. He knows me."

"Mr. Tenzi is not in the office today."

"Listen, honey, this is important. He'll want to hear what I have to tell him."

"If you will leave a number ..."

"I'm leaving nothing. I want to talk to Nick now. Tell him it's about Lou Matchek."

There was a barely discernable pause at the other end of the line. "You can try reaching him at home." She recited a telephone number, Paich copied it with the stub of a pencil.

As he hung up the telephone a hand came down hard on his shoulder. He gave a little squeal of fright.

"Where is he Marty?"

He turned and looked into the face of Lou Matchek. He swallowed to lubricate his vocal cords.

"Where is who?"

"Tenzi. Don't fuck with me, Marty."

"He-he's at his place in the canyon. I don't know the address."

"That's all right, I know it. You're not going to

tell him I'm coming now, are you, Marty."

"I... uh... no, Lou. Not me. I won't tell him anything."

"Yes, you would. But this time you're not going to. Because if you do, Marty, you're dead. Do you understand me?" The mechanic bobbed his head up and down.

"That's good."

From his isolated corner of the jumbled mind the fragment of the man that was still Jack Gannon watched helplessly as Lou Matchek strode out of the wrecking yard onto Santa Monica Boulevard. His movements were lithe and full of purpose, smooth despite the heavy pistol jammed into his waistband. He pulled open the door of the Dodge Raider and climbed in behind the wheel.

Seated in the Dodge, he hefted the pistol. The knurled grip felt right and natural in his hand. Now he was complete.

If only it weren't for the swarm of bees that came and went in his head. The buzzing grew louder now, building to a rush of winter wind through naked branches.

Suddenly it was crowded in the cab. The fading voice of Jack Gannon cried out for recognition. The memories of Jay Baysinger pulled and plucked at him like an insistent child. He pressed the heels of his hands against his temples, trying to quiet angry inner voices that battled for control.

What the hell am I doing? Where am I going?

Why do I have this gun?

Who, in the name of God, am I?

He was suddenly bone tired. The sun was

down, street lights were coming on. How long had he been without sleep? What time was it, anyway?

The questions battered him like rocks thrown by a pursuing mob. The answers didn't matter. They could wait. There were things he had to do now, people he had to see. A debt to pay off.

He fired the engine to life and pulled away from the curb. As he drove down the block, the darkness pushed into his mind. He felt drained, and he would have to be alert for what he had to do now. He had to sleep.

He looked back at the wrecking yard. Not here. Here lay danger. He forced his eyes wide, screwed all his attention onto his driving, and searched for a secluded spot were he could rest and let the rushing wind inside his head subside.

Chapter 18

Nick Tenzi wore an ankle-length silk dressing gown of the kind no longer seen outside of movies from the 1930s and 1940s. He had it specially made by a tailor on Melrose Avenue under the mistaken impression that it made him look tall and suave. Even when he added the white scarf tucked in around his neck he looked short and oily.

Drummer Cahane and Roy Kilgore knew better than to comment on their chief's appearance. Especially when he was in a bad mood. They stood shoulder to shoulder, eyes downcast, as Tenzi paced back and forth in front of them like an inspector general.

"So you missed him," he said. "You *missed* him. You had Lou Matchek right there in your sights and you missed him."

Tenzi's voice was tightly controlled. He spun away as though he could no longer bear the sight of the two men, and stood with his small hands clasped behind him, staring out through the leaded glass window. Outside the front lawn glowed silver under the powerful floodlights. He held the pose for several minutes. Drummer Cahane and Roy Kilgore exchanged a glance and tried to make themselves small.

Tenzi whirled suddenly to face them. "What happened? That's all I want to know... What the hell happened?"

After a moment's hesitation Kilgore spoke up. "It wasn't all that easy, Nick. He spotted us coming up behind him, and he was driving like a maniac."

"But you did have a clear shot."

"Well, more or less."

"More or less." Tenzi stared down at the shiny toe caps of his Italian shoes. When he looked up again his teeth were bared in a nasty smile. "You had a clear shot at Matchek and you let him get away! Will somebody please just tell me—How the fuck could you let that happen?"

"There were people in the park," Drummer offered. "Families. Having picnics and stuff."

"Oh. No shit. People in the park. Imagine that. Are you telling me you were afraid an innocent bystander might get hurt?"

"There was little kids."

"Well, son of a bitch. Do you know how many kids are gunned down by the juvenile gangs in this city? Four or five a week.

The world doesn't come to a stop. That's fucking life."

"And there was a bunch of sheriffs playing softball."

Tenzi ground his teeth. "Oh, beautiful! Let me see if I've got this straight. You heroes chase Lou Matchek into a park where you've got an open shot at him, but you don't shoot because you're afraid you might hit somebody's stinking kid. So what do you do? You run him right into the L.A. County Sheriff's annual picnic. Is that what you're telling me?"

Neither man answered.

"So Matchek is still out there somewhere and now he's mad as hell. And we don't have a clue where the fuck he is."

"He might go back to the broad's place," Drummer suggested.

"Not likely. He knows you had it staked out. I'm surprised he was even with a woman. As far as I know Lou Matchek never got that close to anybody."

Kilgore looked thoughtful. "What if we grab this one and use her to smoke him out?"

"No good. That might work with somebody else, but not with Lou Matchek. He's the coldest sonofabitch I've ever known. We could pull the skin off this woman with pliers and he wouldn't turn a hair. No, you clowns let him get away, and now, somehow, we've got to find him before he finds me."

The doorbell chimed and all three men flinched, looked at each other and at the door.

"Well, answer it," Tenzi said. "You can bet Lou Matchek is not going to walk up and ring the doorbell."

Drummer Cahane peered through the viewer then cautiously opened the front door. Tenzi stood behind him looking over his shoulder.

Outside on the flagstone walk Merlin Ryan was fending off the friendly leaps of the Doberman, who was trying to jump high enough to lick his face. He looked past Drummer in the doorway to Tenzi.

"Hello, Nick."

"What do you want here, Ryan?"

At the sound of Tenzi's voice the dog dropped into a crouch.

The short hair on his shoulders bristled, he growled low and mean.

"I got to get rid of that mutt," Tenzi said.

"I thought we could talk about a one-time friend of yours," Ryan suggested.

"Now who would that be?"

"Lou Matchek."

"What about him?"

"I hear he's on the street."

"Is that a fact?"

"I see you heard it too."

"I heard rumors. Where is he supposed to be?"

"How about if I come inside and we talk about it?"

"This isn't a roust?"

"You know I don't play games, Nick."

Tenzi jerked his head and Drummer and Kilgore vanished into another part of the house.

"Come on in."

Ryan walked into the living room, inventoried it with his eyes, and made himself comfortable in Tenzi's favorite chair.

"So what about Matchek?" Tenzi said.

"I thought you might be a little worried."

"Worried? Me? Why should I be worried?"

"Maybe because he's looking for you."

"Get to the point Ryan."

"Setting Vin Faccio on him was a mistake, Nick. Before that Matchek might have suspected you were the one who set him up, but he wasn't sure. When Vinnie put a blade into him it erased all doubt. Now Matchek's out, and I don't have to tell you what's the first thing on his mind. I wouldn't want to be your insurance man."

"That's all bullshit, Ryan. Faccio didn't talk, and you can't prove a damn thing."

Ryan lit a Marlboro. He looked around for an ashtray and, seeing none, tossed the burnt out match onto the carpet. Tenzi looked pained, but made no move to pick it up.

"No. Faccio didn't talk," Ryan said. "Not after Matchek shoved his nose back into his brain. So I can't prove anything. But Matchek doesn't worry about proof. As far as he's concerned, you're a dead man."

"So why are you here telling me all this?"

"I'm giving you a chance to stay alive, Nick."

"What's that supposed to mean?"

"It means I can offer you protection from Matchek in return for your cooperation."

"Shove it. I don't cooperate with feds. And I don't need your protection."

Ryan shrugged. "It's up to you, Nick. We're going to get you sooner or later. Me or the Bureau, or the IRS, or maybe the local cops. Your kind is finished. You're out of date. You're a dinosaur. You don't scare people any more. Street punks with bandannas and rings in their ears are taking the action away from you. And now you've got Lou Matchek on your case. I don't have to tell you about Matchek, he did some work for you. He's a human shark. A textbook sociopath. He kills without a thought. It's his work, and he's the best at it. If you want to wait around until he finds you, and he will, that's your funeral."

Ryan ground out the cigarette on his shoe sole and tossed the butt. Nick."

"I've made my offer, and I'm through. So long,

Ryan stood up and started toward the door. Tenzi caught up with him.

"Wait a minute. I think I just got this figured out.

You sprung Matchek, didn't you. You're running him. You let that murderous bastard out to get me. That's how you can offer to protect me from him. All you have to do is say the word to pull him off. Am I right?"

Ryan looked at him gravely. "Nick, I'm surprised at you. I am an employee of the federal government. What you are suggesting is clearly a criminal offense. I'm shocked that you would even bring it up."

"I knew it!" Tenzi said. "You bastards can't hang anything on me legitimately so you pull some rotten trick like this. Well fuck you."

"That's your answer?"

"You got it."

Ryan slipped a business card from his breast pocket and wrote on the back of it. "If you change your mind, Nick, you can give me a call at this number. While you're still healthy."

He levered himself out of the chair and held out the card.

Tenzi took it without looking at it.

"I hope you're not counting on those two clowns in the next room for help," Ryan said. "They're not much as much protection against a man like Matchek."

"Just let me worry about that."

Ryan shrugged again and went past him and out the door. The Doberman was waiting for him. The black stump of a tail wagged itself into a blur. Ryan patted the dog's head and walked away.

When he had driven off Tenzi lashed out with a kick that caught the Doberman in the ribs. The dog yelped and whirled to bare its teeth.

"How do you like it, mutt?"

The Doberman answered with an ugly growl.

"Tomorrow you die:" Tenzi snarled back.

He slammed the heavy door before the dog could get at him and tossed Ryan's card into the drawer of the hall table.

Drummer Cahane and Roy Kilgore met him as he marched into the living room. They stood uncertainly, waiting for orders. Tenzi had none to deliver.

"Go on, get out of here," he said. "I need time to think." When they had left the house and he heard them drive away

Tenzi let his shoulders slump. That sonofabitch Ryan was obsessed with nailing him, even if it meant springing a convicted killer. If it was the legitimate FBI on his ass he could cry harassment and he'd have the *LA Times*, the ACLU, and the 9th Circuit Court of Appeals on his side. But Merlin Ryan played by his own rules. He would not personally come gunning, at least Tenzi did not think so, but with Matchek in his pocket he wouldn't have to.

He stood for a minute in the center of the big room and looked around at the period furniture, the heavy oriental carpet, the Moroccan tapestry, the abstract paintings. Carefully he picked up Ryan's match and cigarette but and dropped them into a bronze bowl.

Each piece in the house had cost a bundle, and they symbolized what he had made of himself. Little Nick Tenzi had come a long way from the streets of Cleveland. Nobody gave him shit any more. Nobody, except one crazy killer and a maverick FBI agent. He walked the length of the room to the bar, selected the bottle of Hennessey Five Star, poured a grapefruit size snifter half full and carried it back to his chair.

He swallowed some of the brandy, coughed,

and let himself think for a minute about running. Get the fuck out of here and away. Tell nobody. Not Cahane and Kilgore, and definitely not Helene. Lou Matchek couldn't stay on the street forever; too many people knew him. When he was caught and locked up, Tenzi could come back. Meanwhile, there were plenty of places he could hide. Not only in the U.S., but in Mexico, Brazil, Portugal, Greece. Sure, it wouldn't be any problem, except for one thing. Everybody would know he ran. Afraid of a lone gunman. Once you're labeled a pussy, you were dead in his business. Respect? Forget it. Without respect Nick Tenzi was nothing. If he ran, no matter what excuse he made up, he would have no more respect than Elmer Fudd. There had to be another way.

Outside the wind blew a tall cypress tree against an upstairs window. Tenzi heard it and spilled an ounce of brandy on his lap before he identified the sound.

His nerves were going fast. Pretty soon he wouldn't be able to hide it. Then he'd really be fucked. Somehow, some way, Lou Matchek had to die.

Chapter 19

The sun slanted in through the windshield of the Dodge Raider, piercing the eyelids of the man who slept behind the wheel. He mumbled something in his sleep, his hand brushed at his face, trying to clear away the irritation. Finally he opened his eyes, blinked, groaned, and let the world tumble in.

He remembered the rushing, roaring wind sound in his head that had finally subsided enough to let him sleep. It had dwindled now to the soft, insistent hum of the bees—still an intrusion, but nothing he could not handle.

He straightened up in the seat, stretched his arms and legs, loosening the muscles. He rubbed at his forehead and the tiny scar there that itched like a spider bite. He looked around to see he was parked on a quiet street of small, inexpensive houses and stumpy date palm trees. No traffic, no pedestrians. A spot well chosen for a man who wanted to sleep undisturbed in his car. He looked into the rearview mirror. Two gray eyes like chips of glacier ice looked back at him.

Names, thoughts, memories flitted in and out of his head like images on a television screen when you zapped through the channels. Then one name, one man, one mission took control. Lou Matchek moved the pistol to a more comfortable position in his belt and drove out of the quiet neighborhood.

From a dark, distant corner of his mind Jack Gannon watched mute and powerless. The Jay Baysinger memories were tatters of a fading dream. Lou Matchek was back, and he was in command.

Matchek did not expend much mental energy trying to understand what had happened to him. He knew he felt goods and strong. It was like he had been riding in the back seat, an unwilling passenger, forbidden to comment or complain, while somebody else drove. Now he was up where he belonged—in the driver's seat.

He relaxed as he drove, shutting down the irritating background thoughts, letting instinct take him where he had to go.

His first stop was in Pacific Palisades, an upscale community north of Santa Monica. He slowed and stopped across from a large, Tudor style house with carefully tended grounds, enclosed by an ornate iron fence. A discreet sign at the gate identified it as Crestview Chateau.

He parked the Dodge and walked across the street. At the gate he paused for a minute to survey the grounds. Several people strolled the litter-free paths that criss-crossed the lawn. Scattered among them were several watchful young men who kept a discreet eye on the strollers and the gate. To a casual observer Crestview Chateau might be a small, fashionable hotel, or an exclusive club. Only a closer look at the strollers would reveal that Crestview was something else.

One expensively dressed woman carried on a spirited conversation with herself as she walked. A young man repeatedly tossed in the air and caught a ball only he could see. And a man with a trimmed white beard sat on a stone bench and stared fixedly at a fountain as though waiting for a nymph to rise from the waters. As a matter of fact, he was waiting for precisely that. The Crestview Chateau was an expensive, privately owned, tastefully run mental hospital.

Matchek pushed through the unlocked gate and walked up the main path to the entrance. One of the watchful young men nodded pleasantly, but kept a careful eye on him as he entered the building.

The reception area was furnished and decorated in Victorian maroons and browns. A woman with silver hair and a flawless complexion sat behind a desk. A placard read: *Mrs. Isham*. She looked up and smiled automatically. Then her eyes flicked over Matchek's unshaven face, his rumpled and ill-fitting suit. The smile stayed in place, but her eyes narrowed.

"May I help you?"

"I want to see Katherine Gannon."

A shadow crossed the woman's smooth face. "Are you a friend?"

"A relative."

"I'm sorry. Mrs. Gannon isn't with us any more."

"She died?"

"No, no," the woman said quickly. "I just meant I mean she left Crestview."

"Why would she do that?"

"I really don't think I should discuss it."

Matchek planted his hands on the desk and put his face close to Mrs. Isham's. Very deliberately he said, "I think you should."

Mrs. Isham blinked rapidly three times, then recovered her composure.

"Yes, certainly. I'll just punch it up on the computer."

He waited while she tapped on the keyboard. The computer buzzed and clicked, and white letters appeared on the screen's blue background.

"Mrs. Gannon was transferred in, let me see, in January to the Marquis Convalescent Home."

"Where is that?"

She tapped the keys again. "It's in Hollywood."

He craned over the desk to read the address on Cherokee Avenue.

"Who ordered the transfer?"

More business with the keyboard. "A Mr. Horace Brill made the arrangements. He was the administrator in her case."

Matchek nodded once to the woman and walked out of the building without further conversation. Mrs. Isham drew a deep breath, much relieved to see him go.

* * * * *

Every few years some member of the Chamber of Commerce would propose a complete rejuvenation of Hollywood. There would be newspaper articles with photographs of Hollywood past and present, and an artist's conception of the wondrous Hollywood future. Television reporters would interview local residents and store owners, who would express varying degrees of enthusiasm. Politicians would be photographed with the hillside HOLLYWOOD sign behind them as they made fulsome promises of the refurbishment to come. After a week or two the whole idea would vanish and Hollywood would settle back into the gang-ridden, crime-stricken, sleazy semi-slum it had become in the past three decades.

This was the Hollywood where Lou Matchek pulled the Dodge to the red-painted curb and parked illegally on Hollywood Boulevard. As he stepped out he was immediately approached by a hollow cheeked individual with his hand out.

"Can you help me out for something to eat?"

"Get a job," Matchek advised him.

One look into the ice gray eyes discouraged the panhandler from further conversation.

The sidewalk was crowded with a mixture of teenagers in trendy shoes and baggy pants, drugged out bums in rags, transvestites, kooks, pimps, whores, and bewildered tourists.

There were black faces, brown faces, painted faces. The shops had iron gratings to be pulled across their fronts at night.

They sold marital aids, paperback books, movie posters, burritos, Orange Julius, electronic toys, T-shirts with clever captions.

Lou Matchek ignored the pedestrians and the vendors. With his eyes fixed straight ahead he strode along the sidewalk where imbedded stars carried the names of show business personalities past and present. Even the ugliest of the oncoming crowd made way for him as they sensed in this man something not to be messed with, not even a little bit.

He turned up Cherokee past a string of drab, faceless buildings to the address he had memorized from the computer screen. The building was old and stained with the grime of the years. It dated to the 1920s when it had provided affordable apartments for people in the burgeoning movie business. After a dozen changes of ownership, a wooden sign with black letters on peeling white paint now identified it as *Marquis Convalescent Home.*

Matchek's scowl darkened. He climbed a short flight of steps to the first landing. There he pushed the door open and walked in to a small, bare room. Behind a cracked pane of glass a young black woman with brilliant red lipstick talked on the phone with great animation. She flicked her eyes over the unshaven intruder and dismissed him as another street bum.

Matchek slapped the flat of his hand against the glass, making the entire pane shiver dangerously.

The young woman covered the mouthpiece of the telephone and frowned at him. "You want something?"

"I want to see Katherine Gannon."

"There's nobody here now to take you up. Can you come back in an hour?"

"No. You tell me where she is. I'll find my own way up."

"We're not supposed to—"

"Where is she?" Matchek showed his teeth.

"Second floor, end of the hall, number 21." The young woman reached for a worn ledger. "Uh, you're supposed to sign in."

Matchek turned away without bothering to answer, and climbed the dark stairway to the second floor. The young black woman slapped the ledger shut, told her caller she'd get back to him, and checked the lock on the sliding glass panel.

Upstairs Matchek found a door with the brass number 22 and knocked.

From inside he heard a female voice muttering

too low for him to understand. There was no response to his knock. He opened the door and walked in.

There were three single beds, a couple of mismatched chests of drawers, a kitchen table, three wooden chairs that looked like thrift shop rejects. Women's clothes were draped over the chairs and crumpled on the floor. The room had the sad sour smell of sickness and age.

In one of the beds a fat woman lay on her back with her mouth open, snoring wetly. She had a brown mole the size of a grape on her upper lip.

A very old woman with a bluish white complexion sat at the room's single window and stared out across the alley at the back of another building. She kept up a soft, incoherent conversation with an invisible companion.

In the center bed, propped up on three pillows, looking straight at Matchek was Katherine Gannon.

Matchek grabbed the only chair that did not have clothes on it and pulled it over next to the bed.

"Are you the furnace man?" she asked. He shook his head. "I want you to get that furnace fixed. It's cold in here all the time."

"It's Louie, Mom." He had to force the words out through a constricted throat.

"They were supposed to bring fruit today. Do you see my fruit around here?"

"I don't see any fruit," he said.

"Well, there you are. The bastards lied. The bastards lie to us all the time."

He looked at her closely. She would be, if he had it right, fifty-five. She looked seventy. Her hair, once a rich brown, was thin and mouse-colored. It needed washing. Her skin was pale and damp. Her face was gaunt, but the high cheekbones and straight, narrow nose were reminders of the laughing good looks he remembered from his childhood.

Now that he was here sitting at his mother's bedside, looking at her vacant face, he didn't know what he wanted to say. It was his first visit since... damn that buzzing in his head was starting up again, blurring his memory.

"Louie?" she said. A tiny light of reason showed in her eyes.

"Yes, Mom."

"Louie, you look thin. Are you eating enough?"

Something stuck in his throat. "I'm fine, Mom. How are you doing?"

"Are you the furnace man?" The tiny light blinked out. "I wish you'd fix that furnace. It gets really cold in here. I'm cold all the time."

Matchek tuned out her words and half-closed his eyes so the picture of the sick old woman in the bed softened. He could remember old snapshots of the wild and pretty young girl who had dropped out of high school in Beaumont, Texas, and come west to seek her fortune. In 1950 Hollywood was not the slime pot it was today, but neither was it The Emerald City. Katherine Gannon had found here hundreds of girls wilder and prettier than she. The competition was fierce, even for the carhop and waitress jobs that would tide them over until the Big Break came.

She found also a muscular, tattooed pimp who called himself Zorro. He taught Katherine how to use a heroin needle, and how to sell her body to keep it filled.

Louie's birth had been an accident, coming just

two years after Katherine arrived in Hollywood, but long after she had given up on the Big Break and fallen in love with the needle. At the first sign of pregnancy she made the bus trip to Tijuana.

There she sat in the waiting room of the foul-smelling Clinica Morales with a dozen other unhappy young women waiting for an anonymous doctor to scoop out their insides. Before Katherine's name was called she got up and walked out to hitchhike back to Hollywood.

Zorro naturally dropped Katherine when her belly began to swell and she could not earn her keep. She signed up for welfare, and went through a state-funded program to cure addicts. She managed to stay off the needle through the last five months of her pregnancy. When Louie was born she felt like a real mother, and promised herself repeatedly that from now on her life was going to be different. By the time her baby was a month old she was back on the drug and back on the streets.

Matchek had pieced the story together from old photographs, his childhood memories, and his mother's vague ramblings. It was a fragmented story of arrests, foster homes, strange men, drunken tantrums, drug frenzies, tears, and a growing madness. There also were a few, a very few, moments of real happiness. A day with his mother at the zoo in Griffith Park when she bought them both popcorn and they laughed a lot. Breakfast at the House of Pancakes where he always ordered blueberry waffles and didn't notice that his mother never touched her own food, chain smoking and drinking cup after cup of black coffee. And sometimes she took him to a movie in one of the big theaters that used to line the Boulevard. There the little boy could lose himself in the brighter-than-life technicolor fantasies.

"Louie," said the worn-out woman in the bed. "I'm sorry. I didn't give you much of a life."

"I'm going to take you out of here, Mom," he said.

"I wanted to do right. I wanted to be a good mother live the way people ought to live. I was young and I was dumb, and I couldn't do it."

"It's all right," he said, knowing as he said it that it was a lie. It wasn't all right. It was a rotten shitty deal. Whose fault was it? Nobody's. Everybody's. What difference did it make?

"We were supposed to get fruit," Katherine Gannon said. "Where the hell is my fruit?"

"You'll have fruit," he said, getting to his feet. "I promise you."

The fat woman snorted suddenly and coughed in her sleep.

The frail old woman at the window chuckled at some secret joke. Katherine Gannon gazed at her son with ineffable sadness.

* * * * *

Back downstairs the young woman behind the glass looked up warily from *Daily Variety* when Matchek's grim face appeared at her window.

"Get Mrs. Gannon's things together and get her ready to leave."

"I got no authorization to do that."

"You will have," Matchek told her. "Get started."

She watched tall, slope-shouldered man shove

his way out the door and decided she had better get Katherine Gannon ready to move.

Chapter 20

The office of Horace Brill, attorney-at-law, was high in one of the gleaming towers of Century City between Pico and Santa Monica Boulevards on the west side of Los Angeles. Deep carpets hushed the footsteps of clients. Furnishings of burnished brass and burgundy leather in the waiting room announced to clients that the services of Horace Brill did not come cheap.

The poised receptionist bore a striking resemblance to the female star of a popular situation comedy—a resemblance that was not accidental. Her expression was professionally cool when the tall, rumpled man in need of a shave strode into the room.

"May I help you?"

"Is he in?"

"Sir?"

"Is he in. Brill."

"Do you have an appointment?"

"I don't need an appointment," Matchek said.

"Mr. Brill is with a client now, if you'll please—"

He did not give the girl a chance to finish. As she started to rise he crossed the spongy carpet to a door marked *PRIVATE*, shoved it open and walked in.

Horace Brill was a smoothly tanned man with a nose that needed fixing and a neat gray beard. He wore a diamond on his pinky that could have fed Bangladesh for a year. He was in earnest conversation with a woman of fifty-some whose face had the tight shine that comes with multiple face lifts. He looked up in annoyance at the unannounced entrance.

"What do you—?" Brill froze with his mouth still open as he recognized the intruder.

"Hello, Horace."

It took only a moment for the veteran attorney to collect himself. He flashed a smooth professional smile to his matronly client.

"I'm sorry, Mrs. Gooding, but will you excuse me for a moment?" He continued without waiting for a response. "If you'll be kind enough to wait outside I'll be with you shortly. Thank you."

The woman gave Matchek an indignant up-and-down look, and took herself out of the office. Brill got up from his desk to come around and close the door behind her.

The professional smile widened. Brill's bright little eyes glowed with heartfelt concern. "Lou, this is quite a surprise. I heard you were you were..."

"Dead? You can say the word if you try."

"Exactly. There was supposed to have been a fight of some kind at Folsom back around Christmas. The news story said you died of stab wounds."

"The report was premature."

Brill rose and came around the desk, still smiling. "Well, I can't tell you how glad I am to hear that." He put out a hand. Matchek ignored it.

Brill retrieved his hand. "I'll certainly be interested to hear how it came about." He took a closer look at Matchek's condition. "What are you doing... out?"

"Never mind that. I *am* out is what matters. What I want to hear now is why you took my mother out of Crestview and put her in that Hollywood dump."

The attorney's mind smoothly shifted gears. "The Marquis? It was highly recommended."

"Did you see it?"

Brill eased back behind the desk and sat down, putting its width between himself and Matchek.

"Well, I didn't go over there personally, but—"

"It's a sewer. "

Brill's tanned forehead creased, showing his distress. "That's certainly something to look into. My thought at the time was that, considering our financial arrangement—"

"Our financial arrangement gave you enough money to keep my mother in Crestview and supply her with anything she needed as long as she lives."

"Costs have increased considerably, Lou, in the three years since we handled this."

"Don't shit me, Horace. There was plenty of money to cover any increase."

"You could be right. I'll have to go over the accounts again."

"Go over nothing, Horace. What you'll do is you'll get my mother out of that dump and back into Crestview where I told you to keep her."

"Well, yes, I suppose that can be arranged. In fact, I'll get on it first thing in the morning."

Matchek's hand shot across the desk and his first two fingers hooked into Brill's nostrils. He lifted the attorney out of the chair by his nose, ignoring the feeble attempts to dislodge his grip.

"You'll get on it now."

Horace Brill, his eyes wide, not smiling now, gagged out the words.

"Sure, Lou, if that's what you want."

"It's what I want."

Matchek extracted his fingers from the other man's nose. He pulled a crisp white handkerchief from the attorney's breast pocket and used it to wipe his hand. Brill touched his nose tenderly and examined his fingertips for blood. Finding none, he put on a pale imitation of his friendly smile and punched a button on the built-in intercom.

"Donna, get me the Crestview Nursing Home in Pacific Palisades."

A tense 30 seconds passed. Horace Brill sniffed noisily several times. Matchek's eyes never left him. When the telephone on his desk warbled Brill snatched it up gratefully.

Matchek stood over him while he made arrangements for the readmittance of Katherine Gannon to Crestview. He told them to dispatch an ambulance right away to transport her there from the Marquis. He then called the Marquis and in firm lawyer tones informed them that he was having Mrs. Gannon moved at once, and he was seriously considering action against them in light of disturbing reports on the quality of their service.

"Satisfied?" he asked when he hung up after the last call. "For now," Matchek said. "I don't want to hear that she's been moved again."

"You won't, Lou. My word on that."

"Because if I do, I'll come back for you."

The attorney nodded, his face drawn under salon tan.

"And Horace, you're not going to mention to anyone that I was here, are you."

"Why would I do that?"

"Just make sure you don't."

When Matchek had gone Horace Brill reached into a drawer for a handful of tissues. He blew his nose several times, forgetting all about Mrs. Gooding who still waited in the outer office.

* * * * *

Down in the underground parking lot Matchek climbed into the Dodge and slammed the door. As if it were a signal, the bees swarmed again. Other voices, other people—Jay Baysinger, Jack Gannon—tried to force themselves into his consciousness.

Matchek struggled to hold them back. He had more calls to make.

He was not ready to surrender control. Gradually the other voices subsided. The bees settled down.

Matchek drove out Santa Monica all the way to Ocean Boulevard. There he turned south into Venice.

Once a developer's dream of Mediterranean bungalow and palm lined canals, Venice today was a mismatch of high-rise condos, pricey apartments, funky 1920s houses, and trendy boutiques. The inhabitants included upscale singles, party people, street freaks, and a few long-time residents who still remembered the old days.

Matchek parked the Dodge and walked along the ocean front, ignoring the mutter of conflicting voices in his head. He paid no attention to the panhandlers, the tourists, the sidewalk vendors, or the entertainers doing their pitiful little acts with a hat or a coffee can sitting on the cement for contributions.

A young roller-skater in neon shorts, knee and elbow pads, and helmet rolled toward him. When Matchek failed to leap out of his way as did most pedestrians, the boy swerved at the last moment and fell heavily to the pavement. He sat there swearing softly as Matchek walked on without looking back.

The building where he stopped was a five-story wedding cake of pink and white stone and glass. The parking area was protected by a barred gate that raised and lowered for residents with a magnetized key card. Matchek pulled into a loading zone, left the truck, and walked to the apartment foyer. There a security speaker system guarded the entrance.

Matchek lifted the telephone receiver punched a three-digit number he dredged up from his memory.

"Yes?" A low-pitched female voice that triggered below-the- belt sensations.

"Hello, Denise."

A barely perceptible pause, then, "Who is this?" "Matchek."

"No!"

"Yes. Buzz me in, baby."

A longer pause, then the clatter of the electric release for the door. Matchek pushed it opened and entered.

The elevator smelled of strawberry incense and sweat. The sweat was his own. The hallway on the top floor was wide and bright as sun filtered in through a skylight. Matchek stopped at a door and knocked once. It opened immediately.

Denise Underhill had the look of a well-groomed

graduate of a quality women's college, which she was. She carried herself with the sleek professionalism of a high-priced call girl, which she also was. She wore a black jersey dress, small silver earrings, and the barest touch of makeup. Her hair was a rich auburn, brushed out to frame her face. She was a healthy 34 looked it, and liked it.

"My God, it *is* you," she said.

"I know, you heard I was dead."

"That was the word. Come in here." She took him by the wrists and pulled him into the apartment. He pushed the door closed and she stepped back to size him up.

"You look like hell, Lou."

"I've been busy." He walked past her and dropped into a velour chair of marshmallow white. The chair faced a balcony that ran the width of the room and looked out over Santa Monica Bay.

The woman walked over and stood by the window, looking down on him. After a minute she said, "You want to tell me what happened?"

He rubbed his forehead. The low-key buzzing was giving him a headache. "I'd like to, but I'm a little confused about that myself."

Denise stood in a familiar pose, elbow cupped in one hand, fingertips lightly against her cheek. "Is anybody looking for you?"

"Lots of people. Nobody followed me here, though."

"Do you want to stay?"

"Just until I catch my breath."

"You know you can stay as long as you want," she said. "Like to clean up?"

He managed a grin. "Probably a good idea. Aspirin in the bathroom?"

"In the usual place. I've got something stronger, if you want it."

He shook his head. "Aspirin is as strong as I want to go. I will use the shower, though."

The shower was an integral part of an enclosed sunken tub with blue and white tile and gold plated faucets. A gentle spray of water that hit his body from several directions. Matchek closed his eyes and let the feel of the water and the smell of the woman's perfume in the bathroom recall other times.

Women had never been important in his life. He took one when he felt the need, made no promises, asked no favors. In his line of work it would not be smart to tie up with a woman. The Dillinger Rule, he privately called it. Yet somehow he and Denise had come together and fit like two pieces of a jigsaw puzzle. Neither had interfered with the other's life, yet each could shut out the world when they were together.

The irony of the situation did not escape him. Much as he had hated his mother's life and what she did, he had taken for himself a woman in the same profession. There was, of course, a huge gulf between the frenzied ten-dollar couplings of his mother with the countless men she brought home, and the 500-to-1000-dollar-a-night "dates" that would make Denise a very rich woman before she lost her looks.

No money had ever passed between them. They had never had a serious quarrel. Insofar as either of them could love anyone, Denise Underhill and Lou Matchek loved each other.

He came out of the shower clean, but with the

stubble still on his face. One of Denise's huge pink towels was wrapped around his waist.

She looked him over. "Much better." He nodded agreement.

Denise picked up his wrinkled clothes, holding them delicately in her fingertips. "Too bad we can't do something about these."

She let the clothes drop and came across the room to him.

Her perfume filled his head.

"It's good to see you," she said. "You too."

She slipped her arms around him, kneading the rigid trapezius muscles.

"You're tense." She pulled his body against hers and kissed him.

The feel of her breasts flattening on his bare chest, her pubis pushing forward against him fired more sensual memories. Their lovemaking had been fierce and unrestrained. All the hungers he held inside, and all the real passions she covered with pretense were released in their wild, exhausting encounters.

But much as he wanted her now, he could not react. She drew back and looked at him. "Problem?"

"Yeah." The voice was Lou Matchek, but the speaker was the creation of three days ago, Jack Gannon.

Denise released him. "You can still stay."

"Thanks. But I've got another stop to make." He carried the rumpled clothes back into the bathroom, dressed, and came out again.

"Will you be coming back?"

"I don't think so."

"Well... Take care of yourself, Matchek."

"You too, baby."

Their eyes met and held briefly, then he was out the door and gone.

Chapter 21

It took a full twenty-four hours for Kristy Baysinger to feel the full impact of what happened in the park. Then she started to shake. Her hands trembled uncontrollably, her entire body shivered as though caught in an icy draft.

Someone, two men was all she could tell from the glimpse she caught before Gannon pushed her to the floor, had actually shot at them. Real guns, real bullets. The kind that maim and kill people. She would never again watch the casual shootouts of television cop shows with the same easy acceptance.

And now the card from somebody named Ryan of the FBI stuck in her door. On the back a handwritten note: *Please call me,* and a scribbled telephone number.

Although she drank infrequently, and never alone, Kristy wanted a drink now. She went to the kitchen now and poured herself a full glass of chilled Chablis. It was not quite the blood-warmer she had in mind, but was the strongest thing she had in the house. She downed two generous swallows and stood taking regular deep breaths waiting for the wine to do something. It helped a little. She carried the glass back to the living room and sat down to think about the bizarre events of the past three days, and how they had yanked her well-ordered life out of orbit and set it on a new path.

Jack Gannon was at the center of it. Who and what was Jack Gannon? What was his relationship to her late husband? Why was he the target of gunmen? Would she ever see him again? And if she did, what, exactly, were her feelings about the man? She had seen something emerging that was neither Jack Gannon, the man they had invented, nor Jay Baysinger, whose memories he had somehow absorbed. There was a coldness and a hard sense of purpose to the new personality that frightened her.

She took another sip of the wine. Her hands no longer shook. She considered refilling the glass, but decided that would be excessive. She wanted to be in full possession of her wits when he returned. If he returned.

Had she been foolish to put so much trust in this stranger?

His aversion to the police should have warned her off. She should have immediately gone to them herself and reported... reported what? That a man had come to her door on a Sunday afternoon obsessed with the idea that he was her dead husband? Was there a law against that?

At the very least she should have closed and locked the door once he was gone and forgot about him. But she could not have done that. His insistence that he was Jay Baysinger, and the things he knew piqued her curiosity. But it was more than that.

Kristy refilled the wine glass after all. She sipped the cool Chablis and let herself admit that she was attracted to Gannon, whoever he was. Immoderately, irrationally attracted to him. That was not like her.

Kristy's social life had been minimal since Jay moved up to work and live at Fairhaven. She had channeled her energies into her work at the clinic, not allowing herself to become involved with anyone. She had dated, of course, mostly doctors who put in time at the clinic. Nothing serious had developed, even with the two she had gone to bed with in the past three years. She had begun to think that she had at least achieved mastery over her sexual self, and then Jack Gannon came into her life.

Now he was God knew where, driving her beloved Dodge Raider.

There would be bullet holes and a shattered windshield when he brought it back. *If* he brought it back. She smiled at herself, worrying about the condition of her car, when the other night she had freely given the man her body. Strange how values got shuffled around in times of stress.

The sound of the doorbell chime startled her. Feeling foolishly guilty, she ran to the kitchen and stashed the empty wine glass in the dishwasher. She touched her hair in front of the mirror over the mantle, and peeked through the curtains.

A blocky, heavy-browed man with a fierce moustache stood outside. His posture was erect and formal. With him stood a tall blond man wearing a brown police-like uniform.

Irrationally, she felt like a fugitive, and had to fight down a crazy impulse to run out the back door. Ridiculous. She hadn't done anything wrong. She squared her shoulders, marched to the door and pulled it open, prepared to be indignant about the infringement of her rights.

"Mrs. Kristiana Baysinger?" the blocky man said.

"Yes."

"My name is Gunther Tork. I'm with VA Security." He flapped open a wallet to show her an identity card with his picture and the seal of the Veteran's Administration.

"I'm not sure I—" Kristy began.

"Attached to the Fairhaven Medical Facility," Tork explained.

"What is it you want?"

Tork looked up and down the street as though he feared they might be observed, "Can I come inside, Mrs. Baysinger?"

"I suppose so."

He turned to the uniformed man. "Spencer, you move the wagon somewhere out of sight. Tell Krebs to park the Buick, and you two take a position where you can watch the house."

The uniformed man nodded curtly and marched back toward the street. At the curb waited a station wagon with *Fairhaven* lettered on the door in a flowing script. The guard got in and drove off down the block.

Kristy stood out of the way and let Gunther Tork enter the house. His eyes took in everything with a professional sweep of the interior.

"What is this about, Mr. Tork?"

"Captain," he corrected.

"Captain then. What is your business with me?"

From an inside pocket he produced a thick manila envelope. After fingering through the contents he pulled out a black and white prison photo, full-face and profile, of a lean-jawed man with pale eyes.

"Have you seen this man?"

"Why?"

"Can you just tell me if you've seen him, Mrs. Baysinger?"

"Yes," she admitted.

"Do you know who he is?"

"Suppose you tell me."

"His name is Louis Matchek."

"Is that supposed to mean something to me?"

"He might be going by another name."

"Is he wanted for something?"

"Please answer the question, Mrs. Baysinger. Do you recognize the picture?"

Kristy frowned. She was not surprised to learn that her "Jack Gannon" had been in prison. He had given her enough clues. She could see no profit in protecting him now, yet she would proceed carefully with this Captain Tork.

"He came to my house Sunday," she said.

"He seemed...confused."

"That figures. He was undergoing treatment at Fairhaven." He tapped the side of his head.

"Are you telling me he is mentally ill?"

"I guess you could put it that way." Tork looked toward the rear of the house. "Is he here now, Mrs. Baysinger?"

"No."

"Has he been here?"

"I told you he came to the house on Sunday."

"But he isn't here now."

"No."

"The last time you saw him was when?"

Kristy felt herself blushing, and was angry about

it. "Captain Tork, before I answer any more questions, I want to know what this is all about."

"This man, this Lou Matchek, was at Fairhaven for experimental surgery. He came on a volunteer basis from Folsom State Prison. Matchek was serving a life term there as a convicted killer. He is an extremely dangerous man. It's my job to find him and bring him back."

"You say he's a killer?"

"A professional, cold-blooded killer. He was convicted of just one murder, but there is little doubt that he is responsible for a dozen or so dead men."

"I've talked to him. It doesn't seem possible."

Tork hefted the envelope to show her the sheaf of papers inside. "I have documentation here if you want to read it. Court records, police reports, newspaper stories. We know him better than you, Mrs. Baysinger."

Kristy waved off the envelope. She wobbled for a moment, feeling as though she had been clipped behind the knees. Tork came forward to catch her, but she recovered her balance and stepped back to sink into a chair.

Tork nodded, satisfied that he had made his point, and sat down on the couch without waiting for an invitation.

"I take it Matchek gave you some kind of cover story." he said.

"He came here Sunday saying—I know this sounds crazy—but he said he was my husband."

Tork nodded. "That's more or less what we figured might have happened. When a bank card he stole from one of our people was used in Glendale, we added it up and it seemed likely he'd come here."

"A bank card," Kristy repeated.

"Was the name on it Elliot Porter?"

"Yes, it was."

Kristy tried to assimilate what he was telling her. "Captain, you're going to have to fill me in on what's happening here. I feel like I came late to the party."

He gave her a tight smile. "It's a very complicated medical business, Mrs. Baysinger. I'm not a medical man, and I can't give you the nuts and bolts of it. I only know that Matchek underwent some kind of process up at Fairhaven that involved your husband."

"Involved him how?"

"I really can't say, Mrs. Baysinger. Dr. Vespa up at the facility would be the man to explain it to you."

"It doesn't make any sense. My husband is dead. He's been dead more than two years."

"As I said, I'm not the man to explain it." Tork brushed aside the subject of Jay Baysinger. "The important thing now is that we find Lou Matchek and take him back before someone gets hurt."

"Hurt?"

"He's a violent man. In his present state, nobody can predict what he might do."

"He didn't seem to be as unstable as all that."

"You can't always tell from talking to somebody. Psychos can fool you. Do you expect him to come back here?"

"I-I'm not sure."

She did not completely trust this man with his brusque military manner and the restless eyes. And she did not like him. Still, what he told her about Jack Gannon, or Matchek, or whoever he was, had a chilling ring of truth. And it would explain the uneasy feeling she got around Jack when that other personality showed through. Also his aversion to any contact with the police. Then there was the shooting business in the park. Innocent citizens are not chased and shot at. Not in Glendale.

"I do expect him back, but I don't know when," she said. "He has my car."

"I see." Tork looked grim. "I'd better be here when he comes."

"I don't know how long he'll be."

"We'll give him twenty-four hours. It might be best if you weren't here."

"This is my home. I am not going anywhere."

"If you insist. I have to warn you, if he does come back, he might not want to leave with me."

Kristy regarded him thoughtfully. "Why aren't the police involved in this?"

He answered as though he had the phrase memorized. "Government security matter, Mrs. Baysinger. We try to keep the local authorities out of it if possible."

"Would you object if I called them?"

"I'd prefer you didn't, but I can't stop you."

It was a bluff. Kristy had no intention of involving the Glendale police in what was already a complicated mess.

She said, "Do you think there will be trouble?"

"We hope not. We'll try to take him as quietly as possible, but with a man like Matchek you never know. I still think it would be best for you to find somewhere else to stay tonight and tomorrow."

"No," Kristy said firmly. "I want to be here."

Tork shrugged his powerful shoulders. He gave

her a brief on-and-off smile and settled himself on the couch. He folded his arms and prepared to wait as long as he had to.

Chapter 22

Matchek sat upright and angry in the cab of the Dodge Raider. He was parked along a side street in West Hollywood that was lined on both sides with apartments. The radio was tuned to a soft rock station with the volume low. As he became aware of the music he reached out and snapped it off.

Jay Baysinger's rumpled jacket lay on the seat next to him. Sweat had soaked through Jay Baysinger's soiled shirt. Outside darkness was spreading over the city. The apartment dwellers who passed on the sidewalk glanced curiously in at the man sitting rigidly behind the wheel, then looked quickly away. There was something in his face they did not want to confront.

He worked his fists open and closed, feeling the pull of the tendons in his wrists. With one hand he rubbed at the hairline scar. The bees were back in his head. The last thing he remembered was leaving Denise's apartment building. The thought of Denise brought a pang of loss and melancholy, which quickly dissipated. His memory was a jigsaw puzzle with too many pieces missing.

* * * * *

Lou Matchek had never, as a child or an adult, been troubled with memory lapses. He remembered everything he wanted to remember, And he put away those things which he did not. They were out of sight but could be retrieved when it suited his purpose. This selective retention had served to screen off the ugly events of his life, most of which took place before his twenty-first birthday. And it enabled him to keep sharp in his mind those things that a man in his profession could not afford to forget.

So it was especially annoying to have hours of his life simply disappear. More troubling still was the sense that he had not been alone during those hours. Even now he could sense shadowy presences with him in the cab of the Dodge. They were here, looking over his shoulder, making judgements, whispering urgently into his ear. Matchek shook his head to clear it of these other presences, but managed only to jostle and push them back into a dark corner.

The bees were at rest again. Night was claiming the city. It was time to get on with what he had come to do. It was time to kill.

* * * * *

In the house up in Benedict Canyon Nick Tenzi was jumping at shadows. He found it impossible to sit still. He paced from one end of the large living room to the other, no longer bothering to hide his anxiety. Fuck the image.

Drummer Cahane and Roy Kilgore were not happy about being there. Sitting with Tenzi right now was like riding a target ship through gunnery practice. They stood glumly apart and watched their chief pace.

Tenzi came to a sudden stop and whirled on the other two men. "He bought a gun. That motherfucker

Artie Paich actually sold Matchek a gun."

"I don't guess he had much choice," Cahane suggested. "When Lou Matchek wants something, he gets it."

"Oh, thank you," Tenzi sneered. "Thank you very much for that little piece of wisdom. You know what he's coming after now, don't you, you musclebound fool?"

"I don't like to be called fool, Nick."

Tenzi rolled his eyes to the ceiling.

"Oh, Christ, now he's going to get sensitive."

"We don't know for sure that Matchek's wise," Kilgore said, trying to smooth everybody's feathers.

"He's wise," Tenzi said decisively. "You can bet your everloving ass he's wise. And he's coming here tonight. I can feel him out there now, getting closer."

Cahane and Kilgore looked at each other.

"There's three of us," Drummer said with a shrug, "and only one of him. He's not Superman."

Tenzi snorted contemptuously, then resumed his pacing. "We don't have to stay here and wait for him," Kilgore suggested. "We could get out of town and stay put until somebody gets him, Somebody is bound to get him."

"Are you saying I run?" Tenzi said. "Run like a scared woman from that crazyass gunman?"

"I just thought it would be better than sitting here waiting for him."

"Well, you two do what you want, but Nick Tenzi doesn't run from anybody."

It was bullshit, of course. The one thing Nick Tenzi wanted to do right now was hop a plane and get far, far away from the city where Lou Matchek stalked him. But if he admitted that, if anybody even smelled fear on him, he was finished, and so was what little was left of the organization. And as for telling Cahane and Kilgore to do what they wanted, Tenzi would have shot them both in the back had they tried to walk out the door.

"We just gonna wait?" Drummer said.

Tenzi glowered at him. The big dumb clod was developing an attitude. Once this Matchek business was over he would have to be dealt with. Right now Tenzi needed him.

"Have you got another—suggestion?" he asked with heavy sarcasm.

Outside, well away from the house, the Doberman barked once.

A single sharp bark, then silence.

Instinctively the hands of Cahane and Kilgore jerked toward their weapons.

"Forget it," Tenzi said in a voice that was steadier than he felt. "The mutt only barks at raccoons and me."

* * * * *

Outside Matchek crouched and held out his hand to the dog, palm up. The Doberman cocked its head and looked at him, its eyes reflecting the faint light from the lamppost at the end of the cul-de-sac. It whined softly.

"Hello, boy," Matchek said in a soft, calming voice. "How you doing?"

The Doberman's tail wagged enthusiastically and it approached, presenting its head to be patted.

Matchek obliged, and ran his finger around,

scratching under the collar. The Doberman waggled happily at finding a friend on a lonely night.

Matchek stood up and listened. Traffic noise filtered up from Sunset Boulevard. A night bird hooted somewhere in the brush. No sounds came from the house.

He moved several steps closer, the dog dancing eagerly at his heels. Lights blazed in every visible window on the first floor. Matchek gave the dog a farewell pat on the rump and started forward, keeping low and in the shadows of the shrubbery. The Doberman trotted alongside, looking up at him, anxious for approval.

"Go on home," Matchek said in a whisper. "Oh I see, you are home. Well then stay. Sit. Go somewhere else."

The dog cocked his head, his eyes bright and alert, wanting only to please.

"Ah, hell, come along then, but be quiet."

Sensing that he was accepted, the Doberman prowled happily in Matchek's shadow as the man made his way cautiously closer to the house. He stole silently through a cluster of palmettos to crouch beneath one of the two large living room windows. He waited a minute to be sure he was not seen, then raised up to look.

Three men were inside. One paced the floor, gesticulating as he talked. The other two stood close together, their eyes following the nervous one. Matchek recognized all three of them. The two men standing on the far side of the room were the driver and the shooter who made a try for him in Brand Park yesterday.

The pacer was his former employer and subsequent betrayer, Nick Tenzi.

Possibly he could have shot all three of them from where he stood outside the window. He had the element of surprise, and the range was favorable. However, there had been no time for him to check out the gun, so he could not know if it shot left, right, high, or low. Every pistol had its peculiarities. A missed shot now could tip the odds in their favor, But if he got close enough, variations in the gun's firing pattern would not matter. Shadowed by the Doberman, Matchek continued his circuit of the house.

Through leaded windows he surveyed a dining room dominated by a heavy table covered with white linen with place settings for six. Silk flowers bloomed in a silver bowl in the center of the table. The room had the look of a department store window—a carefully staged setting that would never be used by real people.

Matchek ran in a crouch across a flagstone patio. At the far edge an illuminated Jacuzzi steamed emptily. Beyond it a sparkling blue pool awaited midnight swimmers.

The kitchen gleamed with pastel and chrome appliances that were fitted with more controls, dials, readouts, switches, lights, and timers than a radio station control room. Not a spot of grease or crumb of food indicated that the high tech equipment had ever been used.

Another patch of shrubbery, then a window looking into an expansive master bedroom. A built-in big-screen television set was on, tuned to a desk-and-sofa talk show. Everyone on the show seemed to be having the time of his life.

The bed was king-size plus, and was covered with a snowy spread of white satin. Reclining on the spread was a blond woman in a pink jump suit that was a size too tight. Her head was propped on a stack of pillows. She sipped at regular intervals from a tall glass, and seemed to be paying little attention to the television screen.

Two smaller bedrooms were brightly lighted but empty and, as far as Matchek could tell, unused.

With the Doberman still trotting behind him, Matchek moved quickly past the dark garage and came again to the front of the house.

The dog gave a muffled *whuff*, and Matchek turned to silence him. In doing so he passed through the beam of an electronic alarm he would otherwise have detected.

* * * * *

At the insistent beep of the alarm signal Cahane and Kilgore reached again for their guns. This time Tenzi did not stop them. He crossed quickly to the window, flattened himself against the wall next to it, and peered out past the edge of the heavy drapery.

"See anything?" Drummer asked in a harsh whisper.

"No."

"Maybe it was the dog," Kilgore suggested.

"Hunh-uh. The alarm beam is higher than the mutt could reach. It has to be a man."

Helene came in from the bedroom. Even in the tension of the moment Cahane and Kilgore could not help observing the way the pink jump suit clung to the dips and mounds of her body.

"What is it, Nick?" she asked.

"How the fuck do I know? Go back to bed."

"I wasn't in bed," she said petulantly.

"I don't give a shit where you were, just get the hell out of the way."

"I don't like it when you talk to me like that," she said.

Tenzi turned on her. "Nobody cares what you like and what you don't like. Now get the fuck out."

She started to say something more, then closed her mouth, turned, and left the room.

"Stupid broad."

Tenzi again peeked past the curtain. The three men held their breath. No sound could be heard inside or outside the house.

"Somebody's out there," Tenzi whispered.

"Do you think it's him?"

"How do I know? Drummer, you go out the front, Roy take the back. Whoever's out there, be sure you shoot first."

"Where are you going to be?" Kilgore asked.

"Right here." When the other two men stood their ground, Tenzi took a step toward them and looked each in the eye. "You going out or what?"

They glanced at each other, then after a fractional hesitation Kilgore said, "We're going Nick." A slow three seconds went by before they moved.

Kilgore headed for the kitchen where the back door opened onto the patio. Drummer Cahane undid the locks on the front door, and with a last look back at Tenzi, went out into the night.

Tenzi locked the door behind him, then hurried through the house to secure the back door too.

* * * * *

Matchek stepped back against the rough trunk of a palmetto, becoming virtually a part of it. The Doberman sat attentively ten feet away, waiting for the game to continue. The front door opened and closed softly. Matchek eased the gun out of his belt and held it with the barrel pointing up, muzzle level with his mouth, ready to point and fire in any direction.

It was the dog who alerted him. The cropped ears pricked and the pointed nose swiveled back toward the rear of the house. A moment later Matchek heard the cautious footfall.

The man's shadow appeared around the end of the garage. His hands were clasped in front of him gripping a pistol in combat position. Light from a front window fell on his face just long enough for Matchek to recognize him as the shooter from Brand Park.

He passed just beyond arm's length from the palmetto. As he began to move away Matchek spoke in a low voice.

"Hey."

Kilgore whirled, the pistol stretched out before him, his eyes wide and searching.

Matchek was waiting. He squeezed the trigger and the Colt Trooper boomed. Roy Kilgore's left eye disappeared in a dark splotch. He made a soft, plaintive sound, took a reflexive step backward, and flopped to the ground.

There have been cases where a man shot in the heart was able to empty his own gun, even though for all practical purposes he was a corpse. A hollow-point bullet through the eyeball into the brain left no such post-mortem possibilities. Matchek spent only a moment looking down at the body, then his internal warning bell clanged.

Before he could react, a gun roared close behind him. A hammer blow caught him in the right thigh, knocking the leg from under him. As he fell, Matchek cursed himself for his carelessness. He should have known there would be two of them.

Chapter 23

When Drummer Cahane saw Kilgore walking cautiously toward him, he let go a long-held breath in relief. It meant they had circled the house in opposite directions and encountered no intruder. They would not, after all, have to face Lou Matchek.

Drummer started to grin. He already saw himself and Roy having a drink together, laughing about how Nick Tenzi had the shit scared out of him by a phantom. Never mind that the two of them had been pretty damn scared themselves.

Now they could go back inside and report that there was nobody here. The alarm must have short circuited. Or a blowing tree branch set it off. Or if somebody was here, he was gone now. Whatever the reason, it meant there would be no need for anybody to face the deadly hitman tonight.

Drummer had his mouth open to hail his friend when he heard the soft, almost inaudible voice from just behind Kilgore: "Hey!"

Frozen for the moment, Drummer watched his partner whirl at the sound. He heard the explosion of a gunshot, saw the fiery muzzle blast. Kilgore took an unsteady step backward, and just for a second Drummer thought he was all right. Then he collapsed and hit the ground in the nerveless fall of a dead man.

A shadow detached itself from the palmetto Kilgore had just passed. A man. Drummer pointed his pistol without aiming and fired. The shadow grunted and fell just beyond Kilgore.

The flash from his own weapon dazzled Drummer for a moment. He blinked, trying to squeeze the darkness from his vision. He stood, pistol gripped in both hands, breathing as softly as he could through his mouth. When he could again distinguish forms he moved forward step by deliberate step.

He looked down at Roy Kilgore's face. What was left of it. One wide eye stared up toward him and beyond him. The other eye was gone. Nothing now but a black hole into the brain.

The other body lay crumpled on its side. A revolver lay six inches away from one limp hand. Drummer Squatted down to take a look. In the reflected light from the window he recognized the hard, lean face.

So, Matchek, you're not Superman after all.

If this were the days of the fabled Old West, a time in which Drummer Cahane often wished himself, he would now be considered Top Gun. That was what happened when you brought down whoever was Number One before you. At least that was the way it happened in the old Western movies Drummer loved. A pity that in today's wimpy world he couldn't tell anybody outside his immediate circle. All the same, word would get around. Drummer Cahane would be a man to reckon with.

He stood up again and prodded Matchek's body with his toe. Dead weight. Still, it would be dumb not to make sure. A .45 caliber slug in the back of the head, right where the skull rested on the neck would do the job. He bent forward, steadying the heavy pistol.

A sudden whimper to his left made him jerk upright. He spun toward the sound to see Tenzi's dog standing half in the shadows, looking uncertainly from the fallen Matchek up to him.

"Nick's right," Drummer muttered. "You are one dumb dog." He turned back to put the finishing bullet into Matchek's brain. It took an instant for his own brain to register the fact that the patch of grass where Matchek had lain was empty.

"What the fuck?"

He started to rise when he sensed the whisper of movement behind him. Still in a crouch, he turned his head and looked up into the hot black mouth of a pistol.

"*No!*" screamed his brain before his body could respond. An instant of blinding pain in his eye, then Drummer Cahane's world exploded.

Matchek stepped back away from the falling body. He grunted and shifted his weight, wincing at the pain in his leg. He reached down and touched the wound and the warm wetness of blood on his pants. It was a slow seepage, that was good. No major blood vessel had been severed. He ground his teeth and felt all the way around his leg. Blood in the front, more blood in back. The bullet had gone all the way through, providentially missing the bone. It probably took out a chunk of the big quadriceps muscle, but that would mend. Still, he would need treatment to prevent infection.

During the time Lou Matchek was inside the Valleydale Youth Institute he learned all he had to know about pain. Because of his refusal to defer to the older boys he became a favorite target, especially when they learned he had no juice on the outside. He developed a technique while absorbing those beatings whereby he mentally squeezed all the pain down into a hard, compact blood red ball and stuffed it into a small compartment in his brain that was insulated from pain. He used that childhood trick now to squeeze down the pain of his bullet wound leg as he walked stiffly toward the front door.

* * * * *

Inside the house the three gunshots fell like hammer blows on the ears of Nick Tenzi. The first two came. *BAM! BAM!* One right after the other. Then maybe twenty seconds of silence during which a dozen possible scenarios flashed through his mind. Did they get him? Did he get them? Did those fools shoot each other? Who was left alive out there?

He peered out past the drapery, but saw nothing. He went into the entrance hall and put his ear to the heavy oak door panel. Silence.

The itchy feeling of being watched crept over him. He turned from the door to see Helene standing just beyond the archway into the living room. Her eyes were wide and staring, her arms crossed protectively over her breasts.

"What do you want?" he shouted, angry at the fright she had given him.

"What's going on, Nick?"

He stared at her.

"Are Drummer and Roy out there?"

"Yeah, they're out there."

She waited, finally speaking when he said

nothing more. "What are you going to do?"

"What do you mean *do*?"

"Those were gunshots."

"Don't you fucking think I know that?"

"Do you want me to call the police?"

"You silly cunt. The police would fucking love to be called to a shooting at Nick Tenzi's house. They've been trying for years .to nail me for something. Anything. I wouldn't stand a chance of talking my way out of this."

"Out of what? You don't even know what happened."

"Shut up, will you." He put his ear to the door again.

Something rustled softly. The wind in the palm leaves? Another listener on the opposite side of the door?

"Aren't you going out and look?" Helene said.

He wanted to tell her what an asshole suggestion that was, but the words caught in his throat. He had a sudden mental image of what he looked like crouching here with his ear pressed to the door.

Helene's expression told him that she saw the same picture. She turned away from him, and with a dignity that irked him even more than her questions, walked back toward the bedroom.

"All right," Nick Tenzi said, too low for anyone to hear.

"All fucking *right*."

He lurched over to the table and fumbled in the drawer for the Browning. It felt reassuringly solid and deadly in his hand. He jacked a shell into the chamber. Back at the door put his eye to the tiny lens in the peephole, saw nothing but dark. These fisheye lenses weren't worth shit unless somebody stood directly in front of them. Carefully, willing his hand not to tremble, he undid the locks and grasped the heavy doorknob. He turned the knob and pulled the door open half an inch, an inch. Nothing stirred out there. Two inches.

Wham! The heavy door exploded inward, knocking Tenzi backward as it banged off the wall. Simultaneously something hard and metallic cracked down on his wrist, snapping the bone. The Browning clattered to the tile floor. Tenzi grabbed his damaged hand and whimpered.

Lou Matchek stepped into the house and kicked the door shut behind him.

"Hello, Nick."

Tenzi's mouth opened. And closed. He looked past Matchek at the door.

"Your friends won't be coming," Matchek said.

Tenzi stared into the killer's eyes, cold and gray as the northern seas. He looked down at the blue steel revolver in his fist. He knew what it was like to be a tick of the clock away from death. The front of his pants got hot and wet. He looked down to see he had pissed his pants.

He had to say something. Had to. "I... I... I heard you were out."

"Yeah, I bet you did."

The words burbled out of Tenzi like popcorn out of a hot kettle. They were the frantic, pleading words of a man who is about to die.

"Listen, Lou, I don't know what you think happened, but let me tell you the way it really was."

Matchek cut him off. "I know the way it really

was, Nick."

Tenzi could not stop himself. "The whole thing was a mistake. A fucking terrible mistake."

"You got that right," Matchek agreed.

Tenzi backed step by step into the living room. The mere fact that he was still alive gave him hope. A professional killer like Matchek did not pause for conversation before getting on with business. Maybe there was still a chance.

As Matchek followed, Tenzi saw he was moving one leg stiffly. He looked down and saw the blood. Either Cahane or Kilgore had put one into him before he killed them. The wound did not look serious enough to drop Matchek before he could pull the trigger again, but Tenzi was grasping at even the smallest chance to be spared.

"You set me up, Nick," Matchek said.

"No, no it wasn't that way at all."

Matchek continued as though he hadn't spoken. "You sent somebody to do Niedenfuer before I got there. Probably those two goons outside. Then you had the cops waiting so I'd walk into their arms."

"Lou, I—"

"Shut up. You set me up, but I didn't believe it. Not then. I didn't even believe it when somebody told me about it. Not until your boy Vin Faccio put a blade in my back. Then I believed it."

Tenzi was wet all over—from sweat under his arms and across his back, and from urine down his legs. His mind flashed all the way back to the streets of Cleveland when as a terrified boy of ten he offered to do anything they wanted if the bigger, stronger kids would let him put his pants back on.

"Let's talk Lou. I was wrong, I made the mistake, and I'm willing to pay for it. Just tell me what you want. We'll work it out. Anything, Lou. Anything you want is yours."

"You'll pay, all right," said Matchek, "but not the way you think. You don't have anything I want."

The revolver came up and looked Tenzi in the eye. "Oh, no, Jesus God Lou, don't do it! Don't hurt me! Please! I'm begging! You can have it all. Everything I've got. I'll sign this place and everything over to you right now, I swear! I'll go away and you'll never see me again. Please God, don't do it!"

For an eternity the round black eye of the revolver stared at him. His limbs quivered, the muscles of his face squirmed like a nest of worms as he imagined the bullet smashing through the delicate eyeball back into the gelatinous mass of his brain, there exploding into unbearable, unspeakable agony.

"No!" he screamed.

Incredibly, the gun lowered centimeter by centimeter.

Matchek raised his free hand to rub a tiny reddish scar right at the hairline. The harsh planes of his face changed ever so subtly, as though a shadow had passed over him.

Matchek let the hand holding the revolver drop to his side. Without speaking he turned and walked back through the entryway to the door. He opened it and went out into the night.

Back in the living room Nick Tenzi began to shake. He was soaking wet and he was chilled to the bone. The pain of his broken wrist suddenly hit him. He could not believe what had happened.

Somehow, miraculously, he was alive.

Chapter 24

Nick Tenzi stood as though frozen in the archway between the living room and the entrance hall and stared at the front door.

He could not believe that Lou Matchek stood here and pointed a gun at him, then had walked out that door without killing him. At any moment he expected it to burst open, the hitman to come raging back in to shoot him full of painful holes.

As the seconds ticked by and Matchek did not return, Tenzi's taut nerves began to loosen gradually like over-stressed guitar strings being slowly tuned down. He could feel his muscles start to relax. The cold wetness of the sweat and urine that soaked his clothes made him shiver. Pain from his broken wrist brought a sharp groan. With pain came the return of movement. He scrambled to the door and one-handed snapped the locks into place.

With the danger locked out, anger flooded over him. That sonofabitch! That rotten, bullying, self-loving sonofabitch of a Lou Matchek had walked past his two best men right into his house and had humiliated him like no man in the world should be humiliated.

As his anger swelled, Tenzi wondered for the first time about the fate of Cahane and Kilgore. What the hell had those assholes been doing out there that they couldn't prevent a lone man from busting into the house?

He looked around on the tile floor of the hall, spotted the Browning automatic over against the baseboard. He picked it up, checked the action, and holding the gun in his left hand, crept back to the door. He put his ear to the panel once again. As before, he heard nothing outside.

He gave it a minute. Two minutes. Three. Finally he convinced himself the danger was past. If Matchek was going to kill him, he would have done it. There was no reason for the hitman to hang around outside now waiting for him.

Still, it was not without a bone-deep shudder that he eased open the door and stepped through. A sudden growl made his heart lurch. He spun around to see the Doberman standing behind him, the short fur bristling on his neck.

Tenzi swung the pistol toward the dog. "That does it. You're history, you worthless mutt."

As though he sensed the man's intentions, the dog vanished into the shadows.

All his rage and humiliation was focused now on the dog. "You can't hide forever, you sonofabitch. You're going to die tonight. You hear me?"

The night wind was cold and it pasted the wet clothes against his skin. Leaving the front door open for the light it afforded, Tenzi began walking along the front of the house.

At the base of a palmetto his foot struck something soft and he jumped back as though he'd stepped into a nest of snakes.

He looked down, and in the diffused light from

the window and the open door behind him, recognized the soft thing as a body. Beyond it lay another. The nearer, more bulky one was Drummer Cahane. Dark blood pooled where one eye should be.

Tenzi did not need to see the face to tell him that the other body would be Roy Kilgore.

He felt no emotion for the two dead men other than anger for their clumsiness in letting themselves get killed, thereby endangering him. Had they been better at their job, they would

be alive now and Lou Matchek would be lying here instead.

His instinct, looking down at the two bodies, was to get the hell out of there. Without Cahane and Kilgore, however incompetent they might have been, he was alone and unprotected.

He fought down the impulse to run and moved in for a closer look. He had not the slightest doubt that both men were dead, but in case there were any questions later he had better make sure.

He prodded Drummer Cahane with his foot. Dead weight. He squatted next to Kilgore and saw another blasted out eye. Say what you would, the son of a bitch could shoot.

He stood up, feeling queasy. Nick Tenzi had seen death before, but he had never felt its icy breath so close. He knew that Cahane and Kilgore had never really liked him, and Tenzi had considered them several notches below him in the evolutionary scale. All the same, they were as close as he had to real friends. And in a matter of a few seconds they had both been erased. The realization of how isolated he was hit Nick Tenzi like a fist. For the first time in his life he felt an aching need for another human being to stand with him. He wanted his wife.

Leaving the dead men where they lay, he hurried back into the house. Helene had come back into the living room. Tenzi started toward her, holding out his arms.

"You stink," she said.

He stopped as though he had hit a wall. "Wh-what?"

"You smell of piss and body odor."

Tenzi could not believe what he was hearing. Helene had never spoken such words to him. She would never have dared. Now for the first time he saw that she was fully dressed in a pearl gray suit. A traveling bag stood on the floor at her feet. It took a moment for the import of this to sink in.

"What's the idea?"

"I'm outta here, Nick."

"What are you talking about? Where do you think you're going?"

"Away. Away from you."

"You're crazy. You don't have any place to go."

"Oh, yes I do."

Her icy calm unnerved him more than if she had launched into a screaming tirade.

He said, "It's all right. We're safe now. Matchek's gone."

"I know," she said.

"You know?"

"That's right. I stood right over there and watched you piss on yourself and listened to you beg him not to kill you. I've never seen a grown man get down and beg like that before."

"Hey, what else could I do?"

"You offered him everything you had, remember? Did that include me, Nick?"

"He had a gun," Tenzi said, hating himself for trying to excuse his behavior to this bimbo, but unable to stop. He held up his broken wrist. "I was hurt."

"Too bad."

"Helene, listen to me. The man's crazy. He killed Drummer and he killed Roy. Then he got in here and I didn't know what he was going to do. I didn't want him to hurt you."

"That's a laugh," she said without smiling. "You didn't give a good goddamn what happened to me. You never have. You were so afraid he was going to shoot you that you pissed your pants. I can't stand being around you."

"Helene, you can't do this."

"Oh? Why not?"

"I've taken good care of you."

"Sure you have. And I paid for it. I gave you everything you wanted from me. I figure we're even."

"I'm warning you, if you walk out that door you're never walking back in."

"That's good enough for me." She reached down and picked up the bag.

Words began to tumble out of his mouth. "Helene, don't leave. I don't want to be here alone. I'll give you whatever you want. Things will be a lot better between us. I can do a lot for you, you'll see. I don't want you to go. I... I need you."

"You make me want to puke," she said.

He stood rooted to the floor as she walked past him. She walked close enough that he could have reached out and grabbed her, but he made no move. He knew now it wouldn't do any good. He might have grabbed her, even knocked her down with his one working hand. But he couldn't hold her. Not now or ever again.

At the front door she stopped and looked back. His heart leapt with hope. Maybe she was having second thoughts.

"I'll be back tomorrow for Fritz. Don't let anybody take him." Helene went out into the night and closed the door.

Fritz. She would come back for a fucking dog, but would not give her husband a kind word.

Tenzi stayed where he was until he heard the garage door rumble up and Helene's little sports car drive away and out of his life. He gripped his throbbing wrist and turned in a slow circle. He was alone in the big empty house. His wife was gone, two dead men lay out on the grass and a dog that hated him prowled the grounds. There was nobody left. Nobody to turn to.

Nobody he could even call.

Wait a minute. There somebody he could call. He hurried out to the table in the entrance hall and yanked out the drawer. It pulled all the way out, spilling the contents on the tile floor, He got down on his knees and poked through the ad flyers, old letters, bills, receipts, paper clips, ballpoint pens, note pads, Scotch tape, and other bits of meaningless trash until he found what he was looking for. Merlin Ryan's card with the phone number he had written on the back.

Breathing hard, Tenzi took the card with him back into the living room and punched out the digits on the telephone buttons. He waited impatiently through five rings until a reedy male voice answered.

"Seaview Motel."

"I want to talk to Merlin Ryan."

"What's the name?"

Tenzi repeated it. "He's staying there."

"Just a minute. Okay, right he's in Number Nine. I'll ring him."

An interminable wait as the receiver buzzed three, four, five times. The reedy voice came back on.

"I guess he's not in his room."

"Can I leave a message for him?"

"Yeah, I guess so."

"Tell him Nick Tenzi called."

"What was that name again?"

"Tenzi. T-E-N-Z-I." He gave the man his phone number. "Tell him to call me as soon as he gets in."

"You want him to call you," the man repeated.

"As soon as he gets in. Whatever time it is. Make sure he get's the message. It's urgent."

"Sure, urgent," the man said in a tone that did not build Tenzi's confidence.

He hung up the phone. If there had been such a thing as telepathy, and if Nick Tenzi had the power, he would have sent his plea like an arrow to Merlin Ryan, wherever he was. Suddenly the whole dark world seemed populated with enemies who would smash him like a bug if he ventured out. The one man he could go to was the FBI agent. All he could get in return for his surrender would be years of his life spent in a federal penitentiary. Some deal. If he had possessed a sense of irony Nick Tenzi would have grinned at that.

Something howled outside the window, a broken, offkey wail.

Tenzi jumped. Then he recognized the sound. "That fucking dog."

At last he had something alive and tangible to strike out at. Matchek had shamed him, Cahane and Kilgore had failed him, Helene had left him. They were all beyond his reach now, but the dog who hated him was still here. At least something was going to pay for the pain he had suffered this night.

He retrieved the pistol, eased open the front door, and stepped outside.

A soft growl from somewhere in the shadows. Son of a bitch was black, hard to see him at night.

"Here, boy." The friendly tone did not come readily to Nick Tenzi. It was a tone he never used with man or beast. "Come here, Fritz. I've got something for you."

Another growl. The dog was not buying the friendly approach.

Tenzi moved cautiously in the direction of the growl. He had to carry the gun in his left hand, and his right was useless for bracing the weapon. But no matter, he could still shoot well enough to hit something that wasn't shooting back.

"Come on, Fritz, let's get this settled once and for all." He dropped all pretense at friendship. All his stored up hatred for a hostile world of taller men, contemptuous women, righteous cops, thieving employees was compressed and concentrated on the dog that moved warily somewhere in the darkness.

He caught a shudder of movement off to his left. A shadow blacker than the surrounding shadows. Tenzi shifted his weight, bringing the pistol around in that direction.

A growl. A gleam of canine teeth in the faint light coming from the house. And two eyes reflecting red.

"There you are you hellhound." Tenzi said it softly so he would not startle the animal. "I've got you now."

He squeezed the trigger. The gun boomed and bucked in his unaccustomed left hand. The dog yelped once and vanished. Tenzi heard him whining in the shrubbery a few feet farther on.

"Hurts, does it?" he said to the night. "Good. It's going to hurt a lot more before I'm through with you."

Another slight movement of the shadows. He fired again.

Silence.

"Did that finish you off?"

With the rush of victory tingling throughout his body, Tenzi started toward the spot where he would find the remains of his enemy. He had taken two steps when ninety pounds of black and brown fury hit him from the side.

Tenzi went to the ground under the slashing teeth of the Doberman. He struggled to bring the gun into play but the dog's training took over and he seized the man's wrist between his powerful jaws and crunched down on the bones.

Tenzi screamed as the gun dropped harmlessly into the soft grass. Blood from the dog's wound mingled with his own as the Doberman struggled to reach a vital spot.

As never before, Nick Tenzi fought now for his life. Both his hands now flopped without strength on broken bones. The dog's teeth ripped savage wounds in his arms as he tried to protect his eyes.

The last thing he saw was the nightmarish black face of the Doberman, eyes glowing red, teeth smeared with blood. Then the powerful jaws clamped shut, the teeth biting deep on each side of Tenzi's windpipe. The dog shook him like a stuffed toy. He kept shaking until most of Nick's throat tore away in his teeth.

The dog spat out the ragged flesh and the section of trachea. Bloody froth bubbled from Tenzi's torn throat. When finally he lay still, the dog sniffed at his body. Then he too lay down, dropped his chin on his paws, and closed his eyes.

Chapter 25

While the telephone rang unheard in his room at the Seaview Motel, Merlin Ryan was pulling his rented Ford up to the gatehouse of the Fairhaven Medical Complex. He waited, drumming his fingers on the steering wheel while the uniformed guard came out and walked over to the car. He rolled down the window and held up his FBI identification.

The guard took his time reading it. "I have to ask your business, Mr. Ryan."

"Why? I've been here before."

"Orders, sir."

"My business is with Dr. Vespa."

"The doctor's office hours are from eight to five."

"I know what his office hours are," Ryan snapped. "My business will not wait."

"My orders were—'

"Stuff your orders. Either I see Vespa now or I make a whole lot of trouble."

"I'll call his apartment," the guard said, looking unhappy. He turned his back and punched out a four-digit number. He tried to muffle his voice, but his words were clearly audible. "That FBI guy, Ryan is here, Doctor. I told him your hours, but he says he's got to see you now. Looks like he might be a problem... I see... Yes, sir."

The guard hung up the phone and came back out to the car. "Dr. Vespa says it's okay. Do you know where the living quarters are?"

"No."

The guard squatted beside the car to point the way. "Park in the lot in front of the main building, walk down the path on the right. Dr. Vespa's apartment is in the two story stucco with the bougainvillea out front."

"I'll find it," Ryan said.

The gate swung open and he drove in. He parked the Ford and took a thin sheaf of papers from the seat beside him. Two security guards in front of the administration building eyed him as he got out of the car. It was a little late, he thought, for such vigilance. Lou Matchek was not likely to stroll back in through the front gate.

Following the path that curved back alongside the main building, he had no trouble locating white stucco living quarters.

In the shadows farther along the path someone came toward him. Ryan slowed his pace as he recognized the approaching figure as female. When she passed under one of the bright orange lights that dotted the grounds he saw that it was the receptionist from outside Vespa's office.

Her face was drawn and pale. In the harsh artificial light she aged five years.

"Hello, Miss Fellows" Ryan said as she drew abreast of him.

He got only a short, tear-stained glance before she hurried on. Quite a different Victoria Fellows than the seductress who had greeted him three days ago.

She had no smile to dazzle him tonight, no sympathetic inquiry about his business, no invitation to dinner at her place. He watched her walk on toward the front gate, her heels clacking on the concrete path.

Ryan continued toward the stucco building that housed the living quarters. He flashed his identification again for another guard in the brightly lit lobby and waited while this one too checked with Dr. Vespa. After a short conversation he hung up and spoke to Ryan.

"Go through that door. Dr. Vespa's apartment is at the end of the hall. He'll let you in."

The guard pushed an electrical buzzer that unlocked a door at the end of the lobby. Ryan walked through into a short, well lit hallway. At the far end another door opened.

Armand Vespa stood in the doorway waiting for him. He wore his customary uniform of laboratory coat, white shirt, dark tie. Ryan wondered idly if he slept in the same clothes.

"Sorry about the delay in admitting you, Mr. Ryan, but you weren't expected."

"It was a sudden decision on my part."

"I see. Please come inside."

Ryan walked into the apartment. It was neat and functional, with no visible personal touches. A light burned at a small desk where books and files lay open.

"Apparently I didn't wake you," Ryan said.

"Oh, no, it's still early for me. I get along quite nicely on three hours sleep."

"I met your receptionist going out as I was coming in. She didn't look happy."

"An unfortunate situation that. As part of our tightening security I discovered that Miss Fellows has been relaying classified information about our operations to people outside. Unauthorized people."

"Like Nick Tenzi?"

"You're very perceptive," Vespa said carefully.

"It wasn't that hard to figure out. I saw Tenzi today, and he knew more about Lou Matchek than he should have. Somebody here had to tell him."

"So it turned out. Has your visit to Tenzi anything to do with your business here tonight?"

"I want some straight answers, Doctor."

"To what questions?"

"For one, I want to know why you tried to hide the connection between Lou Matchek and Jay Baysinger."

Vespa's deep-set eyes glittered for a moment. "It seems Miss Fellows was not the only leak in my organization."

"How I got the information is not important. I want to know why the coverup."

"If you know about Jay Baysinger, then I assume you know the pertinent details of his work at Fairhaven."

"I know that he came here three years ago, and that shortly thereafter he volunteered for an experiment that was to transfer portions of his memory to a silicon chip. Apparently that's as far as the experiment went at the time.

What happened to Baysinger afterward is only briefly touched on in the records. Apparently he died a year or so later."

"That is correct," Vespa said. "A laboratory accident. I can produce the reports if you want them."

"I've seen them. Now I'm concerned about the

microchip that held his memory. It's my guess that it was implanted a week and a half ago in Lou Matchek's brain."

"An astute guess, Mr. Ryan."

"Why the delay?"

"I was not ready three years ago to proceed with the second half of my process—the implantation of the chip in a host. More data was required. Also, there was the problem of finding a suitable subject."

"And Baysinger died before you could go on."

"Unfortunately, yes. He was a dedicated and talented researcher, and it was my intention that he would help track the results of the implant and measure the subject's responses against his own."

"That brings me to another question," Ryan said. "After the implant, how much of Lou Matchek is left, and how much is now Jay Baysinger?"

"That was something I had hoped to learn during the post operative therapy. Matchek's unexpected departure has badly upset my plans. I fear that without proper treatment the anti social aspects of the Matchek personality could reappear and overwhelm the gentler but weaker Baysinger element."

"That doesn't sound good. You understand, Doctor, that there are limits to how long we can keep this quiet. If Lou Matchek reverts to type he could do a great deal of damage."

"I have taken steps to prevent that, Mr. Ryan. Right now Gunther Tork and two of his men are at the home of Baysinger's widow. They will protect her while waiting to pick up Matchek."

"I doubt that she is in immediate danger," Ryan said. "Matchek is a killer, no question, but he is not a wanton killer. A more likely target would be Nick Tenzi, the man who tried to have him killed in Folsom."

"I wish we could be sure of that, but an implant of this type has never been tried before. The subject's actions when uncontrolled are not predictable. The unmonitored combination of the two different minds could be an explosive situation. Or a third personality might appear."

"So the bottom line is we'd better get him back," Ryan said. "Definitely. I am directing all my efforts to that end."

"That's not good enough. If you don't have Matchek in hand in the next twenty-four hours, we have to go public, and the search for Matchek has to be expanded."

"That would be disastrous to the program here."

"Tough. I've got other priorities. I want you to have a full, detailed report for me in the morning covering every detail of the Baysinger-Matchek foul-up. And no secret codes this time."

"I'll see to it personally," Vespa said. His eyes were unreadable in their deep sockets.

* * * * *

His mind churning with unresolved problems, Ryan left the living quarters and strode back across the grounds of Fairhaven. He climbed into the rented car and drove out the gate. The guard passed him through without comment.

Back in the Seaview Motel he lay in bed, staring into the dark corners of the room, searching vainly for answers until the telephone jolted him into full wakefulness. The luminous figures on his travel-alarm clock read 3:01 A.M.

He snatched the telephone from its cradle. "Mr. Ryan?" a male voice asked.

"Yes." Who did he expect to be answering the phone in here?

"Got a phone message here I forgot to give you."

"Well let's have it."

"You want me to read it to you?"

"Yes!" Ryan's voice rose with his frustration.

"There's no need to get huffy. It says here, uh, let me see, a Mr. Tenzi called. He wants you to call him back whenever you get in. There's a phone number here for you to call. Urgent, it says."

"Urgent," Ryan repeated under his breath. "How long ago did he call?"

"About eleven."

Shortly after he had left to visit Vespa. Four hours ago.

A lot of things could have happened in four hours. "Sorry about not telling you right away."

Ryan banged the receiver down, then picked it up again immediately. "Dial the number," he snapped when the manager came back on the line.

"What?"

"Dial the number. The one written on the message you forgot to give me when I came in."

"Oh, right. You know it's long distance."

"I know that." Ryan ground his teeth. "You can put it on my bill. Just dial the damn number."

After a series of clicks and electronic beeps Ryan got the burring sound that represented the ringing of the phone on the other end. He let it ring five, six, ten times, then hung up.

"Damn it!" he said to the empty room. "Damn it, damn it, damn it!"

Hurriedly he began to dress.

Chapter 26

The lights of the San Fernando Valley lay spread out far below like sequins on a black dress. The Ventura Freeway was a two-color river, half red, half white, that split the valley east to west. On the right was the commercial glare of electric signs and mercury vapor lamps. On the left the more subdued glow of the residential neighborhoods.

The man who sat in the cab of the Dodge Raider high in the hills with the sparkling panorama spread out below cared little for the view. The pain in his leg and the noises in his head were too distracting.

The digital clock in the dash panel read 4:05. The man shoved his thoughts into place, concentrating so hard it brought beads of sweat to his forehead. After a minute he recognized where he was. On a little used road at the crest of the Santa Monica Mountains. What he could not remember was how he got here. He closed his eyes and searched in the darkness of his mind. Another damned empty chunk of time.

Bits and pieces of the day came back to him—Katherine Gannon in the soiled bed, Horace Brill barbered and salon-tanned in his plush office, Denise Underhill beautiful and sad—like quick cuts on a movie screen. Finally he remembered the bloody business in Benedict Canyon. The hammer blow to his leg. Dead men on the dark ground. Nick Tenzi under his gun. After that the scene fogged over.

He rolled down the window and breathed deeply of the night air. Slowly, methodically he put it all together, remembering even the things he wanted to forget.

His name was Jack Gannon. He knew it was a made-up name.

There was no such person. And yet, it was the name that fit him now. Jack Gannon, incomplete as he was, was the man he wanted to be.

The other one was a stranger. The one named Matchek. The cold, efficient killer who had been in control throughout the day. Jack Gannon had been forced to accompany the stranger

Matchek on the deadly mission to Benedict Canyon.

Bullshit! said the other voice. *There is no Jack Gannon. I am Lou Matchek and you are me. Tonight you-I-we killed two men. Killing is nothing new for us.*

No! cried the Gannon voice. *I am not Matchek! I am no killer!*

The two dead men in Benedict Canyon died while trying to kill him. Tenzi was the target. Under the code Matchek lived by, Tenzi had to die. And yet, when he had the chance, when Tenzi cowered hurt and helpless before him, he had put his gun away and walked out. Lou Matchek would never have done that. Lou Matchek would have killed the man he came to kill. It was Jack Gannon who walked away and let his enemy live.

There is no Jack Gannon, the other voice said again. *You are Lou Matchek with bits and pieces of a man*

named Jay Baysinger crammed into your brain.

I won't accept it. I will not accept it. Lou Matchek, the old Lou Matchek is no more. Leave me alone.

He gripped the steering wheel and ground his teeth, pushing the angry voice back, back into a distant dark corner. His name was Jack Gannon. Beads of sweat pushed out on his forehead as he concentrated. His leg throbbed. The buzzing whirring whooshing in his head swelled to a roar, then gradually lessened. Minutes ticked slowly by. When at last he began to relax the sky was lightening in the east behind the mountains. The Matchek voice at last was silent.

He popped open the glove box searching for a tissue to mop his face. His searching fingers found a red silk scarf. He sniffed it. A gentle floral scent he knew. Kristy. How long ago was it he had left her? Too long. Memories new and old flashed through his mind. Kristy laughing at a children's cartoon. Kristy grieving over the death of a kitten. Kristy running to greet him early in their marriage. Kristy in bed.

Suddenly the most important thing in Jack Gannon's world was to see her again. He keyed the engine to life and headed the Dodge down the hill toward Glendale.

* * * * *

Kristy Baysinger slept fitfully. Troubling dreams of a man in a mask tugged at the edges of her consciousness. She would be in his arms, held close and safe, and then she would look into his face and see a new and frightening mask. She awoke frequently, acutely aware of the man who was sitting silent and watchful out in her living room. Gunther Tork had seemed so ordinary and trustworthy, and he did carry convincing identification, yet something about the man made her uneasy.

Ordinarily, she would never have allowed him to stay in the house, but his credentials were authentic, and his explanation of the Matchek-Baysinger connection all too convincing.

Still, she was not comfortable with a stranger in her house.

In the three years since Jay moved out she had grown to accept the idea of living alone. In the normal course of events, she did not foresee anything she could not handle. But the things that had been happening to her the past few days were anything but normal. A strange man had walked into her life knowing things about her he could not possibly have known. She had gone to bed with the man. Together they had been shot at. When Gunther Tork described the crimes of the man called Lou Matchek, and produced photographs and documentation to prove he and Jack Gannon were one in the same, she had to agree that it would not be wise for her to be here alone if he came back.

Now, twisting restlessly in her bed, she was not so sure she had made the right decision. The memory of their bodies molded together in this very bed was fresh and exciting. While their sex had been uninhibited and even frenzied, there had been tenderness too. Was there, she tried to remember, any hint in his lovemaking that her Jack Gannon could kill as coldly as the man Tork had described? If there was, she had missed it.

She recalled, however, the incident at the bar the day he had arrived. He had slammed a billiard ball into the head of one man and snapped the bones in the arm of another with an icy efficiency. It had seemed totally out of character, and from that moment the little things that reminded her of Jay began fading.

And in the park when the men in the other car fired on them, he had been cool and professional. He had been shot at before.

Much as she fought against the idea, there could be little doubt that the man she had taken into her house and into her bed was Lou Matchek, convicted killer, escaped convict. And yet... and yet she could not set aside the emotions he had revived in her. Emotions she had thought for years were dead.

"What will happen to him?" she had asked Tork before leaving him to his vigil.

"He'll be taken care of," he had assured her. "Nobody wants to hurt him. He has to go back to Fairhaven so they can go on with the treatment that's going to help him. Loose he's a danger to himself and everybody else. Believe me, he'll get the care he needs once we get him back."

Kristy clung to that thought. It was important to her, more important than she had imagined, that Jack Gannon should not be hurt. She rolled onto her side, closed her eyes, and tried to will herself to sleep.

* * * * *

Lou Matchek would have been more cautious in returning to the house on Lemon Grove. He would have seen the black Buick parked across from Kristy's house and recognized that it had not been there before. He would have made a cautious circuit of the block and spotted the station wagon parked on the next street with *Fairhaven* written on the door. And he would surely not have missed the two men who detached themselves from the shadows at when he pulled into Kristy's driveway. Lou Matchek had the jungle animal's instinct for survival that never relaxed. His senses were always alert for danger.

But danger was not a part of Jack Gannon's life. His thoughts were not on who or what might lie in wait for him. His mind was filled with Kristy Baysinger, his only thought was to see her, talk to her, hold her.

He walked to the front door, tried the knob, found it unlocked. That alone would have set off urgent alarms for Lou Matchek. Jack Gannon merely walked in.

The living room was dark and empty. He groped for a light switch, then stopped. The room *wasn't* empty. Something, a slight movement in the shadows, a whisper of sound, a subtle change in the air pressure, told him there was someone in the room. The hair prickled at the nape of his neck. The Matchek part of him stirred, alerted by the unseen menace.

Too late. The sudden light hit him in the eyes. He raised one hand as a shield, saw a lamp with the shade tilted to direct the beam at him. Behind the lamp a blocky figure stood in shadow.

"Hello, Matchek."

Gunther Tork stepped forward to let Gannon see his face.

The heavy moustache was spread in a smile. The dark eyes glittered.

"What are you doing here?"

"Waiting for you. You caused quite a little trouble up at Fairhaven. Now I'm going to take you back. We've got some unfinished business, you and me."

Kristy came into the room and stopped, looking from one man to the other. She wore the belted velour robe, and her face was clean of makeup.

"Kristy, what's going on?" Gannon said.

She looked down at the bloody pants leg. "Your hurt!" Whirling on Tork she said, "What did you do to him?"

"Nothing yet," Tork said. "I just explained that I'm taking him back to get help."

"I don't want any help." Gannon looked into Kristy's eyes.

Her expression was unreadable.

The part of him that was Matchek struggled for release. To Tork he said, "What makes you think I'll go with you?"

"Oh, you'll go," Tork said confidently. "You don't have any choice." He brought his right hand up from the shadows and let Matchek see the gun.

"Is that supposed to scare me?"

"I just want you to know that I have it. I don't want to use it, but I will if I have to."

The hard nudge of metal at his hip reminded Gannon of his own weapon. If he could get it out and dive to the floor at the same time, he might be able to outshoot the overconfident Tork.

Something moved at the edge of his field of vision. "Jack, look out!" Kristy cried.

He saw Tork's eyes flicker as he give a tiny nod.

Instinctively he started to dodge to one side. His wounded leg betrayed him and he staggered, reaching for the gun on his hip. A hard wooden baton hit him a glancing blow on the side of the head. He staggered, spots of light dancing before his eyes. As he went to his knees his shoulder hit a stack of cardboard cartons, knocking it over. With the momentary distraction he freed the Colt from his belt and brought it up in firing position.

"Two seconds to drop it, Matchek, or you're a dead man," said Tork.

He could have put a slug into Tork's heart before it beat again, but the terror in Kristy's eyes froze his trigger finger. He glanced back toward the door to see the two uniformed Fairhaven security guards. The tall blond one held the baton ready to use again. The stocky black guard gripped a regulation .38-caliber revolver. "Hi, fellas."

Spencer and Krebs said nothing. "Please, Jack," Kristy said.

He saw the white spots appear at the corners of Tork's mouth and knew he was an eyeblink from death. He let the Colt drop to the carpet and rose unsteadily to his feet.

The two guards moved in swiftly to seize his arms and haul him to his feet. Tork stooped and picked up his fallen revolver. He sniffed at the muzzle.

"Been busy tonight, have you?" Gannon did not answer.

"You told me he wouldn't be hurt," Kristy said.

"He isn't hurt," Tork said. "That little tap on the skull was nothing."

"What are you going to do with him?"

"Like I said, we're taking him back where he can get the kind of help he needs."

"Shouldn't the police be told?"

"This is not a police matter, lady."

Kristy squared her shoulders. "I think it is. You tell me this man is an escaped convict, a killer. That's something the police should know about." She started toward the telephone.

"Don't do it, Mrs. Baysinger." Tork had turned his head to watch her. The gun rested comfortably in his hand.

"I'm asking you nice."

"This is my house. I do what I want here." She reached for the phone.

"Kristy!"

She stopped and turned at the sound of Gannon's voice. "Do what he says."

"You'd better listen to him, Mrs. Baysinger," Tork said. "He's got the right idea for once."

Kristy saw the look on his face, and the stony expression of the two guards. She dropped her hand and backed away from the telephone.

"That's better," Tork said. He peered up at her from under his bushy brows. "But you know, I'll bet you're thinking right now that just as soon as we're gone you're going to make that call. Is that what you're thinking?"

Kristy was silent.

"You'd better come along with us."

"I'm not going anywhere."

"Mrs. Baysinger, I don't have a lot of time to argue about it. If we leave you behind, you will call the police sure as I'm standing here. That would cause a lot of problems for a lot of people. So why don't you just come along and let Dr. Vespa explain things to you. I think you'll see things different then."

Kristy flashed him a look of raw hatred, but

allowed him to steer her out of the house following the two guards who held Gannon.

They walked out of the house and stopped at the sidewalk. To stocky black guard Tork said, "Krebs, you take the lady with you in the wagon. Spencer and I will bring the hero with us and follow you."

The guard took Kristy by the arm. His grip was light, yet she sensed it could tighten painfully if she tried to pull away. She looked back once at Gannon, her eyes full of apology. He gave her a tight grin, and crossed the street with Tork to climb into the back seat of the Buick while Spencer got in behind the wheel.

In a minute the station wagon turned onto Lemon Grove Street and headed toward the freeway. Spencer pulled out and followed.

Tork nudged Gannon's wounded thigh with his knee, bringing a grunt of pain.

"Just wanted to remind you to behave yourself, Matchek. My orders were to bring you back, but they didn't say in what condition. It wouldn't hurt my feelings at all if I had to mark you up a little. So it's kind of up to you. Now let's just relax and enjoy the ride."

Chapter 27

Merlin Ryan was the last man anyone would call a scofflaw. Even when he was in New York he waited at the corner for a green light before crossing the street. Native New Yorkers jostled him, stared at him, swore at him, made obscene gestures at him, but Ryan refused to jaywalk. He figured if he was destined to die under the wheels of a taxi, at least the taxi would be at fault. In addition to his peculiar pedestrian habits, he always deposited his trash in the proper containers, he did not light up in a non-smoking area, he never parked in a handicapped space or tore the tag from a mattress. However, on the Freeway heading south from Santa Barbara to Los Angeles he ignored traffic laws and fellow motorists alike as he pushed the rented Ford to the 90-mile-per-hour range and darted from lane to lane with abandon. Fortunately, at this early hour traffic was sparse, and no CHP units cruised along his route.

Ryan's sense of trouble, like a cold finger jabbing at the back of his neck, told him as sure as the night was dark that there was bad news waiting for him at Nick Tenzi's house in Benedict Canyon. It was a sense that many career lawmen share, one that often keeps them alive.

So strong was the foreboding that he had dug the belt holster out of his Samsonite 2-suiter and wore it now with the S&W Chief's Special tucked in snugly. In spite of Bureau regulations, Ryan had not carried a gun in two years. He had not fired one, except on the range, in twice as long. This morning, however, the pressure of the iron on his hip felt good and comforting.

When he turned off the freeway at Sunset Boulevard he slackened his speed only enough to allow him to make it through the twists and turns past UCLA without sailing off the road. He turned off at the Beverly Hills Hotel where Benedict Canyon snaked into the hills. Ten minutes later he slid to a stop in front of Nick Tenzi's house as the sky began to lighten in the east.

He paused on the sidewalk, looking up the path that led to the front door. Lights blazed from the windows, yet there was a curious stillness about the house and grounds made him shiver.

He unholstered the revolver and held it ready as he pushed open the low wooden gate and walked toward the house.

His sense of something wrong grew with each step he took.

The first indication was that there was no dog. The big friendly Doberman that Tenzi had unsuccessfully tried to turn into an attack beast was nowhere to be seen. On Ryan's previous visit he had come snuffling and wagging down the path to escort him to the door.

As he rounded a growth of palmettos Ryan saw a vertical strip of light at the entrance indicating that the front door was ajar. Another bad sign. He continued even more cautiously.

A dark mound lay on the grass off to his left.

Ryan did not have to go any closer to know what it was. Even in the dark it was unmistakably a body.

Nevertheless, he crossed the grass to have a look.

He recognized Drummer Cahane, one of the few remnants of the old organization who had helped Nick Tenzi play gangster.

Drummer's single eye, lightly filmed over, stared at nothing. Where the other eye should have been was an oozing black hole.

Ryan moved on to a second shadowy mound lying a few feet away. Like his partner, Roy Kilgore had only one eye now. The shootings had been at close range and the bullets precisely placed. Professional work. The corpses might as well have been signed by the artist: Lou Matchek.

Ryan straightened up and walked back to the front door. He pushed the oak panel gently and it swung all the way open. The entrance hall beyond was empty. He stepped inside, keeping his back to the wall, and looked into the living room. Lamps were on, bottles and glasses sat on the bar, a magazine was spread open on the floor next to a chair, but there was no one in sight.

Room by room he prowled the house. Lights blazed everywhere, but there was no sign of life. In the master bedroom drawers were pulled out and clothes disarranged in one of the walk-in closets, the one that held the woman's clothes. A fistful of hangers were empty. Shoes were scattered on the floor. Signs of hasty departure.

Ryan continued to search the house, being careful not to disarrange anything, until he satisfied himself it was empty of life. His head churned with unanswered questions. Who killed Cahane and Kilgore?

Where was Nick Tenzi? Had he taken his wife and run? But then why the call to Ryan with the urgent request that he call back? So many questions, so few answers.

He returned to the living room and sat down. He closed his eyes and pressed his fingers against the lids. Sometimes when he did that he could picture in his mind a recent violent act that had taken place in the room. It was a psychic kind of thing that he never talked about. The FBI did not approve of its agents indulging in metaphysics.

This time it didn't work. There were no visions, only the shapeless flashes caused by the pressure of his fingers on his eyeballs. There was however a faint smell that did not belong. It took him a moment to identify it. Urine.

Ryan rose and started for the door. Spots on the expensive carpet. He knelt, touched one of the spots. Tacky, like drying paint. Only it was not paint, it was blood. This had been a night of violence in Benedict Canyon.

Ryan stood up and went back outside. He carefully left the front door ajar as it was when he found it. He stood for a minute looking down at Cahane and Kilgore, trying to reconstruct in his mind the last moments of their lives. Which had died first? How much time elapsed before the second was shot through the eye? Impossible to tell in the morning twilight with the naked eye. Anyway, what difference did it make?

He crossed the path and was just starting around the house in the opposite direction when he saw the third body. He had missed it on the way in because it lay concealed by a rose bush.

Ryan approached close enough to see the face

and answered at least one of his questions. Nick Tenzi had not gone anywhere.

Most of Tenzi's throat between his chin and his clavicle was gone. Ripped out, leaving shredded flesh and dangling tendons.

Dark blood soaked his chest and the grass around his head. A pistol lay inches from his hand.

Ryan lifted the pistol, hooking a pencil through the trigger guard. The cordite smell told him it had been recently fired.

However, it was obviously no bullet that had torn Nick Tenzi's throat.

Ryan looked around for another weapon, and he saw the dog.

The friendly Doberman lay at his master's feet, dark-stained muzzle resting on his paws, as though in sleep. But the dog was not asleep. Looking closer, Ryan saw the bullet wound in his side that had killed him.

He could not help but feel more compassion for the dog than for the man. A peace-loving animal, he had been forced into a violent arena where he did not belong. As for Nick Tenzi, his fate had been sealed years ago.

Ryan went back into the house, used the phone to call the Beverly Hills police and report what he had found in Benedict Canyon. He identified himself, but declined their request that he stay at the scene. He promised to contact them later. Right now he had places to go, people to see.

* * * * *

He reverted to his daredevil driving style in covering the fifteen miles between Beverly Hills and

Glendale. By the time he reached Lemon Grove Street, early risers were getting into their cars for the daily commute. The sky in the east was a pale blue, promising a clear California day. Behind him the night hung on grimly.

A muscular 4-wheel-drive Dodge Raider sat in the driveway of Kristy Baysinger's house. Ryan lay a hand on the hood and felt the warmth of the engine underneath. The door of the truck was unlocked. No keys in the ignition. In the glove box was a silk scarf, breath mints, a Los Angeles street map, and a couple of envelopes addressed to Kristy Baysinger.

He got out of the Dodge and walked across to the front of the house. His heart sank. Another door stood ajar. He had seen more than enough of death this early morning, and silently prayed that he would find no more inside.

Kristy's neat little house held no bodies. There were, however, signs that all had not been peaceful here. A stack of cartons had fallen over, spilling the contents. A floor lamp lay on its side. Here, as at Nick Tenzi's house, the occupants had left without turning off the lights.

Ryan pushed aside a stack of magazines and sat on the couch. He stared at the empty room and once again closed his eyes to try get a picture of what had taken place here.

The Dodge outside with the warm engine told him someone had arrived not too long ago. Kristy? What would she have been doing out in the small morning hours? Matchek? More likely.

The bodies of Cahane and Kilgore at Tenzi's place looked like his work. Would he have finished that business then returned here to Kristy's? Not the Lou Matchek Ryan knew. He would be long gone. But as Armand Vespa had pointed out, there were other elements to that personality now.

So go with that hypothesis. Matchek, driving Kristy's car, comes back. Do the two of them then leave? In what? And how did the stack of cartons get knocked over? Unlikely that Matchek and Kristy had fought. Unlikely too that they would leave the door ajar and the lights on. So who else was here?

Tork! The answer hit him like a fist. Of course! Vespa had sent Tork to stake out Kristy's house. Matchek shows up, Tork, probably with help, grabs him. Takes him out of here to return to Fairhaven. Kristy too? Why?

Ryan sprang up from the couch. He had answered as many questions as he could with psychic dialogue. It was time for action.

He sprinted from the house to his car, leaped in, and roared off once again toward the freeway.

Chapter 28

In the chill dawn there was little traffic heading west on the Ventura Freeway. The Fairhaven station wagon and the black Buick bearing Gunther Tork and his prisoner had no trouble staying within a few yards of each other. Both Krebs up front and Spencer behind kept rigidly to the 55 mile-per-hour speed limit, even though the other scattered vehicles heading out of Los Angeles passed them with ease. There would have been embarrassing explanations necessary, had either of them been stopped by a CHP unit.

Up in the wagon Kristy Baysinger was having serious misgivings about the whole operation. Even if Jack Gannon, or Matchek, was everything she had been told, was this Gunther Tork any better? He had virtually forced her to accompany them up to Fairhaven. Her anxiety grew steadily over what the plans were for her and for Gannon/Matchek once they locked behind those walls.

She twisted around in the seat, trying to see what was happening in the Buick. All she could see behind the windshield was the reflected glint of the sun off the blond guard's sunglasses.

* * * * *

In the back seat of the Buick, the man Kristy

knew as Jack Gannon sat with Gunther Tork on his left. His hands were clasped in his lap and his head bent forward. The bees were swarming again, the separate voices in his head fighting for dominance.

The bullet hole in his thigh had stopped bleeding. The cloth of the trouser leg around the wound had stiffened with the clotting blood. The pain had settled to a dull, deep throb that kept time with his pulse.

"Not feeling so good?" Tork could not keep the satisfaction out of his voice.

Gannon made no answer.

"That's what happens to people who play with guns." Tork was enjoying himself. He dug into his jacket and brought out the Colt Trooper Gannon had surrendered back at Kristy's house. "It didn't take you long to get hold of one. Another good argument for handgun control."

He laughed immoderately at this observation and nudged Spencer in the front seat. The guard managed an unconvincing chuckle.

"Who did you use it on tonight?" Tork persisted. "Nick Tenzi? No loss there. You probably made a lot of people happy. If it was Tenzi, you'll have that FBI maverick, that Ryan guy pissed at you. He wanted to nail Tenzi himself, Be a hero like Elliot Ness or somebody. Or maybe it was Ryan you blew away? Was it one of them?"

Gannon turned his face away and stared at the passing scenery.

"Either one is OK with me." Tork was enjoying himself, savoring his position of power. "Ryan was sniffing around Fairhaven, just looking to make trouble.

And Tenzi, acting like he was a big shot gangster. Maybe he would've been in the Fifties. Now the niggers and the beaneaters run the show. Tenzi was just a punk operating on borrowed time. Which one was it, Matchek? Tenzi or Ryan? Or did you blast somebody else?"

He barked a laugh, "But you're not what you used to be, are you. You had the drop on me back there in the house, but you couldn't get off a shot. The old Matchek might have gone down, but he'd have taken a couple of us with him. Never thought I'd see Lou Matchek turn pussy."

His seat mate turned and looked at the beefy captain of security. "Why don't you give it a rest, asshole."

Tork's smile decayed. His heavy face flushed a dark, dangerous red. "You watch your mouth, shitbag. And you just better remember I'm the one with the piece here. Maybe once you were hot shit with a gun in your fist, but now you're naked and you're nothing. Don't forget that."

The lids came down over the ice gray eyes; and Tork did not see the dangerous emotions behind them. He was right about Jack Gannon being powerless without a gun. Even armed Gannon would be no match for a tough professional like Tork. But it was no longer Jack Gannon who sat passively in the back seat of the Buick. Lou Matchek had returned.

Gunther Tork did not know that. As far as he knew, he was riding next to a one-time tough guy who had given up his gun without a fight as soon as somebody drew down on him. He was just a little disappointed. Lou Matchek's reputation had let him to believe he was bringing in one hardass sonofabitch. He would have enjoyed much more killing that Lou Matchek than this sorry imitation.

Whatever Armand Vespa had in mind for this man, Gunther Tork was determined he would find a way to kill him. Matchek had cost him his reputation and his job with the DEA. Matchek had made him and his Fairhaven security people look like incompetent fools. He had diminished Tork in the eyes of his employer; brought him down to a level where Dr. Vespa could not respect him. There was only one way to settle that debt. Matchek was going to have to die.

Sitting next to him, head down again, hands clasped, Matchek knew Tork was planning to kill him. It was something you could smell on a man, blood lust. He figured his chances of getting back to Fairhaven alive were no better than even money. And if he did get there safe, what then? Armand Vespa digging back into his head to screw around some more with his brain? Of the two options, Matchek preferred to die somewhere on the road. But not unless he had to.

Jack Gannon would have accepted his fate. Gannon was not without courage, but he lacked cunning. He did not have the cold steel core of suppressed pain and anger that drove Lou Matchek.

The Jack Gannons of the world were the well-meaning heroes who ran after a punk who had just snatched an old lady's purse, only to be shot in the face for their trouble.

Jack Gannon would have sat stoically in the back seat of the Buick fighting down nausea from the pain in his leg, and silently, impotently cursed his fate. Lou Matchek's mind was racing ahead of the car, searching for a way out.

Tork fell silent after a few miles, tiring of the one-sided conversation. Without moving his head Matchek's eyes skipped around the interior of the Buick. Barry Spencer up in front kept his eyes fixed on the road and the station wagon ahead of them.

The door handle on Matchek's right had been removed. The seat backs, extended by the head rests, discouraged any thought of climbing into the front seat before either Tork or the driver put a bullet into him.

On his left Gunther Tork sat relaxed but not careless. His suit jacket was unbuttoned, his right hand rested within easy reach of his shoulder holster. Matchek's Colt was in the jacket pocket on Tork's far side. The door handle over there was in place but unreachable unless he went over or through Tork.

The station wagon carrying Kristy and Leon Krebs peeled off the freeway just south of Santa Barbara onto the old 101. The Buick followed. From all outward appearances the man sitting next to Gunther Tork was a defeated, dejected Jack Gannon, his hands clasped, his head down. Actually, Lou Matchek's muscles were tense, his nerves taut. His eyes behind half-closed lids missed nothing.

After five miles they left the highway and turned up the narrower county road. The forest pushed close on each side. Both the station wagon and the Buick slowed as the road began to twist and climb into the hills toward the Fairhaven access road.

Matchek chose his spot. Spencer braked to ease the Buick into a sharp-angled turn. Letting the centrifugal force take him, Matchek slumped over against Gunther Tork with a convincing grunt of pain.

Instinctively Tork seized him by the shoulder to push him off. Matchek's left hand dived between Tork's solid thighs and found his testicles. He clamped them in a powerful grip and twisted while his right hand fumbled inside Tork's jacket for the gun.

Tork squealed like a gut-ripped pig. His hands flailed at Matchek. Spencer hit the brake, fighting to keep the Buick on the road while he tried to see what was happening behind him.

The car fishtailed, and the back half slammed into a yellow guard post, jamming the fender panel in against the tire.

Matchek got his fingers on the butt of Tork's revolver. He continued to mash the man's balls in his fist as he tried with his right hand to free the gun from its holster. Unable to get any leverage in his arms in the cramped back seat, Tork leaned forward and sank his teeth into Matchek's wrist. With tears of pain streaming from his eyes he clamped his jaws together and tasted a salty spurt of blood.

Matchek released his ball-busting grip and knuckled Tork at the hinge of his jaw, yanking his right hand free as the teeth loosed their grip. Giving up on the gun, he hit the door handle. He gathered his strength and dove over the doubled-up Tork and out onto the shoulder of the road as the door sprang open.

Spencer had his gun out as Matchek rolled to the edge of the berm where the forested hill fell steeply away from the road.

The guard looked at his boss, who had both hands cupped between his legs.

"Shoot him, you idiot!" Tork cried in a strangled voice.

By the time Spencer had pushed open the front door and climbed out, Matchek had rolled over the edge and tumbled down the bluff through the thick underbrush and out of sight. The guard looked back helplessly at his captain, who was breathing hard through his mouth as he climbed, still bent over, out of the car.

Up ahead Krebs had stopped the station wagon. He came running toward them with his revolver unholstered.

"What happened?"

Tork stood with his hands braced on his knees. He looked up at Krebs, blood from Matchek's bitten wrist speckling his chin. "Go on up to Fairhaven."

"What about the woman?"

"Take her. Dr. Vespa will know what to do."

Krebs stood uncertainly. "What about Matchek?"

Tork looked down into the thick forest that fell away from the road. "Spencer and me'll take care of him."

The two guards exchanged a look their captain did not see. After a moment Krebs holstered his gun and jogged back to the wagon. Tork jerked a thumb toward the lip of the bluff. "Let's go..."

Spencer looked over the edge, then back at Tork. "Down there?"

"Hell yes, down there. Don't worry about Matchek, he's got a slug in his leg and I've got his gun. Get going, I'm right behind you."

Reluctantly Spencer sat down at the edge of the slope and began half-sliding, half-stumbling toward the bottom. Tork made sure his gun was securely holstered, then followed.

* * * * *

Matchek's descent had been more violent. He had rolled and tumbled out of control down the steep wooded slope. He did what he could to protect himself, tucking in his chin, drawing up his knees, and folding his arms across his chest. Barbed thorns snatched at his clothing, small boulders and tree trunks thumped and battered him as he tumbled down and down. After what seemed a long, long time he slammed into a rotted log and came to a stop at the bottom of the canyon.

For a minute or so he lay motionless, waiting for the impact of a bullet. When there was none, he opened his eyes and blinked out the dirt and the pine needles. The road far above him was obscured by trees and brush. There were only patches of the bright morning sky visible through gaps in the foliage. Slowly, painfully, he began to unfold his body and take inventory.

He was bruised and scratched and scraped on every unprotected part from his wild tumbling fall. The bullet wound in his thigh was open and oozing an unhealthy yellow-white fluid. The crescent of Tork's bite mark was purple and bleeding. He cautiously tried each limb separately, decided nothing was broken. So far so good.

But what next? He had not thought beyond disabling Tork and getting out of the car. He was a city boy born and raised on the concrete. Making his way safely out of the wilderness with only one working leg was not going to be easy. In his favor was the probability that Tork was as out of place in the woods as he was, so would have no easy time tracking him down. Because

Tork would come after him, of this he was sure.

He pulled himself erect and swayed for a moment, light headed. The bullet wound throbbed like a hot iron jammed into his thigh. Matchek knew he was not going to travel any distance with this leg.

He cocked his head listening. Gradually he became aware of the tiny sounds of the forest. A bird called overhead and was answered by another farther off. Something skittered unseen among the dry dead leaves. A squirrel scolded him from the branch of a tree and disappeared in a flash of gray.

From up toward the road came an irregular thump-bump.

Matchek tensed as a grapefruit-sized rock bounced and rolled down the path his body had made and thudded to rest against the same rotted log that had stopped his fall. He heard a shout somewhere above him, but could not make out the words.

Tork was coming.

Chapter 29

As he drove north at an excessive speed on the Ventura Freeway, Merlin Ryan allowed himself to wonder briefly if he might be wrong. What if his reconstruction of the action in Kristy Baysinger's house had been faulty? Lou Matchek could be still back in the city, stalking somebody else. The woman might be, well, anywhere. Tork could be following Matchek, their paths leading to a final violent meeting somewhere. Meanwhile he, ace FBI Special Projects Agent Ryan, would be chasing phantoms up into the mountains behind Santa Barbara.

Angrily he rubbed out the negative thoughts. To the exasperation of the Bureau, Ryan had based many of his decisions through the years on naked hunches like this one. He had seldom been wrong.

He turned off the freeway onto 101, then to the narrow county road that snaked up into the mountains. He swerved around the tight corners with an unaccustomed recklessness. As he rounded an especially tight curve he saw the black Buick up against a guard post and hit the brakes. A few feet beyond the Buick was a steep dropoff into a forested canyon.

Ryan pulled up behind the Buick and got out. He peered inside and saw blood smears on the back seat. Stepping past the barrier, he Looked down the slope and saw the path of newly broken brush and dislodged stones leading into the green tangle below. Somebody had left the car in a hurry and taken the swiftest way down the hill.

No doubts clouded his thinking this time. He zipped up his jacket as protection against the undergrowth and began a controlled sliding descent into the forest canyon.

* * * * *

It was slow going for Matchek through the scrub pine and thickets that carpeted the canyon into which he had fallen.

Under the best of conditions his progress would have been slow, and his wounded leg impeded him even more. The flesh around the bullet wound was puffy and painful when the fabric of his pant leg rubbed it.

From time to time he stopped to listen. Behind him Tork made no effort to muffle the sound of his approach. Why should he? He knew Matchek was hurt and unarmed. It was a matter of time until he caught up. Matchek knew this too, and he began to ponder alternatives to flight.

He was leaving a clear trail of broken brush and blood spots. No way to avoid that. Gunther Tork, healthy and armed, was going to overtake him, probably in minutes. Since he could not hope to escape, and stood little chance in a fight, his only option, other than surrender, was to surprise his pursuer in an ambush.

The thick brush and close-growing trees offered

ample hiding places. But at best, hiding would only delay discovery. Tork would soon find him, and he would be back in the same predicament. A weapon was what he needed. A weapon with which he could strike before Tork realized he was no longer running.

One which would do enough damage to ensure that Tork would not get his gun into action.

He searched his pockets. Nothing of any possible use, except the ring with Kristy's keys. If he got close enough, these could be gripped so the shafts stuck out of his clenched fists. A blow with them could do considerable damage, even blind a victim. The trouble with that was that Tork was unlikely to be careless enough to let him get within punching range. And with his damaged leg, he was not going to spring very far from his hiding place.

A bird cried angrily back in the direction he had come from, marking Tork's progress. He had no time to waste on attack methods that could not work. Time to get organized. First, a hiding place. He continued several yards through the heavy chaparral, making no effort to conceal his path. On the contrary, he made sure the broken twigs and the scuffed up ground would point the way. Then he retreated ten yards back along the broken trail and moved off to the side at a spot where he could stand upright, yet remain hidden from the trail by a clump of laurel. Behind him the sounds of Tork's approach grew louder.

Next, a weapon. He scanned the ground, kicking away the carpet of pine cones and dead leaves. He hefted a rock the size of a coconut. If thrown accurately enough to strike a vital spot on Tork's skull, it might do the job. However, the laurel branches that offered him the hiding place would hinder the sweep of his arm necessary for that kind of a throw. And if he missed, he was finished. There would be no second shot at it.

He tossed the rock aside and dropped to his hands and knees, looking for something, anything, that would offer better odds.

Everything he found was too small, too rotted, too heavy, or in some other way unsuitable as a weapon. He could now hear the steady crunch of Tork's approach. He had very few minutes remaining to come up with a plan.

Matchek got out the keys again. If it came finally to a hand-to-hand fight, he would give it a try and at least inflict some damage before he was shot to death. The thought brought a grim smile, which quickly faded.

He stood up to position himself as best he could behind the sheltering laurel. As he did his eye fell on a spar of a dead branch thrusting a blunt, broken end at an angle toward the sky. The other end was lost in a waist-high thicket. He grasped the branch and pulled. The other end was entangled in new-growth roots and resisted his efforts. With the sound of his pursuer growing louder and closer, Matchek wrenched and twisted the branch until at last it came free in his hands. It was thick as his forearm and as long as he was tall. Opposite the blunt, heavy end was the stump of a "Y".

Gripping it near the narrow end, he tried a tentative baseball swing. The "Y" caught in the surrounding bushes and it took several seconds to pull it free. He tried to break the branch over his knee to shorten it into a more useable club. The wood refused to crack.

He could hear the heavy huff of breath now as

Tork closed in on him. In another few seconds he would pass on the other side of the thicket where Matchek was hiding. Then, a few yards farther on he would see where the broken trail ended, and come back.

Carefully Matchek slid the branch through the thick brush, poising the blunt end at the edge of the trail. The branch rested there horizontally like a pool cue on a bridge. This left the "Y" with about 2 feet of branch at eye level on his side. He gripped the crotch with his right hand and waited.

In less than a minute there was a grunt and a muttered curse as someone stumbled in the broken trail. Matchek poised his branch and strained for a glimpse of the pursuer through the thicket.

The brush was too thick to make out more than a shadowy silhouette, pushing aside the foliage, intent on the trail left by Matchek. When the man's head moved even with the blunt end of his ram, Matchek put his full strength into his arm and shoulder, and shot it forward. He heard the satisfying crack of the butt end of the branch hitting a skull, and the thump of a body falling into the brush.

Matchek leg go his grip on the ram and struggled back out through the brush to the trail. As soon as he saw the man lying face down, blood seeping from his head, he realized his mistake. "Freeze, asshole." Gunther Tork had his pistol leveled at Matchek's ear from a distance of five feet. "Hands behind your head. Now! You know the position."

Matchek raised his arms and laced his fingers behind his head. Tork flicked his eyes down at the fallen guard then back up at Matchek.

"Added one more to your list, hey, scum bag?"

"The wrong one."

"Kind of chickenshit, isn't it, clubbing the guy from ambush like that."

"You do what you have to."

"Well, you've done your last, Matchek." Tork showed his teeth. "Your last, ever."

Keeping the gun steadily aimed at Matchek, Tork stepped over Spencer's body. With his free hand he drew the six-foot branch out of the thicket and hefted it. "Not bad," he said. "A little clumsy for close work." He jabbed it toward Spencer. "But effective."

Matchek shrugged, watching Tork closely for any little lapse that would give him an opening.

"Not thinking of grabbing the stick out of my hands, are you, asshole?"

Tork gave the branch a sudden thrust, ramming the split end into Matchek's thigh, right on the suppurating bullet wound. "Maybe Rambo could do it, but this isn't a movie, asshole, this is real life."

Matchek grunted in pain. He lurched to one side and his hands came down from his head reflexively.

"Keep 'em up," Tork snapped. "Or you're a dead man."

Matchek obeyed, clamping his jaws to keep from groaning. He stood supporting his weight with his good left leg.

"Think you can make it back up to the road? Might be a little rough climbing with that leg."

"Fuck you," Matchek said through clenched teeth.

Tork hit him again on the wound. Pain howled up into his brain and he went to his knees.

"No," Tork said. "It doesn't look like you can

make it. But I can't just leave you here, now can I. That wouldn't be sporting." He was enjoying himself now. "Not sporting at all."

Matchek tried to rise again, but his leg wouldn't support him. He fell back to a sitting position on the trail.

"No," Tork said again, "No way I can leave you sitting here.

Why who knows what might happen? The ants might get a whiff of that hole in your leg and start chewing on you. A hungry coyote might come along and take a bite for himself. And there are probably snakes in these woods."

He stepped forward and kicked Matchek in the thigh. For a moment the world turned crimson as the pain clanged up into his head.

"Or," Tork went on, "there might be a miracle. That leg might all of a sudden get better and you'd walk out of here and cause me more trouble than you have already."

Matchek shifted his butt on the trail, trying to move his wounded thigh out of kicking range.

Tork dropped the heavy bantering tone. "No, you've caused enough trouble, Matchek, for me and for a lot of other people. Now you've gone and killed one of my men. You really don't leave me any choice."

He sighted down the barrel of the pistol. Matchek braced for the corning impact.

The sound of the gunshot was strangely muted by the surrounding trees.

Chapter 30

Merlin Ryan slid, stumbled, tumbled, and fell for what seemed to him half a mile before he came to a stop in a heavy growth of chaparral at the bottom of the canyon. During the fall he had kept his knees bent and his arms in close to his body, protecting his face with his hands. He removed his hands now and looked up. The road was not visible through the tangle of greenery. Only small patches of sky showed through. The sudden shocking silence gave him the sense of having fallen down Alice's rabbit hole. He rose gingerly to his feet and looked around. Nothing but trees, brush and shadows. He began to wonder what the hell he had expected to do once he was down here. This might be one for the bad idea book.

He parted the thicket, drawing a painful scratch down the back of one hand, and saw a rotted log that had been dislodged from its long-time resting place, leaving a matted brown impression in the grass crawling with bugs. There were also several red-brown smudges on the ground and on the foliage spots that could only be blood. The blood spots led off through the brush where tramped-down grass and broken twigs clearly marked the recent passage of human beings. Ryan set off following it.

After five minutes he slowed and listened. There

were sounds up ahead, a thrashing and crunching, that were not made by any forest creature. Ryan proceeded cautiously. At first he made an effort to move smother the sounds of his approach, then decided nobody would be listening for him anyway, and pushed on as swiftly as he could, heedless of the noise he made.

A sudden shout up ahead of him brought Ryan to a stop. He heard voices. The tone was definitely not friendly, but he could not make out what they were saying. He moved forward more slowly.

So suddenly that it startled him, Ryan pushed aside a heavy evergreen branch and saw up ahead the broad back of Gunther Tork. A short distance beyond Tork he could see Lou Matchek standing crookedly with his hands clasped behind his head. Matchek's stance, coupled with the tension in Tork's back muscles, told him there was a gun between the two men.

He let the branch fall back into place as he moved off the broken trail and inched forward through the brush to a spot where he could observe the entire scene. For the first time he saw the third man, a guard in the uniform of Fairhaven Security, who lay face-down on the grass, the blond hair on one side of his head matted and bloody.

Now that Matchek's full length was visible Ryan saw the reason for his off-center stance. The right leg of his pants was crimson wet with blood. Tork indeed held a pistol leveled at Matchek. In his left hand he gripped a long club-like branch.

As Ryan watched, Tork stepped forward and kicked Matchek in the bloody leg. Matchek's breath hissed out in a harsh *Aaaahhh!*

Ryan started to shout but choked it off in

his throat. You don't yell *Freeze!* at a man with a gun unless you're pointing a gun of your own at him. Ryan fumbled at his hip, trying to free the butt of his Chief's Special from a grasping thorn bush.

On the trail Tork said, "You've caused enough trouble, Matchek, for me and a for lot of other people. Now you've gone and killed one of my men. You really don't leave me any choice."

He lowered the gun so it was pointed at the fallen man's head. Ryan could see Matchek's eyes narrow as he tensed for the impact.

Forgetting caution, Ryan tore the revolver free of his holster and the sharp thorns. He fancied he saw Tork's finger tighten on the trigger before he got his own gun around into position and fired.

At the sound of the shot Tork's reflexes took over. He jumped sideways, whirled and aimed at the spot where the shot came from. He squeezed off four fast rounds and dived for cover on the opposite side of the trail. While Tork was occupied, Matchek scrambled on hands and knees into the brush, biting his lip to keep from crying out with the pain in his leg.

The bullets crackled through the leaves all around Ryan's head. Crouching behind the thicket, which now seemed barely adequate protection, he cursed the times he had avoided pistol practice. With a free open shot like he would never get again, he had missed.

"Throw out your weapon," he called, using a voice of authority he had never before employed. "This is the FBI."

Tork smiled grimly. He aimed carefully at the voice and fired his last two rounds.

Ryan felt the last slug hit him like the kick of a mule in the upper chest. He sat down hard in a tangle of branches. His revolver went flying back over his head. His right arm went numb, and the fiery pain hit him as air was sucked into the raw bullet wound.

For several seconds Tork did not move. He heard the other man grunt and fall, but after that there was no sound. In all probability he had been hit, but Tork could not be sure.

Cautiously he made his way back onto the broken trail.

Spencer the guard still lay where he had fallen, but Matchek was gone. Tork swore under his breath and turned in a slow circle. Nothing moved in the thick growth of brush and trees. No sound reached him. He had emptied his gun, and was at the mercy of anyone strong enough to ambush him.

With no attempt at stealth he crashed back over the beaten down grass until he came to a spot where the slope of the hill seemed less forbidding than elsewhere. Grabbing handfuls of brush he scrambled and slid back up the seemingly endless bluff to the road.

Several yards farther on he saw the Buick still wedged against the concrete post. Parked behind it was a nondescript Ford that probably belonged to the FBI man. Tork rested for a moment on the edge of the bluff, listening for sounds of pursuers. He heard none. Still breathing hard, he jogged up to where the two cars stood. He first looked in the Ford to see if the keys were there. No luck. He returned to the Buick and squatted to examine the fender where it was pushed in against the tire. There seemed to be no displacement of the wheel. Gripping the edge of the metal with both hands he heaved backwards and managed to pull it an inch away from the rubber. Enough to make the car driveable.

With a last searching look down into the canyon, he was satisfied that nothing was coming after him. He got in the Buick, cranked the engine, and drove off toward the Fairhaven Facility.

* * * * *

Back down on the floor of the forest canyon Lou Matchek remained motionless for long minutes after he heard Tork retreat back up the trail. Gradually the fiery pain in his leg subsided to a dull throb that he could handle. He pulled himself up by a juniper branch and tested his weight on the wounded leg. It held, barely. He made his way back to the trail. Spencer lay there as before. He saw no sign of the man whose timely arrival had saved his life.

Matchek parted the brush over where he thought the shot had come from.

"What kept you?"

The voice was hoarse and breathy. Matchek pushed aside an alder bush and saw Merlin Ryan reclining with his head resting against the base of a Douglas fir. The right side of his Red Sox warmup jacket glistened with blood. His left hand was pressed to an area high on his right chest.

"Where's your gun?"

Ryan looked back up and over his shoulder into the heavy foliage. "Back there somewhere. I lost it."

"Some G-Man."

Matchek made his way to Ryan's side and squatted next to him. "Let's have a look." He grasped Ryan's wrist and gently pulled his hand away from the wound. The bleeding had lessened to a trickle.

"You'll probably live," Matchek said. "You'll hurt for a while, but you'll probably live."

"Oh, thank you, that really makes me feel—" He broke off in a fit of coughing and spat up a light pink foam.

"You're chances will be better if you shut the hell up." Ryan nodded and wiped his mouth.

At a sudden sound behind him Matchek lurched upright, his hands out to ward off an attack. Nothing there. Then a groan sounded from the other side of the alder bush. He picked his way back to the trail. Spencer was sitting up, retching and holding his head in both hands.

He looked blearily up at Matchek. "Am I shot?"

"You're the only one here who isn't. You took a good knock on the head, though. Sorry about that. We've got another one hurt behind the bush there. Think you can help me bring him out?"

"Are you the one who hit me?"

"Yeah. I thought you were Tork."

"Jesus."

Spencer got to his knees, then tried to rise. He made it to a crouch, then fell back with a groan. He tried it again with the same result.

"I can't get my balance," he said with a tinge of panic. "Shit. Well, sit still. I'll see what I can do."

He limped back into the brush where Ryan sat breathing raggedly.

"Can you get up?" Matchek asked. Ryan shook his head.

"No strength."

"Shit."

Matchek moved to Ryan's shoulder. "Hold on,"

he said, and as gently as he could, pushed the upper part of the wounded man's body forward. He shifted his feet again and hooked his hands under Ryan's arms. Step by painful step he dragged the FBI man out of the thicket and set him alongside Spencer, whose head lolled down on his chest.

Matchek stood back and looked at the two of them.

"You're supposed to be under arrest," Ryan said, and started coughing again.

"Oh yes, you're going to take me in."

Then Matchek got serious. "Since I seem to be the only one of us who can stand up, I guess I'm going to have to walk out of here and get help."

"Are you in shape to make it?" Ryan said weakly. "Who knows. I wish you'd held on to your damn gun."

Ryan tried to shrug and grimaced in pain. He waved a hand toward the trees. "It's out there somewhere."

"Yeah, well, I'm not going to thrash around looking for it."

He cupped a hand under Spencer's chin and raised his head.

"You didn't have one?"

The guard blinked, trying unsuccessfully to focus his eyes. "Left it in the car."

Matchek stepped back and shook his head.

"Fine pair of professionals."

Ryan coughed. Spencer slowly lowered his head again. "Well, get comfy, boys. I'll see you when I see you."

Matchek turned and started away.

"Lou." Ryan's soft call stopped him.

"Yeah?"

"Car keys. Right hand pocket."

Matchek knelt beside him, fished into the pocket, and brought out the keys. He jingled them in his hand, nodded once to Ryan and disappeared back up the trail.

Spencer rolled his head to one side and looked at Ryan. "You know him. Do you think he'll come back for us?"

The FBI man wiped his lips with the back of his hand. "No." He sensed rather than heard the groan of the other man. "But then, you never really know about anybody."

Chapter 31

Armand Vespa's eyes glowed angrily in their deep sockets as he listened to Leon Krebs's recitation of Matchek's escape.

"And what was Captain Tork doing while Matchek made his way out of the car and into the woods?"

"Like I said, Doctor, I was up front with the lady in the station wagon and couldn't see what all happened back there.

Near as I could tell, Matchek got the captain in the, uh, vitals, and immobilized him while he went over the side."

"Tork recovered sufficiently to go after him?"

"Seemed so. Him and Spencer."

"And Matchek was wounded?"

"Looked like he was shot in the leg."

"So chances are good that my two able-bodied security men will bring him back."

Krebs looked off at a corner of the ceiling. He had seen a look in Matchek's eyes, a look he remembered from fighters who were at there most dangerous when they were hurt. But he new what the director wanted to hear. He said, "I'd say they'll get him."

"They had better," Vespa said darkly. "Bring in the woman, but stand by."

Krebs went out and came back immediately with Kristy Baysinger. She pulled her arm free of his grasp and marched to Vespa's desk. There she planted her feet and glared across at the director.

Vespa had never been comfortable talking to women.

Especially angry women. He liked to be in control at all times, and he could never be sure of which direction an angry woman would jump.

"I want to know why I was brought up here," Kristy said. "What right do you have to hold me?"

Vespa made an effort to keep his voice within a range of normal speech. He did not want a shouting match.

"As Captain Tork should have told you, it's a security measure. Once you understand the full extent of our operations here at Fairhaven, their importance to the country, you will see why precautions had to be taken to ensure that you would not reveal details of our work prematurely."

"You can cut out the bullshit, Doctor. I was pushed around in my own home and brought here in a car by an armed guard against my will. That's kidnaping. And that can bring you more trouble than you ever imagined. So start explaining."

Vespa sighed deeply and turned his skull eyes on Leon Krebs, who stood at lumpish attention beside the door. Krebs heartily wished he was someplace else. Anyplace else. Why did he catch all the shit details?

"I apologize for any excessive force that was used. If disciplinary actions are called for, you have my word they will be carried out."

Yeah, carried out on guess who, thought Krebs.

"Fine," said Kristy. "So either start explaining, or take me home."

Vespa's hands danced lightly on their fingertips. "What, exactly, is it you want explained."

"You can start with the real story of what happened to my husband."

"You were told all about that two years ago. A tragic but unavoidable accident in the chemistry lab—"

"I bought that at the time," Kristy said. "Now I want more details."

Vespa's hands fluttered into the air. "My dear, I don't understand."

"I never saw Jay's body. He was in a sealed coffin when I got here."

"Believe me, you wouldn't have wanted to see it. The mutilation caused by exploding chemicals is not easy to look upon."

"Let that go for now. What about this man Matchek? Who is he? What was he doing here?"

Vespa settled into his lecture-room tone. "Louis Matchek is a seriously disturbed sociopath. He came to us as a volunteer from Folsom Prison. We were conducting an experiment that I hoped would correct his anti-social deviation by overriding the violence syndrome in his brain. Unfortunately, he fled from the facility before the program was completed."

"If he's so dangerous, why was there no report of his escape in the news?"

"I had hoped our people could reach him and return him here without fanfare. Had the news gone out it might have triggered a violent confrontation."

"What was Matchek's connection to my husband?"

"It's rather difficult to explain in ordinary terms."

"Try me. And use any terms you want."

Vespa formed a diamond with his thumbs and forefingers. "Do you know anything of memory transference?"

Kristy frowned. "I know there have been experiments with rats using chemicals. Ribonucleic acid was drawn from the brain of one and injected into another. There was some indication that the second rat remembered things the first rat was taught, but nothing conclusive."

"I'm impressed, Mrs. Baysinger."

She waved away the compliment, impatient for him to continue.

"The experiments to which you refer were conducted at Stanford University. However, they are primitive compared to what we are attempting here. We have married the biochemical concept to state-of-the-art computer science and microelectronics. When it was determined that the seat of long term memory could be found in the temporal lobes and hippocampus, the next step was to—"

The door opened suddenly and a thin, middle-aged woman who had replaced Victoria Fellows stood uncertainly in the doorway. "What is it, Miss Schaeffer?" Vespa said in the irritable tone of a professor whose lecture is interrupted.

"I'm sorry, Doctor, but Captain Tork is outside. He says it's urgent that he talks to you."

"Tork? Who is with him?"

"No one, sir. He's alone."

Vespa's face clouded. "I see. I won't need you

any more today."

The woman nodded, stole a timid glance at Kristy, and went out.

Vespa spoke sharply to Krebs.

"Find a room for Mrs.

Baysinger in the infirmary."

"Wait a minute—" Kristy began.

"I'm sorry, Mrs. Baysinger, but I have business. We'll talk later."

With a flip of his hand he told the guard to get her out of there. Krebs took her arm, and after a momentary resistance she let herself be led away.

Vespa leaned back in the leather chair. His hands picked at each other like tiny monkeys searching for fleas. In a moment Gunther Tork entered. There were deep scratches on his face and hands. A rip in his trousers bared a scraped knee. One sleeve of his jacket was torn completely off.

"Where is he?" Vespa demanded. "Where is Matchek?"

"There was an accident," Tork said.

"Krebs told me about the accident. He said you and Spencer followed Matchek into a ravine while he brought the Baysinger woman here."

"That's right. We—"

"Where is Matchek?"

"He's still down there at the bottom of a cliff."

"You lost him."

"The guy's not human. He had a bullet in his leg, so I didn't think he was going anywhere. Then he rolled all the way down this steep bank into a bunch of trees, and I thought that would finish him. But he was waiting for us. He brained Spencer, but I got the drop on him. I had him, and I was bringing him out."

"Well?"

"Somehow that redheaded FBI guy, that Ryan, must have followed us. He showed up from nowhere and started shooting."

"And what did you do then?" Vespa asked in a deceptively mild tone.

"I returned his fire."

"And?"

"I brought him down, but during the action Matchek got away."

"Again," Vespa said darkly.

"I had my hands full what with Spencer down and Ryan blasting away at me. I emptied my gun, and when I couldn't find Matchek I climbed back to the road and came here."

"You ran," Vespa translated.

"Jesus, Doctor, it's thicker than a jungle down there. You couldn't see somebody three feet away. If Matchek would have got to me, there'd be nobody to come and warn you."

"Ah, yes, very considerate."

"I did the best I could," Tork mumbled.

"Perhaps." Vespa's fingers wove themselves together. "So you left three men at the bottom of this canyon. Tell me again, what was their condition."

"As far as I could tell, Spencer's finished. Probably Ryan too. I know I hit him. I can't be sure about Matchek. He had that leg wound to begin with, and it wasn't getting any better."

"You know what it will mean to us if anyone comes out of that canyon alive. No coverup will be possible."

"Let me take a couple of men back there and I'll guarantee nobody comes out alive."

"No more men," Vespa said.

"It's your responsibility. You go and take care of it."

"I'll need a piece. Something heavy," Tork said.

"Get it. You know where the weapons are kept." Tork pivoted and marched toward the door.

"And don't worry about bringing Matchek back alive," Vespa called after him. "He's of no use to us now."

Tork smiled tightly. He said, "That's what I've been waiting to hear," and continued out of the office.

Armand Vespa sat looking after him. Tork's usefulness was ended. The best possible outcome would be for neither him nor Matchek to come out of the canyon. And considering Matchek's proficiency as a killer, that was a good possibility. The doctor allowed himself a minute to savor the prospect, then he sobered.

There was still the woman to deal with. Naturally, she could not be allowed to leave and spread the story, even what little she knew, of what went on at Fairhaven. The facility would never survive even a cursory investigation.

When it was determined she was missing, there would be a search. But from what Tork and Krebs had told him, no one could know she was here. The woman appeared healthy and bright, so she could be of some value in the laboratory. There were aspects of the female he had long wanted to explore.

* * * * *

Gunther Tork went first to his own quarters

where he changed into a heavy camouflage jacket and pants. Then he jogged across the grounds past the infirmary to the building that housed the gymnasium.

The weight room, sauna, and showers were empty with the staff placed on alert status. Tork hurried to the far end of the building where a heavy door was labeled *EQUIPMENT ROOM*. He opened it with a key from his ring and stepped through, pulling the door closed behind him. Only he and Dr. Vespa had keys to this room, which was in fact the Fairhaven armory. The doctor's prohibition of guns at the facility was real enough, but he was not blind to the possibility of an emergency.

Tork switched on the bare overhead light and scanned the collection of rifles and handguns in racks along the wall. He selected a Savage semi-automatic 12-gauge shotgun that had been sawed off just in front of the magazine and just behind the pistol grip. The alteration turned it into a powerful mankiller just 15 inches long.

He pulled open the ammunition drawer He dropped a box of double-ought magnum shells into a jacket pocket. Each shell contained 12 pellets, the size of small peas. A blast at close range could blow a man in half. And it did not need careful aiming. He scooped up two loose shells from the bottom of the drawer and loaded them into the magazine.

He slung the weapon through a belt loop and left the armory, locking the door behind him. Once outside, he hurried to the parking lot in front of the administration building, climbed into the battered Buick, and drove off toward the front gate.

"I'm coming for you, Matchek," he said through

clenched teeth. "You don't know it yet, but you're a dead man."

Chapter 32

Jack Gannon gripped the wheel of the rental Ford and fought to keep the car on the road through the switchbacks and hairpin turns on the road up the mountain to Fairhaven. The bullet wound in his leg kept up a steady throb. His face felt hot. Fever, probably, he thought. Sweat soaked his clothes as his body fought the infection. He had to keep his mind cool and functioning. It required a fierce concentration to drive as the conflicting personalities within him battled for control.

This is crazy, said the ice cold Matchek voice. *I should be heading in the other direction. You' re driving me straight into trouble without even a gun. And for what? A woman I don't even know.*

That's not true, said the fading voice of Jay Baysinger. *I do know Kristy. I know her as only a man can know his wife. I love her. I know I was not the husband I should have been. I should help her now, I know that... I would help her, but I'm hurt. Get help for my leg, then I can see about Kristy.*

Shut up, both of you, said Gannon silently. *I'm doing what I have to do. This is where it started, and this is where it's going to end. One way or another.*

And there was Merlin Ryan to think about, and the injured guard, Spencer. Without his help they would die at the bottom of the canyon. Matchek would not care, Baysinger would deny responsibility, so it was all up to Jack Gannon. So many people depending on him, so many voices battling for dominance. And he was not even sure who he really was.

So intent was he on stifling the inner turmoil that he was a fractional second late in seeing the other car as it swerved around a curve coming straight toward him. He hit the brakes at the last moment and slid onto the loose rock at the side of the road.

"Watch it, you crazy son of a bitch!"

The Ford banged off the facing wall of granite as the Buick slewed past. With a clear mind Gannon would have recognized the black Buick. Without the demand on his total attention he might have looked into the other car and seen the hate-twisted face of Gunther Tork.

He righted the Ford and sped on. Behind him Tork fought the wheel and cursed as the Buick fishtailed on down the mountain.

He searched desperately for a spot on the road wide enough to turn around.

Gannon wheeled into the private road and floorboarded the gas pedal the final two miles. The tall gates were closed. No one was in sight, but there would be one of Tork's men in the gatehouse.

He hunched his shoulders, braced his arms, and aimed the car at the center of the double gate. He hit the wrought iron grillwork at 50 miles an hour with a shriek of torn metal and splintering glass. The center lock snapped and the gates parted, flying inward like great broken wings.

The uniformed guard ran out of the gatehouse.

He gestured and shouted as the car roared past. Gannon ignored him and cut across the lawn toward the administration building. After a stunned moment, the guard gave chase, running between the twin furrows of flattened grass left by the tires.

The Ford bounced up the three low concrete steps leading to the entrance to the main building and crashed through the glass door, jolting to a stop against the reception desk. The startled security guard sprawled out of his chair to the tile floor. By the time he recovered and started to clamber to his feet Gannon had the front of his shirt in a steel grip.

"Where's Vespa?" It was the diamond hard voice of Lou Matchek that spoke into the face of the helpless guard. A voice that said beneath the words, *Answer fast or die.*

"End of the hall... on the right," croaked the guard. His eyes flicked toward the telephone.

Gannon hit the guard once with the hard edge of his hand just behind the right ear, then caught him as he fell forward and lowered him to the floor. It was the combat sense of Lou Matchek that knew exactly where to hit him, but it was the gentler Jack Gannon who caught the man before he cracked his skull open.

He ran limping down the hall past the closed doors on both sides to the last on the right. He pushed it open, ignored the empty reception desk, and shoved his way into the office labeled *Dr. Armand Vespa, Director.*

Vespa was seated in his high-backed swivel chair, turned to look out the window. He pivoted when Gannon entered. The skull face barely twitched with surprise, then a smile quirked the narrow lips.

"Welcome back, Mr. Matchek. Or is it

Baysinger?"

Gannon was momentarily confused by Vespa's calm. He said, "You were expecting me?"

"I knew you'd be back. I'll admit I didn't expect you to come alone."

For an instant the room wavered. The bees rose in a swarm.

There was an itch somewhere under his scalp. Under his skull. He rubbed at the hairline diamond scar.

"Headache, Mr. Matchek?"

"Go to hell. Where is Kristy Baysinger?"

"Well, well, Can it be that Lou Matchek the heartless killer has one after all?"

"Just tell me where she is, butcher."

The two spots darkened over Vespa's cheekbones. "You don't want to call me names, Mr. Matchek."

Gannon planted his fists on the dark wood desk and pushed his face close to Vespa's. "I'll call you what you are, you son of a bitch. Where's the woman?"

The doctor's long fingers traced the edge of the desk. The flash of anger subsided, but something more dangerous took its place. Gannon for the first time saw in the shadowed eyes the fire of madness.

Vespa said, "Apparently our experiment has already met with some success. The Lou Matchek who was brought here in December would never risk his own neck for a woman. Nothing in his history shows he considered women more than a convenience."

Gannon struggled to control the growing tumult in his head. He took a step back from the desk, grunting at the pain that now throbbed the entire length of his leg.

Vespa caught the reaction and looked down at the bloody pants. "We'd better take care of that."

The buzzing in Gannon's head grew to a rushing wind. Deep under his scalp the itch got worse. "Later. What have you done with Kristy?"

"Mrs. Baysinger is resting. I know you are concerned, but I'm afraid you're not completely rational. Your face is flushed. Your speech is slurred. Clear symptoms of septicemia. Why don't you let me have a look at that leg. You really shouldn't be standing on it."

Vespa's deep, gentle voice was hypnotic. His leg did hurt terribly, Gannon realized, and he knew Dr. Vespa could ease the pain. A part of him wanted very much to relax and give himself over to this man. The part that was Jay Baysinger still admired and respected him. The force of Vespa's will was like a firm, gentle hand on his shoulder.

"Let me give you something for the pain. Clean out the wound. You'll feel much better. Then we can talk."

Gannon closed his eyes, pulled in a deep breath, and summoned the cruel strength of Lou Matchek. "Take me to the woman, Vespa, or..." Here he faltered.

"Or what?" Vespa said softly. "Violence doesn't come easily to you any more, does it?"

Gannon felt the hairs quiver on the backs of his arms. The son of a bitch was right. Where Lou Matchek would have calmly reached across the desk and punctured an eyeball when Vespa stalled, he found he could not even give voice to the threat.

Take over, Matchek!

Without haste he turned and walked back to the case beside the door that displayed the antique surgical instruments. With his left fist he smashed the glass panel, ignoring a deep scratch one of the shards gouged across the knuckles. He took a moment to look over the selection, then chose a bronze surgeon's knife with a thin four-inch blade.

Vespa rose from his chair, but Gannon was back at his side before he could move. With his left hand he seized the doctor's left wrist and levered it up between his shoulder blades. At the same time he pricked the flesh just below the jawbone with the point of the knife, bringing a bright bead of blood. Vespa reflexively reached for Gannon's knife hand, but relaxed when he felt the blade bite into his throat.

"Now," Gannon said, "let's go get the woman." Vespa allowed himself to be guided to the door.

"Apparently," he said, "we did not cut out enough of the old Matchek."

In the hallway they were met by the guard from the gate. Behind him, holding a hand to the back of his head and looking groggy, was the lobby guard. When they saw the blade pressed against Vespa's throat they stopped as though they had hit a wall.

"You fellas go inside and make yourselves comfortable. If I see either of you again your boss gets a new mouth."

The gate guard looked to Vespa. The lobby guard forgot his aching head and gaped.

"Do as he says," Vespa ordered.

The guards went in. Gannon added a little pressure to his grip on Vespa's arm.

"Got a key?"

"I don't lock my office," Vespa answered tightly. "Then I guess you boys are going to have to be on your honor." Gannon waved them on, and the two guards continued into Vespa's office.

"Remember," Gannon said, "I see either of you and it's *kkkkkkk*." He pantomimed slashing the doctor's throat and both guards flinched.

He kicked shut the door to the inner office and steered Vespa back out to the hall.

Lou Matchek was in full motor control now as Jack Gannon pulled back into the observer position. He could only hope that when the time came he could push Matchek back into the closet before some unfixable damage was done.

They left the administration building through a back door and walked along one of the pleasant paths toward the infirmary. Gannon kept a friendly hand on the arm of Dr. Vespa as they walked. The scattered strollers on the grounds nodded politely and passed on. What they could not see was that Gannon's thumb rested on a nerve just above the doctor's elbow where a minimal pressure could cause paralyzing pain. The surgical knife he kept concealed in his free hand.

They entered the infirmary, where the admitting nurse nodded pleasantly to Dr. Vespa as they passed. The sharp antiseptic smell of the hallway brought back vivid impressions to the Matchek mind.

"Where to, Vespa?"

"She's on the second floor."

"For your sake, she'd better be all right."

"Of course she is," Vespa said. "I simply had her brought here because I thought she would be comfortable."

"Save it, Vespa. I've got a low bullshit tolerance."

They continued to a room not far from the one Matchek occupied when he was transferred from Folsom. Vespa unlocked the door and pushed it open.

Kristy sprang up from the chair where she was sitting to face them. Her eyes flashed with a mixture of anger and fear When she saw Gannon she gasped audibly.

He showed her the bronze knife. "It's all right, Kristy.

The good guys are in control."

"Jack, thank God. I didn't know what happened to you." She dropped her eyes. "Is your leg—?"

"It's all right," he interrupted. "I'll fill you in later. Right now we're getting out of here. I'm supposed to send help for a couple of people at the bottom of a canyon."

"I don't know why you're being so melodramatic," Vespa said. "This is not a prison."

"I'm not sure what this is," Gannon said, "but it's time somebody took a close look. Now let's walk nice and calm, three old friends, back to the parking lot where I left the car. And believe me, Dr. Vespa, if you talk out of turn, there's enough of Lou Matchek left in me to slice you're windpipe without a thought."

"I believe you," Vespa said.

They walked three abreast, Gannon in the middle, back along the side of the administration building to the small parking lot in front. They rounded the corner and looked into the muzzle of Gunther Tork's sawed-off shotgun. Ranged behind him were the two guards they had left in Vespa's office.

Gannon thumbed the nerve in Vespa's upper

arm. The doctor squealed in sudden pain. Gannon shoved Kristy to one side and yanked Vespa in between himself and Tork. He brought the surgical knife up to eye level.

"Put away the cannon, Tork."

Tork hesitated a moment, then swiveled the shotgun so the black muzzle looked at Kristy's stomach.

"Want to see the woman splatter? he said. "You got five seconds."

Despite Gannon's grip on his arm, Vespa turned his head enough to show him the skull smile.

"Now we find out who is really in control."

Chapter 33

Cut his throat, the Matchek voice rasped inside his head.

They're going to kill the woman anyway, You've got one chance in a hundred of getting out of here. Drop the knife and your chances go down to zero.

From far back in the corner of his mind the Jay Baysinger voice pleaded, *Don't let them hurt Kristy. Dr. Vespa is a scientist, trust him. Do what they say, don't make trouble, and it will be all right.*

He looked over at Kristy who stood frozen, staring at the shotgun Tork held leveled at her stomach. It would be the first time she ever had a gun pointed her. It was a terrifying sensation, seeing violent death just a trigger jerk away. "Tell him to get the gun off her," Gannon said.

"You overestimate my power over Captain Tork," Vespa said. "Tell him or you die."

"Do you really think you would gain anything by killing me? If you do, now is the time to act."

A crucial three seconds passed, a lapse that would never have occurred had the Lou Matchek of old been in charge.

Vespa recognized the hesitation. He said, "There is no need to make more of this situation than it is. All

I want is for Fairhaven to continue. With post-operative therapy we can clear up this confusion in your mind. As for Mrs. Baysinger, my only concern is that she understands what we're doing here. Once it's made clear to her, I'm sure we can all agree on the future. So you see, we'll all start over again if you simply give up the knife.

He's lying, said Matchek. *Kill him and get out.*

No! cried Baysinger. *Your only chance is to do as he says.*

It was decision time for Jack Gannon. Slowly the fingers gripping the bronze handle of the knife relaxed. He released his hold on Vespa's arm. The knife fell to the pavement with a soft clang.

Tork moved in at once, jabbing Gannon in the breastbone with the muzzle of the shotgun. "Not so tough now, are you."

"Lock him up," Vespa said.

Tork seized his arm and pushed him roughly, falling in behind with the sawed-off ready.

Kristy recovered from her paralysis. "What are you going to do? His leg needs attention." She started toward Gannon.

"Stay where you are, Mrs. Baysinger." Vespa's voice was soft, but there was a steely threat in the words. He bent and picked up the fallen surgical knife, balancing it in his palm. "A clumsy instrument by today's standards," he said, "but serviceable."

"You said I could go," Kristy protested.

"Of course you can," Vespa said in the same ominous tone. Kristy took a step toward the gate.

"But not right away." The knife did tricks in Vespa's long, sensitive fingers. "First we have things to talk about."

Gannon looked back over his shoulder. Tork jabbed him in the spine with the shotgun muzzle.

Vespa said, "Be careful, Captain. We want to help Mr. Matchek, not injure him."

"Sure," Tork growled. "Let's go, *Mister* Matchek."

They walked back along the side of the administration building, Gannon struggling as the pain ballooned in his thigh, Tork prodding him with the shotgun if his step faltered.

They entered the infirmary. Tork balanced the weapon easily in one hand while he unlocked a door on the first floor with the other.

"Inside," he ordered.

Gannon entered and Tork snapped on the overhead light. The room was small, about eight-by-ten, the walls and ceiling painted hospital white. The only furnishing was an examination table and a metal stool. The room had no window.

"Think you'll be comfortable here?" Tork said with clumsy sarcasm. He looked around the room. "We could have some real fun here, you and me."

He thrust the gun forward suddenly, prodding Gannon in the wounded leg. Taken by surprise, Gannon gasped with the pain.

"The thing is, I don't know how long you're going to last. That leg looks pretty bad."

Gannon showed his teeth. "What's the matter, Tork, embarrassed about letting a cripple get away from you?"

"I'll tell you one thing, asshole, it won't happen again."

"Or maybe you're still feeling bad that you couldn't handle a simple protection job back in Miami."

Tork's rage bubbled almost to the surface. He pushed it down and forced a smile. "No, I don't think you're going to hold up too well. In fact, your woman will probably last longer, no matter what we do with her."

Gannon's jaw clenched.

Tork saw he had hit a nerve. "Hey, you didn't really think she was going to walk out of here, did you?"

"You are a piece of shit, Tork."

"Oho, now we're calling names, are we?" The blood pumped into his face, turning it a deep blotchy red. "All I ask is one thing, give me an excuse to splatter you. Try to get past me now, why don't you, big man? Look, I'll hold the gun down like this. If you're fast enough you could grab the gun, use it on me, run out of here on your gimpy leg and save the girlfriend.

Be a big hero. Try it, Matchek. Please try it."

The knuckle whitened on Tork's trigger finger. The tendons stood out in his right arm, straining with his eagerness to blow a hole in the other man.

Gannon did not move.

"I thought so," Tork said. "You're chickenshit. Big man with a gun in your hand, chickenshit when your on the other end. You make me want to puke."

He swung the barrel of the shotgun up without warning and whacked it across the bloody part of Gannon's thigh where the flesh was already swelling enough to make the pants tight on his leg.

It was not difficult for Gannon to scream with the pain. He staggered and started to fall forward. Tork stepped back to let him hit the floor, and for that instant his grip on the shotgun slackened.

Gannon turned his fall into a dive. With his left hand he clamped onto the shotgun barrel just in front of the trigger guard. He drove the stiffened fingers of his right under Tork's breastbone and dug for the diaphragm.

Tork's breath blasted out through his mouth. He stumbled back against the wall, fighting to keep his grip on the gun. In eerie silence the two men grappled, muscles straining, sweat greasing their faces. The only sounds in the small room were their grunts and harsh breathing, the scuffling of their shoes on the composition floor.

For long agonizing seconds their faces were inches apart, teeth bared, eyeballs bulging. Four hands gripped the shotgun in a grotesque parody of little boys tossing a bat for first ups.

Their bodies pressed together like lovers in a last sensual dance.

The explosion of the gun was sudden and stunning in the confined space. The light was blotted out for an instant.

Gannon's ears boomed with the echo of the shot. It took him a beat to realize that if his ears were ringing, he was alive.

Then his sight returned. Four hands still gripped the shotgun. The men's bodies were still pressed together. But now Gunther Tork had no face.

Then suddenly, like a marionette whose strings have been cut, Tork crumpled. His back hit the door, pushing it closed as he fell. He pitched forward and the blasted front half of his head smacked the floor like a split melon. A pool of blood spread lazily outward.

Gannon spent only a moment looking down at the dead man.

The sound of the shot would bring someone on the run. He had to move and move fast. He took a second to concentrate on the fiery pain in his leg. He willed it down into a hard compact knot of agony that he could carry as long as he kept it from exploding.

He jerked open the door against the dead weight of Tork's body and stepped into the hall. A hoarse shout came from the direction of the entrance. Gannon saw uniformed guards, at least two of them, pushing in through the door. He aimed the shotgun at the ceiling and fired. The weapon boomed and echoed in the corridor. A light fixture shattered and rained down in a fine sprinkle of glass. The guards dived back out the door.

Gannon took off run-hopping the other way in the corridor. There would be no time for Tork's men to have covered the rear exit. He sent a tiny prayer that the door would not be locked.

It wasn't. Gannon ran out and down across the sloping lawn to where the stream wound past. There were no sounds of pursuit, and he did not want to slow down to look. He splashed into the stream and across, limping on the far side into the aspen grove.

Now there was shouting from the infirmary building. More guards milled around. Gannon could see even from this distance that most of them were armed. So much for the no-gun policy.

He turned to continue through the shallow aspen grove when the world tilted abruptly. He stopped, grabbing a tree trunk for support. He was feverish, his mouth suddenly dry.

Not now! his mind shrieked. *I can't pass out now.*

The dizzy spell faded, but the fever remained. He looked back across the stream, fighting down a crazy desire to wade back in and cool his burning flesh. Through the leaves he saw guards pointing this way. They would be coming soon. He had to move.

He started out of the aspen grove toward the wall which lay 100 yards away. His wounded leg betrayed him and he stumbled forward, almost falling. He felt himself caught under both arms and pulled upright. He struggled, but his strength was fast draining away.

With the scene shifting and blurring before his eyes he turned, expecting to see the faces of Tork's guards blazing with lust for vengeance. The faces he saw were empty of emotion. One of them was chillingly familiar—a fleshy, pale-haired man of undetermined age. The other was an old, old woman with gaping toothless mouth who gripped his arm with surprising strength.

Droolers.

One of them, Gannon could not be sure which, tried to take the shotgun. He managed to clutch the weapon to him as the world swam in and out of focus. His fevered brain tottered on the brink of delirium.

They were propelling him, half-carrying him across the grounds now, heading for the North Annex. Gannon tried to dig in his feet and stop them, but he had not enough strength left. It took all his concentration to keep from blacking out.

The North Annex door opened before them and Gannon was hoisted inside by his two escorts. The dormitory smelled of clothes and bodies. He blinked rapidly and brought it into focus. The droolers—twenty, thirty, however many there stood ranged in front of him. Their idiot stares told him nothing. They made a low mumbling sound that was not words. They seemed to be trying to communicate, but had not the power.

The two who had him by the arms walked him across the room toward the far wall. From somewhere within he summoned the last of his strength, and with a shrug of his shoulders threw them off. He wheeled the shotgun into firing position and swiveled it slowly back and forth over the droolers.

"Hold it right where you are. Nobody move."

He might as well have spoken to the aspen trees outside.

The threat of the gun was beyond their understanding. They continued to shift around until they had him circled. Then they started to move in.

"Get back, damn it!"

His shout had no more effect than the shotgun. Slowly, mindlessly, they shuffled closer, reaching for him. Their wordless babble blended with the swarming bees. He could smell their sour breath as they closed the circle.

Desperately, he pointed the shotgun at the ceiling and pulled the trigger. The hammer clacked down on an empty chamber.

That stupid son of a bitch Tork had loaded only two shells.

The droolers reached him. He felt their hands on him. He no longer had the strength to fight.

Chapter 34

Gannon closed his eyes and hunched his shoulders. To his surprise, the hands that touched him were tentative, even gentle. He opened his eyes. Looking into the mind-blasted faces surrounding him, he saw a spark here and there in the vacant eyes, not of hostility, but of compassion. And ineffable sorrow. The tension drained suddenly from his body, and he would have fallen had he not been supported by many hands.

The pale young man who had helped bring him into the building moved in front of Gannon now. It was the same man who had pulled the toothless woman away from him on his first visit to the North Annex, which seemed such a long, long time ago.

There was a sharp pang of recognition, and suddenly he knew who the man was and why he was so familiar.

"Hello, Jay."

Jay Baysinger's only response to his name was a vaguely puzzled look. He put out a hand and touched Gannon lightly on the cheek.

Gannon looked into his eyes. "What did that brain butcher do to you, Jay? And to the rest of these people?"

The question was rhetorical. No one in the North Annex could answer him.

Something banged against the door. Gannon looked over and saw that a heavy trunk had been pushed up against it on the inside, barring the way to whoever was out there. The faces turned to him, childlike and open, eager for approval.

A wave of dizziness hit him again. He waved a hand weakly. "That's good," he said. "Thank you."

Another series of thumps battered the door from outside.

Then Armand Vespa's voice, amplified by a bullhorn.

"Matchek. Come out. No one will harm you. I only want to help."

The people—he could no longer think of them as the droolers—looked to him for a response. He limped across the bare floor to the door, assisted by Jay Baysinger and another man. He put his mouth close to the wooden panel. "Vespa?"

"I hear you, Matchek. Are you coming out?"

"Go to hell."

There was a rising babble behind him. Gannon turned, afraid for a moment that he had turned the people against him. What he saw was thirty or so faces contorted into a wild assortment of smiles. Their wordless prattle had a joyous tone. Some of them brought their hands clumsily together in an attempt at applause.

"Listen to me, Matchek. You have no chance of escape. I give you my word, if you come out now you won't be harmed. If we have to come in after you, I promise you will regret it."

Gannon turned away from the door and scanned the eager, empty faces. Their eyes were on him, waiting.

Their heads bobbed, their bodies jerked, but they were waiting for something.

"What do we tell him?" Gannon said.

From thirty mouths came three blurred syllables. They formed no words, but Gannon recognized a childish echo of his own response: "Go to hell!"

Silence for a moment, then Vespa's voice on a rising note of anger: *"I have the woman, Matchek."*

Kristy. The son of a bitch still had Kristy. Got to think of something.

Gannon pressed the flat of his hands against the door and tried to organize his thoughts. The bees swarmed. His legs failed him and he started to slip to the floor. He was caught and carried back out of the way and supported by many hands.

From outside came a crack of static as Vespa killed the bullhorn. His unamplified voice could still be heard clearly through the door.

"Break it down!"

Boom. Something heavy hit the door outside. The panel shuddered, the trunk slid back an inch.

Boom.

In Gannon's fevered mind the battering at the door became a physical pounding on his head. He pulled free of those who supported him, staggered a few feet toward the door, and started to fall. Once again the hands of the North Annex people caught him.

Boom.

They steered him, half-carrying him, back away from the door.

Boom.

He was eased into a chair. The people ranged themselves in a rough circle facing him. In Gannon's disoriented mind they were a team waiting for the coach to tell them what to do.

Bleary as he was, he still saw the absurdity of the image. A fevered, delirious coach and his band of mindless droolers squaring off against a healthy, heavily-armed foe. He could not suppress a wild, irrelevant laugh. His team echoed him—a babble of manic mirth.

Boom.

A door panel splintered. *Crunch.*

Another panel went. Hands reached in through the broken door and pushed the trunk back and away. The door swung wide.

Leon Krebs and two other uniformed security guards stood shoulder to shoulder in the doorway. Behind them, his long white laboratory coat slapping his legs, was Armand Vespa. His hair was wildly disarranged, his skull teeth bared, his face distorted with violent emotion.

Leaving Gannon in the chair, the North Annex people ranged themselves between him and the door, facing Vespa and the guards.

The doctor stepped forward and spread his arms wide, Moses parting the Red Sea.

"Get back. Out of the way, you dribbling fools."

A murmur rose from the people, but none of them moved. "Go in there and get him," Vespa ordered his guards.

First Krebs, then the other two stepped inside the building, their weapons ready. The droolers moved forward to meet them. Something like a growl came from their many throats. The guards hesitated a moment, then took a step back.

"What are you doing?" Vespa cried. "I said go in there and get Matchek!"

With agonizing effort Gannon pushed himself to his feet.

The pain from his leg enveloped his entire body like a flame. He tried to go forward, but his muscles would not respond.

The Annex people reached the doorway. With Jay Baysinger taking the lead, several of them went through to the outside. Krebs and the other two guards continued to retreat.

Vespa was shouting now, his arms windmilling, his hair whipped into a tangle.

"Shoot them down! Shoot, you imbeciles!"

The guards looked at each other, then at Krebs.

"We can't do that, Doctor," Krebs said. "They're unarmed. They're sick people. We can't shoot them."

"Then give me that gun!" Vespa snatched at the .45 automatic Krebs carried and wrested it from the surprised guard. "If you can't do your job, I'll do it for you!"

"Dr. Vespa, don't!" cried Krebs. He reached for the pistol, but backed off when Vespa pointed it at him.

"Get away! I don't need you. Any of you."

Krebs raised a hand. He and the other three guards moved off slowly.

Vespa fired once over their heads. The gunshot was shockingly loud. In the sudden silence that followed one of the guards brought his rifle around. Krebs slapped it away.

"Don't!"

The guards backed away, slowly at first. Vespa fired again, into the ground this time. The two armed guards turned and broke into a run, crashing through the aspen grove into the stream and up across the slope of lawn on the far side. Krebs stood his ground until Vespa leveled the pistol at him, then he followed the others.

As more of the Annex people came outside, Vespa turned back to face them.

"Move out of the way, you brainless fools!" Craning over their heads he shouted, "I'm coming for you, Matchek. I warned you."

The Annex people muttered wordlessly, but did not give way.

Vespa waved the pistol at them. "Move aside! I'm ordering you! I'm the only one who can ever make you well. If you want my help, get out of my way!"

Jay Baysinger shambled toward the doctor. His head swung back and forth, but his eyes never left Vespa. His mouth tried to form words, but all that came out was gibberish. His hands reached out as he approached the doctor.

Vespa shot him four times in the chest. Jay continued to come on, his body shuddering with the impact of each bullet, until the fourth burst his heart.

He went to his knees. Bright blood bubbled out of his mouth. In the last moment of his life the long-dimmed light of intellect flickered in his eyes. He stretched out his arm, pointed a forefinger at Armand Vespa, and died.

For the Annex people that was the trigger. With all the pent-up rage and pain of the years suddenly released, they cried out their fury and surged forward. Vespa looked up from the body of Jay Baysinger. Before he could react the droolers were upon him. He did not get off another shot.

From the doorway where he supported himself against the jamb, Gannon saw the people swarm over the doctor. He saw the flapping white lab coat go down under the wave of bodies. He heard the screams, the rip of cloth, the snap of breaking bones. Emotions flashed like starbursts through his fevered mind. In rapid succession he knew the cold indifference of Lou Matchek, the tragic disenchantment of Jay Baysinger, and the helpless horror of Jack Gannon.

The wind roared in his ears, the world dimmed and blacked out. He did not feel the floor as he hit it.

* * * * *

A minute... an hour... a lifetime? Later, Gannon opened his eyes. All the pain was gone. He was floating free on something soft and billowy. A cloud. An angel watched over him. No, not a cloud. He was on a bed. And the angel was Kristy Baysinger.

And still there was no pain.

Slowly, jerkily, the world took shape. Gannon looked around him and he remembered. Tork. Armand Vespa. The sad, angry, mind-crippled people. He rolled his head on the pillow. He was in the North Annex, lying on one of the narrow beds. He looked down at himself and saw that his right trouser leg had been cut away, and his leg wrapped with a clean white bandage.

He tried to speak, but his vocal apparatus was slow in responding. He looked past Kristy, out the open door. Efficient looking young men in the uniform of the Ventura County Sheriff's Office moved in and out of the frame. An ambulance was backed up close to the building, and two white-coated attendants were loading a body bag inside.

Jay Baysinger had found peace.

A second body, covered with a beige hospital blanket, still lay on the grass. A dark stain had soaked through the blanket. The skeletal fingers of one hand reached out, still clutching the ground in an agony of death. Gannon switched off the mental image of Armand Vespa's last minutes.

"Welcome back," Kristy said.

Gannon raised a hand that felt weighted with lead. Kristy took the hand and held it to her cheek. Gannon's gaze moved around the empty dormitory.

"Where are the people?"

"They're being held in the infirmary," Kristy said. "They'll be taken care of."

"They're not really dangerous you know."

"I know."

"They saved me."

"Yes. After ..." she gestured vaguely at the doorway, "... what happened to Dr. Vespa, they just stood quietly and waited until the sheriff's men got here."

The next words came hard for him. "Do you know ...?"

"About Jay?" she helped him out. "Yes. I saw him. But it wasn't really him. For all practical purposes, Jay Baysinger really did die two years ago. I don't think I want to know what happened since. I have my memories."

He looked up at her. "So do I." He saw the quick flash of pain in her eyes and went on. "Why doesn't my leg hurt?"

"The paramedics gave you a shot. They're going

to take you to a hospital in Santa Barbara for further repairs." He had a sudden thought. "Ryan."

"The sheriff's rescue team has already gone for him and the guard you left in the canyon. I told them as soon as they got here."

"Good." His enthusiasm faded. "The trouble is, Ryan will probably send me back to Folsom."

"Don't be too sure. You're not the same man you were, Jack."

"Maybe not," he said. "But, Kristy, who am I?"

Before he heard her answer he started to float away, up and out the door and off over the countryside. Kristy held tightly to his hand. It would be nice, he thought, if she could come with him.

Chapter 35

Gannon maneuvered down the corridor of All Saints Hospital in Santa Barbara using a cane and walking stiffly on his bandaged right leg. He nodded to the medical personnel who hurried by.

They responded with cool professional smiles. He had argued with the nurse, who wanted to roll him out of here in a wheel chair.

Hospital policy, she explained, to cover them in case a patient fell on the way out and subsequently sued. When he signed a release they finally agreed to drop the wheelchair requirement. They may have had to carry him in, but Gannon was determined to walk out of here under his own power.

A hand came down on his shoulder and he flinched instinctively. When he turned he saw a tall man with a half shaven head of blond hair and a gauze bandage over his bare scalp.

"Remember me?" It took a minute, then the voice and face clicked in. "Sure. How's the head, Spencer?"

"No lasting damage they tell me, but I'm going to look goofy for a few weeks. It'll play hell with my social life."

"Sorry about bashing you. I meant to hit Tork."

"Forget it. You owed me one. I'm just glad you

didn't have a gun."

"Yeah. Well, take care."

"Sure. You too." Spencer turned off and headed for the elevators. Gannon continued down the hall to a private room where the door was propped open.

The room was as cheery as a hospital room can be. Warm sunlight streamed in through the window. Fragrant bouquets of flowers bloomed in vases on the bedside table and the window sill. A basket of fruit sat within reach. A smiley-face floating balloon was anchored to the foot of the bed.

Gannon limped through the door, trying unsuccessfully to look jaunty with the cane he had not yet mastered.

"Still malingering at government expense?" he said. "No wonder taxes are so high."

Merlin Ryan was propped up on a stack of snowy pillows. A hanging IV bottle dripped its contents slowly into a vein. The hospital sheet and blanket were turned down just enough to expose the top of the wide white bandage that circled his upper body.

Seated in the chair next to the bed was a dark haired young woman with liquid brown eyes that brimmed with love for her man.

"Hi, Gimp," Ryan said. To the woman at his side he said, "Linda, meet..." the hesitation was only a fraction of a second during which the two men exchanged a glance that said everything, "...Jack Gannon."

She stood up and took Gannon's hand. "You are the man who saved my husband's life. Just to say thank you seems... not enough."

"It's plenty. Besides, I think we're about even in

the life saving race."

"All the same, thank you." She squeezed his hand and returned to Ryan's bedside. She leaned down and kissed him lightly on the mouth. "You two will have things to talk about. I'll come back in a little while."

Linda smiled again at Gannon and went out. "Nice lady," he said.

"Yes, she is. Sit down , Jack."

Gannon took the chair vacated by Linda. "No more 'Lou'?"

"Lou Matchek is dead," Ryan said. "There's a death certificate and everything."

"I wish that was true," Gannon said. "I mean I wish he was wiped out, but he's still there in my head. Waiting."

"I want to talk about that. But first, fill me in on what's happened at Fairhaven. I've been getting my reports in tiny bites."

"It's pretty well wrapped up. Vespa's dead, Tork's dead. The rest of the staff is being questioned. They rounded up the people who were kept in the North Annex, the ones they called the Droolers. They'll get real care now, in legitimate hospitals. I don't know if they can be helped, but they're sure as hell better off."

"I know Tork caught a shotgun blast, but nobody wants to say exactly how Vespa died."

Gannon looked down at his hands. "I didn't see it. I was out of it by that time. I hear he had a heart attack. The excitement or something."

"So be it," Ryan said. "What are you going to do now?"

"First I figure out who I am. Then decide where

I'm going."

Gannon said it lightly, but the smile did not reach his eyes.

"How would you like to work with me?"

"FBI? You're kidding, right?"

"You wouldn't be on the rolls, officially. You know I operate outside the Bureau's limits. I'm getting the credit for busting up Vespa's freak factory, so right now I can swing a little weight in the right circles."

Gannon watched him carefully.

"Just what kind of work are we talking about?"

"It would depend on what I'm working on. And there's no point in going into detail until you decide to do it."

"You aren't talking to Jack Gannon, are you. The guy you want is Lou Matchek."

The two men traded stares. Ryan was the first to blink. "All right. You said Matchek was still there, waiting. Some of the jobs I have to do are, well, untidy. I could use a Matchek on the side of the good guys for a change."

"Jesus, I don't know. Right now Jack Gannon, the invented man, is in control. I like it this way. To turn things over to Matchek again would be unchaining a pit bull. It might be a very bad idea."

"It might," Ryan agreed. "There's no way of knowing for sure. Just one more point—Lou Matchek still has a large debt to pay. This is one way he might start settling up."

Gannon's eyes narrowed to chips of gray ice. "People could get hurt."

"Some people deserve to get hurt," Ryan said.

Gannon got out of the chair and limped over to

the window. He looked three stories down at the world. Cars rolled past on the street. People walked by on the sidewalk, singly and in pairs. Two small children ran by, their laughter floating lightly up to the open window. A young couple strolled hand in hand. Everybody down there had someplace to go, someone to go to. Where was he going? Jack Gannon was not real. Jay Baysinger was dead. Lou Matchek was dormant. At least for now. He turned back to the red haired agent in the bed.

"I'll think it over."

"Do that. Whatever you decide, I've started the machinery to provide you with authentic Jack Gannon ID. By the time the job is finished, he'll have a more solid background than I have. You might want to think about some work on that face."

"Thanks. I'll still think it over."

"You know how to contact me?"

"I can find out."

The men nodded, one to the other. They did not shake hands.

Gannon left the room. Ryan reached for an apple.

Across from the elevator was a small waiting room for visitors—a sofa, couple of chairs, magazine rack, television set. Linda Ryan and Kristy Baysinger were seated in the chairs talking when Gannon came in. Linda rose immediately, said her goodbyes, and hurried back to her husband's bedside.

"She really loves that man," Kristy said.

"I guess she'd like to see him in another line of work."

"No, that's not true. If this is what he wants to do, then it's what she wants. I told you, she really loves him."

Gannon rubbed absently at the hairline scar. "Let's get out of here. Hospitals depress me."

They rode down together in the elevator and walked out of the building. At the entrance they stood awkwardly silent.

Kristy was the first to speak. "What do we do now, Jack?"

"I think you pick up your life where it got derailed, and I try to build one."

"You mean separately."

"Kristy, I owe you more than I can ever pay back, and I'd a hell of a lot rather walk away from here with you than alone, but it can't work. There are a couple of people standing between us."

"I don't understand."

"There's Jay Baysinger and Lou Matchek."

"Jay's dead."

"No, he isn't." Gannon tapped his head. "Part of him is in here. Memories. Things I have no right to remember. But he's there."

Kristy said nothing. Her eyes were moist, but she did not turn away.

"And you've seen enough of Lou Matchek to know he is not a nice man. I've got him out of sight now, and out of the driver's seat, but I can never be sure he won't take over again."

They stood for a minute close together before Kristy spoke again. "I'll miss you, Jack. I'll miss you a lot. But I know you're right."

"Being right doesn't make it any easier. I'll miss you too, Kristy. I've got some memories that are mine alone."

She pulled his head down and kissed him once hard on the mouth. "Good bye, Jack."

She turned and walked briskly, heels clack-clacking on the concrete, to the parking lot. Gannon stood looking after her, half-hoping she would turn and call to him. If she had, he would probably have run to take her in his arms and hold her there forever.

But she did not look back.

* * * * *

Gannon walked slowly away from the hospital. He looked up once at the floor where Merlin Ryan lay. He could see nothing but the reflected sun on the glass panes.

With his hands sunk in his pockets he walked on. Since he regained consciousness in the hospital, he had been Jack Gannon, and no one else. There had been no conscious effort on his part, but the Baysinger memories were in shreds and the Matchek persona had stayed submerged. Maybe he was going to be all right.

As the thought brought a smile to his face, a soft thrumming began in his head. It swiftly grew louder into a whirring, buzzing, thumping din. He put his hands over his ears, feeling for a dreadful moment that his control was slipping away.

Than a shadow passed over him. He looked up and saw the helicopter with the big red cross on its belly whopping down toward the hospital's rooftop landing pad.

He gave the copter a rueful grin. Whatever direction his life took, it was not going to be easy.

The helicopter landed, the thrumming stopped. Jack Gannon walked on alone.

THE END